BREAKER AND THE SUN

LAUREN NICOLLE TAYLOR

BREAKER & THE SUN

ISBN: 978-1-63422-242-6

Cover Design by: Marya Heiman
Interior Format by: Courtney Knight
Editing by: Cynthia Shepp

For more information about our content disclosure, please utilize the QR code above with your smart phone or visit us at www.CleanTeenPublishing.com

TO THE SUFFERERS OF NOSTALGIA, SOLDIER'S HEART, SHELL SHOCK, BAT-TLE FATIGUE, COMBAT STRESS REAC-TION AND FINALLY PTSD. MAY YOU FIND YOUR PEACE.

BREAKER

1

THEIR FACES BELONG ACROSS THE SEA.

I spit on the ground and gaze steadily at my shoes as I walk. *Not here in New York.* A heavy-footed brawl dances inside me—the war between who I used to be and who I'm trying not to become. Man versus soldier.

Little Red whines as he tugs on my sleeve. "We're totally lost!"

I shrug. He doesn't even realize how right he is.

Briefly disconnecting my study of the cold concrete, I look up, trying to get my bearings in this huge city. My eyes refuse to rest on the slash characters climbing up neon signs in front of me. The pictures of steaming noodles in red and pink bowls that stream down banners in every other doorway. Instead, I stare ahead, the Empire State Building glowing like an American beacon several blocks away.

Little Red bounces up and down, eyes full of candy. He stares into every crowded store window, fingers streaking across the hot glass where animals hang from hooks with hollow, barbecued eyes. My eyelids streak with ash, my nostrils reluctantly smell burning flesh, and my heart dips. A flash of green. That feeling of losing control...

Elbows dig into my sides from two soldiers. "Try it! Hey man, you only live once," Slats urges with a knowing grin.

I shudder, watching the man squat over a pile of ash, spots of red coals peeking through four charred, still furry legs. "Have you ever?"

Grims laughs. "Yeah. Tastes like pork. A puppy pork chop!"

My teeth clench and my stomach turns as I watch the man poke at the pile of coals with a stick. I can't…

The man presents me with a piece of shaved meat on a plastic picnic plate, his eyes imploring. He jerks it under my nose, and I know I have to try it or I'll offend him.

I hate that I have to do this—be here, put food in my mouth, and smile even though I want to vomit. I hate it. I hate it. I hate it. Here.

My palm starts to burn. I pull Red away from the windowpane, catching the owner's dark, curious eyes. I quickly look away, feeling split down the middle like the duck dangling in the window.

Why did I think this visit would be a good idea?

Hugging myself, I think of home and its isolated bareness. The comfort of rarely running into anyone like *them* anywhere. I sigh, weaving through China-town like it's a minefield. Careful to avoid bumping shoulders or making eye contact with anyone. Because their faces act like bombs in my mind. They explode the violent memories and destroy the good ones.

I keep the Empire State Building in my sights.

I rub my temple with one hand as I drag Little Red down the sidewalk. My headache is building like a forest fire. I need to escape.

"Maybe we should stop and ask for directions?" Red asks, coming to a halt and pulling my arm backward.

Shaking my head, I mutter, "I can't," in an irritated, scratchy tone.

"What do you mean by *you can't*?" he asks, confusion floating in his dark blue eyes.

Because this version of me, the one I left Vietnam with, can't look at an Asian face without twisting in pain. Without points of knives tearing stomachs open while grown men scream. He sees only their death and his fear in their eyes.

My jaw clenches, and I try to think of an answer that would satisfy my ten-year-old brother. "I just can't."

Red slams his hands in his pockets and mumbles to the ground. "The old Breaker would have asked for directions."

The old Breaker is gone. I buried him. In a grave as deep as a salad bowl. Hoping maybe one day, he'd scrape his way out. That he'd find me. It was only when my split boots touched home soil did I remember I'd left him behind.

But by then, it was too late.

Grabbing a smoke, I light up. It burns my throat nicely. I try to smile down at my little brother who looks scared. Of me. I drag in and exhale. "Do you wanna go up to the top of the Statue of Liberty or to the Central Park Zoo?" I ask, desperate to flip the page. Trying to force my eyes to click over to a new shot, a color one that's not dipped in red.

He jumps up, trying to grab my cap from my head. "The zoo! The zoo!"

I chuckle carefully. Concerned if I laugh too hard my last shred of decency will fall away from my body. "Okay, the zoo it is."

Ruffling his hair, I step away from the neon lights and the faces I can't look at, and the earth shifts beneath my feet. Mom was wrong. This little bonding trip was a mistake. Normal can't be forced back into someone. I'm a cage that's rusted shut. I'm too changed. Too broken. And I'm keeping all my demons locked inside.

I stare up at the sky, the sun almost touching the tips of the highest skyscrapers. Soon, it will set. The calming night will come.

I don't mind the blanket of darkness. It's the sun I can't stand.

Because before the sun rises, I can forget where I am. Who I am. Once the light spreads across the sky, I remember. And it's another day I have to live like this.

Sunny

2

Coffin-like blackness encases my thoughts, and I lift my arms just to check that I'm not actually trapped. They reach to the sky and flop back down on my duvet. I'm not in Saigon. I'm a normal, breathing girl, lying in my bed in Sundown, New York State, United States of America.

This is a typical reaction to a traumatic event. But it's frustrating. My heart has dealt with the pain, but my brain won't let go. There's a lock on the door in there, and it's blocked by debris. *I just want to feel normal again.*

I pinch my eyes and my fists tighter, then relax. Reliving when dust clogged my nostrils. The taste of ash on my tongue. The feeling of my limbs pinned under broken concrete and giant timber beams split in half like matchsticks is so real. *Too real.* There were acres of dust. Most wouldn't think a building that big and solid could be reduced to particles. To pieces swept from a chair before sitting down.

But I guess everything can be reduced to its most basic of elements. Even people.

Trembling, I tune my ears to the noises outside my bedroom door, reaching out for them to pull the string back to reality. The TV hums, volume so low I'm sure Gung can't hear it. The flush of a toilet. The patch of floor that always creaks. The doll that squeals *Mama.* It's something. But it's not enough. The ghost of debris still presses on my chest, and I can't breathe. I can't hold on. I can't… Air whistles from my lungs like it's the last air to ever live there.

Maybe I'll never feel normal. Maybe, like once a tumor is removed, the brain can only heal around the hurt. Not replace it. Fill it in.

Sitting up, I shake the imaginary rubble from my clothes and swing out of bed.

I need air. I need roofless, wall-less, empty sky.

Shrugging on my coat, I pad down the low-lit hallway. A gold cat on the hallstand waves goodbye to me with unimpressed eyes.

The bath is running, and Ama's soft, off-key singing pushes through the keyhole with the light. If I'm quiet, I can avoid explaining where I'm going, why, how long, and whether I'm wearing enough warm clothes. I roll my eyes and creep like a fog over fields.

The lounge is empty, so I switch off the TV. I follow the sweet, pungent smell of tobacco that curls like a dead arm from the back porch.

Hovering in the night is the warm, orange glow of Gung's pipe. My eyes adjust to see him sitting hunched like a walnut shell on the steps, looking out across the vacant lot behind our house. He doesn't say anything, just nods and watches me slip on my boots. I wander into the scratchy grass laid out like a cheap carpet before the thick woods.

Each step I take away from this little box of a house releases rocks and rubble from my body. The dust pours down my arms as if I've arisen from a sand dune. I feel real untainted air entering my lungs. Air not heavy with nightmares and trauma. It doesn't smell like blood and gunpowder. It doesn't feel like death and bony fingers.

I step into the trees and feel them close around me like a curtain. My heart calms as I walk forward.

It's ugly. Twisted. With lumps and bumps that seem unnatural for a tree. Turning my back to its enormous trunk that's almost as wide as a car, I imagine it cradles me in its arms. I nestle into a nook between the trees roots. Its ugliness is comforting. Its gnarled, brittle branches bring me home.

I look up like I always do. Searching for light.

A diamond of sky, twelve little stars caught in a frame of trees branches. It's a halo to settle over my anxiety. Because when I was trapped beneath layers of rubble and twisted bodies, blood dripping slow like a leaking tap… When I had run out of screams and tears, there was one thing that stopped me from giving up and melting into the heaped ground with the rest of them. One diamond of sunlight, then moonlight, then sunlight again, cast over the steady concrete. Floor or ceiling, I couldn't really tell. It meant there was still a sky. It hadn't been torn down and sold for scrap. There was still hope that someone would find me.

I held onto that diamond of light for my life, for my heart. I still do.

BREAKER

3

"It's been months now, Breaker," Mom declares to her stack of ironing. The way she says *Breaker*, it's like a groan, a word cut into pieces. "Don't you think it's time you got a job? *Or* you could apply for college like you planned. Get your degree. The money you saved while you were away should go to some good use." Her voice gets higher at the end like she knows she really is just talking to her ironing. She might as well be.

I shrug, which feels like an effort.

"Where are you going now?" she asks, watching me from the corner of her eye while I put on my army jacket and pat the pocket to make sure my smokes are still there.

"Out," I manage.

Little Red mimics me, "Breaker's goin'...out!" he says in the deepest voice a ten-year-old can manage. I stomp over and scruff up his hair.

"I won't be long," I say, attempting to smile when he holds up a picture of his newest invention, combination dinosaur and robot. It guards the house and vacuums.

I can't muster a real smile or any real emotions because I'm not sure I have any.

Patting my pocket again, I know *something* beats

under the layers of clothes and scarred skin. I'm sure I had a heart once. Now it's buried, beating faintly under wet leaves and boot prints in the jungle.

As I hit the front step, I shove my hands in my pockets. I don't know where I'm heading, just *away*.

This town seems so mundane, so ordinary compared to where I was. When my boots stomped through ramshackle towns that looked like they were made of cardboard and glue, mud splashing, heat seeping into our heavy jackets. Everything was new. Different. I don't know if exciting is the right word, but I didn't mind that. Those were the best parts. Curious eyes, sometimes grateful, beautiful porcelain faces. At the beginning.

Is it strange to miss it? Miss it and hate it at the same time?

Contemplating that little mystery is bound to give me a headache, so I let it fall out one ear.

I fumble with my matches and light up a smoke. It gives me something to do, to hold as I charge down the street. Head down, eyes following the river system of cracks in the sidewalk. This way, I can't see faces. I don't want to. If I look up…if I see one of *them*. Anger crackles through me like a severed power line. I'll shiver and stare with eyes so dead and hard it will frighten them. *It frightens me.*

So, I dip my head. Stare at my boots. Keep my shaggy hair close around my eyes as a shield.

In Sundown, they're easy to avoid. It's a tiny town, made up of gravel driveways and babbling brooks running past front porches. There are far more trees than people here, and I barely see anyone, let alone one of *them.* It's only around tourist season that it might get tricky. I grit my teeth and kick stones as I walk along the dirty road. Busloads of people coming to see the wild beauty of the Catskills will descend on this place in the spring.

Maybe I'll go hide in the woods somewhere. The idea doesn't seem that appealing as I'd have to pack, get supplies… I exhale loudly getting tired just thinking about it.

I cough from cold and smoke and shake my head, my eyes focusing on the brittle trees of the woods that border the whole town. It doesn't remind me of the jungle. These trees don't strangle each other. They give each other space like polite acquaintances. Everything about the jungle was claustrophobic, wrapped tight. Leaves slapped my face, thick as leather. Everything was dripping wet, vivid green.

Flicking my cigarette butt on the ground, I turn sharply. Heading between two log cabins, I crunch over old leaves that are ready to sink into the ground and wait for winter.

Mom's words line the path as I push deep into the woods. *Get a job. Go to college.* I don't know how to explain it to her. It took everything. *Everything.* I don't think there is enough of me left to give to work or study.

I clench my fists and knock against my legs. *I'm a stranger in my own body.*

The sun begins to talk to the trees, sinking lower, whispering quietly as it welcomes the night.

Shadows grow. But the woods call. *Walk on. Forget. Let yourself go.*

I grunt and push on, buttoning my coat and lighting up another smoke.

Soon, all I can see is the orange glow at the tip of my fingers and the spare light of the tiny moon.

It's dead quiet, again reminding me of the difference. The jungle was never quiet. The rain deafening. The insects loud and insatiable. My skin prickles just thinking about all the bites and itches. Green light. Heart dives…

Richie giggles like a girl. A high-pitched squeaking as if someone is poking him under his arms with a skewer. The others laugh at him as they swat their faces. Squatting in the mud, we look like khaki-colored frogs, our plastic skin shimmering under the torchlight. The chirping is deafening, as is the zipping of bugs flying by my ears.

"Fuck! Rich, will you shut up?" I warn, turning my light toward him with a grin on my face. There's a mosquito right above his eye. I reach out and slap his face. He topples. The group ripples with laughter, water spraying from our camouflage. Something moves out the corner of my eye, and I press my fingers to my lips. Eight terrified pairs of eyes stare out into the milky dark. Eyes that remind me of home and Mom and Little Red.

No one breathes.

I shake my head. Drag a hand down my face.

I'm lost.

Looking for something.

Following the sounds of water, I edge into a small clearing.

An enormous, squat-looking tree sits at the edge of the spring, its gnarled roots dipping into the rushing water.

When I flick the butt into the water, it makes a tiny sizzling sound, I jump over the stream and catch myself on its thick trunk, feeling lumps and bumps like tumors all over its skin.

This is far enough.

Sinking down, I press my back against the old tree. It accepts me like it's been waiting. I light up and sigh, watching the cigarette burn down to the filter without taking a puff.

I wish I could burrow into the center of this tree and just rest.

Sunny

4

The acrid smell of cigarette smoke creeps around the tree like Kaa from *The Jungle Book* about to swallow Mowgli. My heart jumps. Someone is here.

I plant my hands in the earth, ready to spring up and run, my ears straining to hear.

A deep sigh. A voice carved into the wood. "It would be easier," he whispers.

The man sounds young. Sad. I shouldn't speak. I should just sneak away before he notices I'm here, but… "What would be easier?" I ask, my hand going to my mouth way too late.

The air grows even colder. Layers of ice sinking down, down, down.

Leaves rustle as the smell of smoke dissipates. I think maybe he's gone. Or I imagined him, but then the man speaks again, a roll of anguish in his voice that hurts me. "To just disappear," he answers.

I open my mouth to speak, though I don't really know what I can say. Silence settles over the place, and it's a good half hour before I hear him tramping through the stream away from me.

Finally, my senses return and I jump up, walking quickly back to the house.

When I reach the edge of the field, I have to shield

my eyes as white light bounces spastically in front of me. Ama stands waist high in dying grass, shining a torch light in my eyes like an interrogation lamp. "Wher you go? We worry about you walking all alone in woods," she scolds as I catch up to her, taking the heavy torch from her thin hands before she throws it on the ground.

I glance up. Gung hasn't moved from his position, planted on the porch steps like a garden gnome. He doesn't look too worried. "Sorry, Ama," I say, bowing my head. She pinches my arm and scuttles inside beneath the stream of light I give her.

When I reach the steps, I bend down and kiss Gung's cheek. I feel his smile as his cheekbones tighten. "Night," I whisper.

He nods. Everything about him is quiet, considered. Each word is chosen and thought about carefully before it is used. "You need space," he says. Or asks, I'm not quite sure.

I close my eyes, letting the peace from my shard of sky settle over me like a new sweater. "*Oui*. Yeah, sometimes."

He hums. Rocks back and forth until he is standing. The cough that comes from deep inside seems like more than just an old-man cough.

He places a worn hand on my back and ushers me inside. "Inside now. It's cold."

We step inside, one after the other, ready to get whipped into Ama's tornado of nonsense. But before she can start, the splash of water in the tub makes me run to the bathroom. I've been gone at least an hour, but the tap is *still* running. Ama's eyes follow me curiously as I burst into the bathroom only to find the tub has only an inch of water in it.

"What the...? How can there only be an inch? It's been running for over an hour." I tip my head to the side and stare at the water sloshing gently against the side like a subtle lake.

Ama comes up behind me and cackles, poking the top of my head with her hard finger. "Cold air make you crazy! You gone only five minute."

I shake my head. I must have imagined the tap running before, or maybe it was the bathroom sink.

Ama grasps my arm and yanks me from the bathroom, pulling me to stand under the living room light so she can yell at me while seeing me clearly.

BREAKER

5

Her voice was as frightening as the whir of a bullet past my ears. Torn palm leaves, burning flesh.

Her voice was a song. Soft as a petal.

The accent was subtle and mixed with other things, but I could hear it. I've been trained to hear it like my life depended on it.

Strangely, when I heard it—four words, one question—hate didn't bubble from where it has built up, from my toes to around the middle of my heart. The anger stayed where it was. Just floating like a cloud holding onto lightning. Maybe because I didn't see her face, I could keep it from rising. Maybe it was because the accent was subtle… *I don't know*. I'm so exhausted from trying to find reasons for all the shit that's wrong with me.

I stumble through the woods, trying to keep in line with the way I came in. I walk straight into a low branch, which scratches my forehead. I touch my skin. It's wet. In the dark, I can't tell if it's blood or sweat. I swear. Only the owls and squirrels can hear me here.

Maybe I imagined it, I tell myself as I strain to see streetlights through the trees.

I could be going crazy. I think Mom and Little Red think I'm crazy.

I'm not crazy.
I'm just...stuck.

It takes me hours to get home. Next time, I'll remember to bring a torch. I decide that there *will* be a next time. And for once, the planning of something doesn't drain me like water from a broken dam.

Pulling open the door, I see Mom and Red sleeping on the couch together. My little brother's head is awkwardly nestled in Mom's armpit. The TV is on with the volume turned down, lighting their faces to pale and ghostly. Buddy Hackett is on *The Tonight Show starring Johnny Carson,* looking all beady eyed and jolly. Not what I'm in the mood for right now.

I swallow my sigh. I'm so jealous of their peace. Just a small sliver would be enough.

Bending down, I scoop Red into my arms, careful not to disturb Mom. He snorts and presses his drooling mouth into my chest. There's a knock on the inner chamber of my heart. Somewhere in there beats a reminder that I love my brother. I love my mom. That I'm capable of those feelings.

Red's arm hangs limply as I carry him to his room. A glorified broom closet. I fold him over and squeeze him into his matchbox of a bed. Pulling the covers up, I think about kissing him on the forehead. I don't.

When I return to the lounge to get Mom, she's already awake. "What time is it?" she asks, bleary eyed and disoriented.

"I don't know," I reply, offering her my hand. She

takes it, and I pull her from the sofa. "It's late."

She wipes her eyes and wraps her arm around my middle, squeezing the dead parts and trying to bring them back to life. "We waited for you to come home, hon. Must've fallen asleep watching Johnny." Her sleepiness is making her a lot more affectionate than usual.

I lead her to her room and make sure she crawls into bed. "Goodnight," I say, almost saluting her.

She yawns and nods in response.

I wander back into the lounge, switch off the TV, and check that the doors are locked.

Then I go to my room, sink to the floor, and try not to sleep.

Sunny

6

"I knew a man who was eaten by bear," Ama says as she straightens already straightened copies of *Seventeen* and *Vogue* on the coffee table. They look ruffled since she always tears out any articles she deems unwholesome and inappropriate. The *Vogue* cover model, Lauren Hutton, looks like she feels very sorry for me. Ama holds up one bony finger and shakes it in my face as I try not to laugh at her. "No! Bitten. Not eaten. He has no foot, and all night he screams with bad dreams."

Gung has taken his leave. Their bedroom door closes quietly.

"I'm very careful, Ama," I say, trying futilely to reassure her.

Her powdered white face is going a strange shade of pink. "I don't care for careful." She throws her arms up animatedly. "You know, in Malaysia, there no bears. No bears that can eat you."

No. Just tigers, cobras, and malaria-infected mosquitoes. And I'm pretty sure there are bears too, actually. I'm about to open my mouth to tell her this when Gung's dark face appears in the narrow opening of the bedroom door. "Come to bed," he orders softly. Ama glances at him once with her intense dark eyes and squints.

I can see the dark clouds clearing a little and she leans into me, pressing her soft cheek to mine.

"I want you be careful because you are precious. You are our precious darling girl." She cups my face in her sesame-scented hands. "We so lucky they find you. We praised God. We thought we lose everyone, but you…you come back to us. You understand?"

Still holding my head, she forces me to nod.

"I do, Ama."

Gung watches us with a softly stern expression. Finally, Ama gives in. "All right! I'm coming," she says in mock anger.

When she's at the door, she turns and warns me. "You look tired. Dark circles like panda. Get some sleep." She shoos me with her hand.

If only it were that easy.

7

The door thumps into my stiff back, and Little Red's bright face pushes through the gap. "Breaker," he says, his voice starting to crack. "Mom's left breakfast, and you've gotta drive me to school."

He keeps shoving the door, trying to slide me along the carpet. I grunt in response and lean back, careful not to trap his little fingers. My eyes adjust to the dim winter light, and I rub them. I must have fallen asleep against the door again. I look up at my perfectly made bed. Hospital corners. Sheets stretched tight over the mattress. Funny the things that stick. Memories like this are wedged uncomfortably in my brain like the coin they used to bounce off the bedding.

"Breaker!" Red complains.

I stand up and step away from the door. He catapults into the room. I catch him around his middle and lift him off the ground, his legs kicking in dinosaur pajama pants and an *Escape from the Planet of the Apes* t-shirt. I've missed the last two *Planet of the Apes* movies. It's something Red is insistent I must get up to date with before the next one comes out.

Throwing my skinny little brother on the bed, I stand over him, hands on hips. He glances up at me with three parts adoration and one part poorly disguised fear.

"Just let me get changed, okay?"

Red scrambles from the bed, leaving wrinkles in the gray bedspread and in my forehead, because I don't want to straighten it later, but I know I'll have to. He punches me lightly in the arm and runs out the door. "Okay, but I don't want to be late. Mr. Delquin can be such an asshole if you're even a second late."

Grabbing his shirt, I pull him back to me. I lean down and try to catch his eyes. "Hey Red," I say shaking my head. "Don't curse like that."

He looks down at where I've scrunched his prized shirt, and I let go. "You curse all the time," he says, his chest puffed out in defiance.

I stumble back in surprise. "When have I ever?"

He swings back and forth, eyes rolling around like he doesn't want to make eye contact. "Every night, you curse. F-this and F-that. I hear you at night."

I guess I must be getting some sleep then…

I sigh, a weird gulp traveling up my windpipe and lodging itself in my throat. "Oh." Red looks worried. I hate seeing him like this. "I'm sorry," I say, and he shrugs and runs to the kitchen.

So sorry.

One day, this car is going to disintegrate while I'm driving it. I'll be left gripping a steering wheel, sitting in the middle of the road like a crazy person.

The truck rattles like it's taking its last breath. Little Red braces himself against the dash as we turn, his eyes wide with jittery excitement. I tighten my fists around the wheel, feeling the heat creep into the backs of my eyes. I don't want to see *them* today.

We pull into the parking lot, and I glance at the clock at the same time as Red. "Sorry, Little R."

He crosses his arms and stares out the window. "We're late. You have to come in and sign something. Or I'll get detention."

I really didn't want to have to get out and go in.

Grabbing my army jacket from the backseat, I pull it on before the freeze bites my arms. Red looks up at me, his face screwed up with disapproval. "Do you *have* to wear that?"

I roll my eyes. "It's freezing out."

He just grunts, and I start to worry that I'm rubbing off on him.

There are a few other stragglers running across the lot, arms hugging their chests. Little kids with backpacks too big for their tiny bodies. Red yells out at a kid running toward the building, a black head of hair barely visible above a large blue backpack that's trying to swallow him. "Jake! Wait up."

Jake turns around and I'm shoved in the chest, falling back, back, back through layers of time. It's hate. But it's also fear. Regret. It's like hands slipping from wheels, and hearts suddenly sinking into stomachs, dread and a curtain of green.

They see our helmeted heads popping up through the fields, and they stare. Stare at us foreigners. Looking sort of amused at our presence knee deep in their rice paddies. They don't understand our warnings. We shoo them with our gloved hands, point our guns toward safety, but still they stare. Or worse, smile and wave.

I blink. Blood and tiny limbs sinking into the mud of a rice paddy. Small, small faces. Innocent faces.

What are we doing here? I bite the back of my hand to keep from screaming. I can't see any more of this. It's turning me over. Flicking some switch I didn't know was there.

Someone laughs, and my stomach turns. I don't want to laugh. But if I don't...if I don't short-circuit these feelings, I might as well join them.

I think about joining them. All the time.

Red impatiently tugs my arm, and I snap out of it. His friend Jake stares at me, his mouth twisted like he's not sure whether to laugh or frown. His almond eyes and jet-black hair are a curse to me.

I cough. Avert my eyes. Try to remember that this kid is not *them.* He's not a part of my nightmare. But I can't stand to look at him all the same. I hate myself for how it makes me feel, and I hate *them* for making me feel this way in the first place.

Jake turns and heads inside. Thankfully, we head in a different direction.

I think of the girl in the woods, her lilted but obviously foreign accent. It's like a lifeline dangling just out of reach. I should have snapped. Should have spiraled into the spin of helicopter blades cutting razor shadows on the wild green floor. But I didn't.

Sunny

8

I smell morning before I open my eyes. Morning is omelets, French toast. Butter. Lots of butter. I lick my lips and just lay there, waiting for the thickly scented air to wrap me in warmth and coax me from the bed.

A thought rattles me from buttery dreams, and I hear his voice. *Just disappear.* His voice, sad and angry but mostly resigned. Like he has already started to disappear, and he's waiting for it to really take hold.

It would be easier…

Concrete crushes my lungs, and I wiggle beneath it.

The Maplewood door opens gradually, softly. Gung always gives me time to get up, to prepare. He pokes his head in and wearily smiles. A gray haze hangs around him like a cloud of pipe smoke. He looks washed out. "Sunny," he says in his heated, gravelly voice. "Come eat breakfast."

I sit up, watching the wedge of imaginary concrete slide to the ground and evaporate. "Kay," I mumble, rubbing my eyes.

His eyes soften as they trace my worn-out expression, and then land on my feet pressed up against the end of my tiny bed. "I make you new bed," he says, pointing.

I go to protest, but his hand is already up to stop me.

"New bed. New dreams," he says with his back to me, shuffling down the hallway. Linked, as I am, to the smells wafting from the kitchen.

He makes my heart hurt. With guilt, with love, with worry. Being raised by my grandparents is like taking a long vacation that I'm not sure I'm going to return from. He's old—they both are—and it scares me.

I pull on a robe and gallop toward the kitchen, taking my place at the counter while Gung sits at the table. It's perfectly set for him, folded cloth napkin and everything.

We never eat together. And we always eat together. Gung at the table, Ama in the kitchen as she samples bites and sips from ladles, and me at the counter, a bridge between the two.

Ama slaps two slices of French toast crusted in sugar and cinnamon on my plate and winks at me. "Open your mail," she urges. Her bright black eyes focus on the small pile of white envelopes on the mustard-colored counter, tipping toward my elbow.

I take a forkful of toast and talk with my mouth full. "The mailman has already been?" I say with surprise.

Ama shakes her head. "Gung go to post office early this morning and tell postman to give mail to him." Then she slaps my hand with the dirty spatula. "Don't talk with food in your mouth!"

"Aie!" I withdraw my hand, which is splattered with fat, and swallow my food. I turn to Gung. He's hunched over his plate, casually flipping the newspaper page over slowly.

"Open! Open!" Ama shouts, poking me with the still-hot cooking utensil.

I stare at the pile like it may burst into flames.

Some are thin. Some are quite thick. I go for the thin one first.

It's from Harvard.

I feel Ama's hot eyes on me as I tear open the envelope.

We regret to inform you…

I slide it over to Ama for her to read. She scrunches it into a ball, throws it in the trash, and then turns to me, waving a knife in her hand. "You too good for Harvard. Bah!"

I snort. *Who's too good for Harvard? Er, no one!*

I'm not crushed with disappointment. It's not the one I wanted anyway. The one I really want sits at the bottom of the pile.

"Next!" Ama shouts as she slams the fridge door and pours me some orange juice.

We open two more rejections before we get to the two fatter envelopes.

I open the NYU one first, smiling widely as I read the acceptance and offer of a scholarship. I beam and reach to hand the letter to Gung, nearly toppling from my chair. "*C'est Fantastique!* I got into NYU."

Gung nods. "Of course you did."

Ama repeats his words but in a 'someone lit a fuse at her feet and she's about to explode out the roof' kind of way. "Of course you did!" she shouts, spatula pointed to the ceiling.

The Stanford envelope gleams like a wounded

white bird in front of me, spattered with oil stains.

I open it carefully.

"I got in," I whisper, tracing the words. All the extra classes I took that I'd already passed in Vietnam were worth it.

The kitchen curtains seem to sway, oranges and apples shuddering at the change in the air. "Eh?" Ama's shoulders rise and fall.

"I got in!" I jump from my stool and crash into Gung, hugging him and releasing smoky smells from his clothes.

He pats my hand and says again, "Of course you did."

I turn back to Ama's frowning face. "Stanford? Stanford in California." She points out the window, parting the curtains with her weapon, her hand tracing a curve. "On other side of country." She shakes her head. "Too far. Too far. Isn't it, George?"

I bite my lip and try to remember how much I owe them. How much I *love* them.

Gung clears his throat and unhurriedly folds his paper over. I stand between them. Electric current rolls from Ama's eyes and is absorbed by Gung's calm countenance. "Sunny decide where she want to go. She work very hard. Annie, it's her choice." He stares her down, and she glares at him with her hands on her hips. I feel like I should sink to the floor and crawl like a commando out the door before bombs start going off and blood is shed.

Ama hisses. A powdered white cobra about to strike.

"*Écoutez*. Look," I say, thinking I don't have time

to get out before the bomb explodes so maybe I should try and diffuse it. "I don't have to decide right now. I have at least two months before I need to mail my acceptance letter."

Ama breathes in and seems to relax. At least she puts down the spatula. "NYU is better school. I know it."

"Annie..." Gung growls a warning.

Ama throws her hands up in the air and leaves the room. Then she runs back, throwing her arms around me and squeezing me tight for three whole seconds. "You very smart girl," she whispers. Then louder, "You take from my side of family! All Gung's brothers are stupid!"

Gung snorts with anger, but she's not silly. She runs out the front door and down to the neighbor's house before he can retort. I cover my mouth, but a laugh slips out.

This moment is pretty much exactly what I thought it would be like. With them. There's just the tip of a wish. A small ache as I imagine what it would have been like to tell my parents this same news. My heart drops, held up by the elastic of two people who always believed in me.

But I guess if they were still alive, I wouldn't be here in Sundown at all. The moment would be different. In a different time and place. I can't undo my life as it is, nor their death as it was. I pat my chest and remind myself how lucky I really am.

BREAKER

9

The walls are the same pale, vomit green they were when I went here. I run my hand over the bubbling paint, withdrawing when I touch something sticky. I wipe my fingers on my jacket with a sour look.

Red looks up at me and rolls his eyes. I'm embarrassing him. I blush, trying to smooth my hair down and look less like a bum. Grabbing my elbow, he starts to steer me toward the office. He needn't bother. I'm pretty familiar with its whereabouts.

The woman behind the counter looks me up and down, clearly uncomfortable. She mutters, "Thank you for your service," so quietly I'm not entirely sure she said it before her gaze slides down her nose and lands on Little Red, who's squirming nervously. I smack him lightly in the back, and he straightens.

"My brother said I need to sign something so he doesn't get detention," I say, avoiding her eyes.

Sifting through the mess of papers on her desk, she finally finds a pink sheet. She hands it to me just as a man in a sport coat comes to the office door.

"Mr. Van Winkle!" Mr. Delquin exclaims. "Look at you all grown up." His extends his arm, palm upward as if holding a plate, as he takes in my scruffy appearance. Like… *Ta da! Look how disappointing you are.*

Crossing the distance between us, he offers his hand. I take it reluctantly.

He turns to the receptionist. "Grace, this is Breaker Van Winkle. Back when I taught at the high school, he was one of the most promising students from the class of sixty-nine."

She giggles at my name, ineptly trying to cover her mouth with her polished fingernails, but only managing to get lipstick all over her fingers.

"Hey, Mr. Delquin. Good to see you," I manage. Little Red looks at the both of us in horror.

Then Mr. Delquin winks at Red and ushers him along. "Don't worry about the tardy slip, Grace. Red, why don't you run along to class?"

Red doesn't need to be told twice. He disappears before I can blink, a streak of red sneakers and jeans. Delquin is still smiling at me, broadly. Piano teeth I'd like to knock in.

This is what I get for wearing the damn jacket. Pity. Fascination. Sometimes outright anger. Or in Delquin's case, misplaced admiration.

He opens his arm wide and tries to sweep me into his office. His hand presses into my back and I'm suddenly standing in the room, cold sunlight streaming through his window and showing the dust collecting on his desk.

"Sit down, sit down," Delquin urges, still with an awkward smile dripping from his lips. I don't think it wants to be there anymore. It's hanging from his mouth, ready to jump.

I sit down and clasp my hands in my lap. "If this is about Red being late, sir, I promise, it won't happen again," I say to my hands. They are clenched so tight my knuckles have gone white. *Why do I feel like a kid again?*

He laughs, his black hair flopping over his eyebrows. "You're not in high school anymore, son. In fact, I'm sure we can both agree that you've probably done a lot of growing up in the past few years."

I want to throw his gold nameplate at him. I don't feel 'grown up'. I feel undernourished, not growing, stagnant and straining to survive. I stare at his desk—at the fancy multi-colored paperclips and stained coffee mug.

Delquin clears his throat, and I look up. "I just wanted to say I respect what you've done. Serving your country and all. You know I did my time in Korea." It's his turn to look down. To get pulled back into the violent memories that dig into a soldier's back and live between his ribs. Parting. Parting.

My feet start to sink into mud. My body begins to warm from the tropical climate, the thick, thick air.

"You know, it was a brave thing to do, enlisting so you could pay for college. It's a shame you've given up on it. You had such a bright future ahead of you." He rubs his stubbled chin and glances up. "You know, Breaker, it's not too late."

I nod. I know. It seemed like the perfect plan. Twelve months' service would pay for my whole college tuition. But then the bright future turned dark.

I do connect with his eyes, just for a moment, and understanding passes between us like a secret. A note in class. A confession in custody. "Thanks, Mr. Delquin, but I think it's too late for me. Right now, I just feel lucky to be alive," I say, toying with the dog tags around my neck. "To be home." In that sentence, I do sound grown up. I sound like a grown man with too many regrets and not enough time to make them up.

Delquin sighs and leans back in his chair. "Amen to that."

I would like this conversation to be over before we both get stuck in a memory and start crying, so I rise from my chair. "I have to go." My eyes dart to the exit.

Delquin gets up and reaches for my hand again, shaking it firmly. "Look, Breaker, you were always such a smart kid. I know it can be hard to, um, get used to civilian life after what you've seen and done, but I want to offer my help. If you ever decide you do want to go to college, let me know. I can help you with your applications."

I try to smile, because it really is a nice offer. But what's left of me doesn't know what to do. So, I just say, "Thank you, sir."

And I leave.

I want to think, *Maybe*… But, *never* is a stronger, easier word right now.

I can't imagine that life—going to college, getting my degree. I can't imagine five paces in front of me that isn't buried in mud.

I left Sundown eighteen months ago. I have been back for a few months, but I'm not really here.

Scraping my hand along the lockers, I remind myself of time and place. Metal lockers and posters about hygiene are not found in the jungle.

The door to outside calls like a mouth ready to spew me out. I don't ever want to be late again.

As I rattle my pack of cigarettes, I realize there's only one left. I light it up and walk past my truck, heading down the street toward the convenience store on the corner that's lit up all cheery and sunshine yellow.

10

"Ama," I shout as I pull on my yellow smock and quickly button it to my neck. "I need you to drive me to work."

Struggling with my long dark hair, I twist it into a clumpy knot at the nape of my neck. My head jerks back as Ama pulls the knot out and teases the hair with her sharp fingers. "Stand still!" she orders.

I freeze, scared she's going to yank me backward again. Quickly, like the lash of a whip, she has my hair braided and tied. She pats my head. Slaps it, really. "There. Very pretty."

I turn and kiss her cheek. "Thank you, Ama."

She slips on her shoes and slings her purse over her arm. "Let's go."

The pale blue Cortina is already warming as we climb down the steps. The garage door is open and Gung is pulling lengths of timber down from the roof, being careful not to bang into any of the dollhouses and rocking chairs that line the interior walls.

As I climb into the car, I shout, "You don't have to do that, Gung."

Gung just nods, slips his glasses down over his eyes, and pulls a pencil from his pocket.

Ama drives like a distracted demon, reminding me again that I need to go for my license. She waits until the last moment to turn and then pulls the wheel hard, swinging the car out and making me feel like my lungs are strapped into the backseat and my stomach is hiding in the trunk. I hold the side arm of the door and clutch my heart for the full half-hour journey.

When we arrive at the grocery store, she slams the handbrake up before applying the footbrake. We lurch forward and then shoot back into the headrests. Once parked, she turns to stare at me, her teeth showing streaks of red lipstick. She holds out her hand. "Give me discount card," she demands.

I fish it out of my wallet with a sigh. "You can't bargain at the grocery store, Ama. Okay?"

She fixes her hair and slaps the steering wheel. "*Ah baik*! Too many rules from you. Can't bargain. Can't go to college in New York. Can't sleep."

I roll my eyes with my back turned. I know it's hard for her. As a consulate brat, I spent a great deal of my childhood traveling with my parents between Asia, England, and France. But my grandparents had lived their whole life in Malaysia until the incident. And although they jumped at the chance to come here, I don't think they realized how different it would be.

I think my mother always bridged that gap for them. The one between the Western world and their own.

I instantly feel bad for rolling my eyes and link my arm with hers. She leans her head on my shoulder briefly before charging ahead. I trail after her, always scared of what she might do next.

My manager gives me a wary look when we walk through the doors. He knows Ama all too well. He follows a few paces behind her, ready to stop her squeezing the peaches too hard or testing the bounce of the citrus.

I catch Cara's eyes as she looks up from her cash register, and she gives me a quick wave and a smile. Her eyes are questioning. I try to somehow communicate with my eyebrows that I got in to Stanford. She adds up her customer's total, hands them a docket, and then looks back to me. I nod, grinning widely.

"Oh my God!" she shouts, covering her mouth and apologizing to the man trying to pay her. She giggles and hands him his change, making all sorts of strange, excited faces in my direction while she bounces up and down at her station.

I go out the back and punch in my timecard, one eye on Ama through the window in the door as she fills her trolley with out-of-date frozen yogurt.

When I come out, a tall, scruffy man bumps into my shoulder. He doesn't look up or even apologize. Just keeps walking down the aisle like he didn't even see me.

I'm about to yell out when I notice his army greens, and I suppress my reaction. Bursts of light shatter before my eyes and I blink, trying to shake that rubble from my hair. I reach out to steady myself against the shelf laden with Lucky Charms and Coco Pops and take a deep breath. The cool white wire shudders under my grip, and I cough. Dust. Blood. Light. One arm clad in army green, reaching for me, pulling me up and out of the hole.

I squint and focus on the normal things. The monkey on the cereal box. The little leprechaun waving his golden spoon…

Kez, the manager, clears his throat behind me. "Sunny," he says, his voice brushing away the dust and bringing me back to fluorescent lights and beige linoleum floors. "I need you at the checkout."

Shaking my head, I whisper, "*Désolée*. Sorry, Kez." I wipe the sweat from my forehead. "I'll be right there."

He pretends to rearrange stock nearby as I collect myself.

I take a deep breath, glance once more at the friendly cereal leprechaun, and move to the front.

Once I'm sitting on my stool, staring at the cash register, I feel okay. I need to focus on the good things. NYU. Stanford. A new bed.

Cara slams the drawer shut on her register and checks for customers, then turns to me. "Did you get the scholarship?"

I grin, my smile a half moon hooked over my ears. "Uh-huh."

Cara wiggles in her seat and squeals. "Yes! I knew you would, ya smart cow!"

I snort.

Ama sidles up to Cara's register. "At least she no sound like stuck pig!" she says with a wicked grin as she pokes Cara in the side with her pointy fingernail, tickling her between her ribs.

Cara squeals some more, and she does kind of sound like a pig.

"Oh, Annie, stop!" Cara giggles while trying to reach for the yogurt.

Ama cackles like a witch and leans in to pinch Cara's plump face. "Such nice dimples!" Then she shoots me a nasty look. "Sunny too thin for dimples." Like dimples are a necessary feature and I've done something wrong by not having them.

I ignore her and ask Cara, "So what about you?"

Cara laughs as she packs Ama's groceries into a bag. "Vassar, baby!"

"That's so great, Cara." After I congratulate her, I wait for Ama to respond.

She doesn't, which means I'm going to hear about it later. Vassar is in New York. Just over a hundred miles away as opposed to thousands.

Cara blushes. She's worked really hard, and I'm proud of her. "No scholarship or anything, but still… My folks are super happy about it."

Ama pats Cara on the shoulder. "I been tutoring you for one year now with your French, and you smart girl. You good girl, good daughter too, Cara. Staying close to your family."

And there it is.

I'm about to snap back at her when the guy in army greens approaches Cara's counter. Since she's still busy counting through Ama's pile of quarters, I wave him over. He shakes his head and holds his place. Ama turns around and faces him, and he takes a step back from her.

"Sir," I say with a smile. "She's going to take a while. Let me serve you."

He sighs loudly, his broad shoulders pulling up and releasing violently. Reluctantly, he comes to my counter, slamming down a loaf of bread, milk, and a bunch of candy bars like they are about to bite him.

Staring at the black strip in front of us, he mutters, "A pack of smokes."

"Which brand?" I ask.

"Any," he snarls.

I jump a little, and he looks up at me. It's a quick flash of regret balled with sadness that turns to fire like the click of a lighter. I find it hard to look away, his hatred linked to my gaze in chains. I grab a pack of Marlboros and add it to the total. "I, uh, that will be seven thirty-six, sir," I stutter. "Do you want me to bag...?" I don't get to finish as he's already thrown a ten on the counter, grabbed his stuff, and is stalking toward the front door.

"Keep the change," he spits.

The air feels heavy, not with dust for once, but with hate. Cara stares at me, and Ama is starting to turn red hot.

I clench my fists and relax them, clench my fists and relax. I'll never get used to it. The hate thrown at me simply because of the way I look. I swallow dryly and click the drawer closed, separating out the change and putting it in the tip jar to share with the others.

Ama tries to catch up to him, running out the open door, but I can see out the glass that he's almost running down the street. Like he can't stand to be within a mile of someone like me, like both of us.

Tears burn the back of my eyes. I kick the inside of my counter, bruising my toes. I can't let this get to me. *I won't.*

Ama gives a rude gesture to his disappearing back, and I laugh at the image of this little Chinese woman standing in the parking lot, flipping the bird with a bag of out-of-date yogurt in one hand.

I shout out to her, "Ama. *Arrêtez* ! Stop! He's a vet," and watch her lower her arms slowly, rigidly, her temper flaring like wings wanting to fly.

BREAKER

11

What hell is wrong with me?

I should be better than this. *Why can't I be better than this?*

Her face. So smooth, so hurt. She looked like the lost one. The sorry one. I fumble for my smokes and pull the pack open too roughly. Cigarettes scatter on the icy pavement. I swear, squatting down to collect them. As I'm down there, someone throws a dollar bill onto the pile of smokes. Because that's what I look like. A homeless guy. A loser. A bum.

Her voice slips into the back of my mind as I try to shove the dirty smokes back into the pack, breaking and bending them. The strange accent. Kind of French. Kind of Asian. With a little American thrown in there. It's too distinctive to be anyone else. Tobacco crumbles in my hands and sprinkles over the ground.

She's the girl from the woods.

I stare back at the supermarket. Part of me wants to go back in and apologize, but a larger part of me can't stand the idea of seeing her face again. Can't stand the effort of figuring out what to say, how to say it.

Seeing any face like hers again.

Those fine features, delicate and brush-stroked, are devastation. They break apart to reveal blood in the dirt. The sounds of gunshots and children screaming rattles in my empty skull.

I grab my ears and try to shut it out, but I only manage to shut it in.

Breathe, Breaker.

I thump my chest hard. *Breathe, damn it!*

Finding a bench, I crawl onto it. I light up a smoke, letting it smooth out my crumpled nerves.

The girl's voice waves through me like a lullaby. It doesn't push me into bad memories as her face did. It lays a hand on my chest and empties it of the bad things.

I need to hear that voice again.

Sunny

12

"You know I don't think of you like that, right?" Cara asks, nudging me with her rounded elbow. Her long blonde hair waves like yellow silk over her shoulder.

I nod. Cara is easy to figure out. She wears her whole personality on the outside of her clothes, blaring like a neon light for everyone to see. I like that about her. She's a walking advertisement for herself.

"You're my girl!" she sings to the windshield.

I smile. One small piece of armor sliding from my body. "You're a good friend, Cara."

She speeds up to overtake someone and winks at me as she slides in front of the car. "Your Ama must be so proud, right?"

I shrug. Who knows? Right now, she's just super pissed at me. "Maybe."

"Oh, screw her if she isn't!" Cara shouts proudly as she turns onto my street.

My eyes widen, and I bite my lip. I pull Cara apart and put her back together, making sure I remind myself that her family is very different to mine. She is made of the same things as me, skin, bones, neatly packed and organized organs. But her life, her family…it's like they're made up of some other element I haven't heard of. She talks back, she mouths off, and they laugh. I don't know if Ama would actually strike me hard, but I'm too terrified to even test it out. Visions of her waving a fireplace poker in her hand flash across my mind. Cara speaks to her parents in ways I would never even dream about.

"Ama just doesn't want me to move across the country," I say in her defense. *"Elle va me manquer."* She'll miss me.

Cara snorts. "What's that, Frenchie? You're doing it again."

I smile; the slip is delicious like crème pâtissière. It reminds me with a nudge of the tongue that I'm so much more than what the man at the store saw. "Sorry. I said she'll miss me."

Cara parks her olive-green station wagon a mile from the curb and touches my arm. "What about your grandfather?"

Gung would never say it, but I know he'll miss me too. I think about leaving him alone with Ama and shudder. She's too much for any one person to handle. "Gung just wants me to be happy."

I want that too. I just don't know how to figure out what will actually make me happy. I touch my chest. Not until the concrete shifts.

"Out you get!" she says, shoving me toward the door. "See you tomorrow?"

I nod again and exit the car.

Before she leaves, she winds down the window and says, "And hey. Don't worry about that jerk from this morning. He's a jerk with a jerk face and a jerk filling!" She grins and speeds off, leaving me to ponder 'the jerk' from this morning and whether she's right.

Because he's also a veteran, with an unknown filling, and an unknown reason for his behavior.

Walking up the stairs, I pause and bend down, plucking some stubborn weeds from the hard earth. I shake the dirt from them and look at the struggling roots before tossing them in the garden bed. *Is he just a jerk?* Seems like there must be more to it than that. At least, that's what I'd like to believe.

I sigh, wishing I could be like Cara sometimes. To stop searching for the reasons behind things and just accept the world for what it is and all the jerks in it.

The smell of garlic and peanut oil seeps from the front porch, luring me inside and throwing my thoughts into the frying pan. I walk up, my foot hovering over the last cracked bit of peeling concrete. I open my ears and smile wide as I listen to the cackling and coughing coming from within.

"You love my voice, eh?" Ama shouts as metal clatters in musical harmony.

"I love you to shut up!" Gung grumbles.

Ama starts humming out of tune. I can picture Gung's surly expression. His eyes following her around the room like they're trying to decipher one tiny particle of the code that makes her, but then he'll give up. We always give up.

I take off my shoes and open the door.

I'm looking at my rainbow-striped socks when a white china bowl comes flying at my knees. I jump out of the way, and the bowl hits the doorframe and bounces off without breaking. "Ama! What the he…heck?" I manage to avoid saying hell before my intensely religious grandmother slaps me.

"See, George! Doesn't break." She throws another bowl my way like a Frisbee, and I sidestep as it skitters across the cork floor with a clanging marble kind of sound.

I giggle and step into the lounge, kissing Gung on the cheek, inhaling his sweet tobacco smell just as he runs a hand through his thinning hair and shouts at Ama, "You crazy woman!"

"It's Corr Relle!" She says it like it's two words, not one, and like that should explain her throwing crockery. My eyes turn to the kitchen and the dining set strewn across the floor. Ama stands on her tiptoes in the small spaces between the overlapping plates and bowls, knees bent as if she's considering jumping out of the mess she's created.

I put my hand up to stop her. "Ama, let me help you pick all this up." I kneel and start stacking the plates.

"Twenty-five percent off, Sun," she whispers, squatting down on her haunches to help me. She has the balance of a gymnast, leaning her thighs against the back of her calves with ease. Whenever I try to do that, I fall backward. But that could also be because she usually tries to knock me over with the end of a broom.

Ama grins, all red lipstick and white powder, and I smirk. She looks half like a Geisha and half like a forgotten Beatle with her died black hair and pageboy cut.

Gung coughs and strains his ears to hear us. "How much you pay for all this?"

Ama winks at me and lies, "Ten dollars the lot."

He accepts this, although I'm sure he suspects she's lying.

After we rise, she places a bowl in front of me at the counter, serving up some sweet corn soup. I lift the spoon to my mouth.

She asks, "How was rest of day at work. Make any tips?"

"Only from that one guy, you know, the weird one," I mumble.

She shrugs, turning her back to me to rattle a frying pan on the hob.

I take a sip, swallow, stall…

I reach for my spoon again, and Ama grabs my wrist. "You mean the army man who gave you hating eyes because you Eurasian?" she asks, narrowing her eyes at me.

I wonder what she'll say. I never know with her. What side she'll pick.

"Yeah, that one," I start, looking to Gung. He has angled his whole body my way, but he hasn't deemed this conversation worthy of getting all the way out of his chair. I feel more comfortable addressing him. "Though I don't think it's because I'm Eurasian, Ama. I think it's just because I look Asian."

Ama snaps to attention, grasping my chin and pulling it toward her fierce eyes. "Nothing wrong with way you look. You beautiful Eurasian girl." She traces under my eyes with her wrinkled finger. "Eyes like watermelon seeds…"

I smile and try to pull back. "He's a Vietnam veteran. Maybe I reminded him of something bad," I mutter, defending the guy. "Anyway, it doesn't matter. I doubt he'll come back in again, and I got to keep his change."

Ama turns to Gung and says proudly, "I gave him my finger. The middle one! But then…he is soldier."

She sighs very loudly. Everything exaggerated. "Maybe we can be generous to him."

I roll my eyes. Gung rolls his eyes too. The way she flips back and forth is exhausting.

"Are you all right, Sun?" he asks.

I shake my head. "Nothing a Douglas can't handle," I say proudly, sitting up straighter in my seat.

"I saw you roll the eyes at me, Sunny. Rolling around like marble in bowl." Ama waggles her finger at me, dangerously tipping into a temper. "American soldiers save your life. You should be grateful."

I know. I remember.

But it wasn't this exact soldier. It wasn't his hand that reached for me in the rubble.

"Maybe when you doctor, you fix all the soldiers," she announces, and I bow my head to look like I'm agreeing with her.

First, I need to fix what's wrong with me.

Gung flicks on the TV, turning up the volume and trying to stop the conversation from happening. The one about college and where I'm going to go, but Ama's not that easily distracted tonight.

She comes around the counter to stand in front of me. I look up from where I sit on my stool.

"Ama. *S'il vous plaît*. Please. Can we not have this conversation? I don't have to decide just yet."

Gung clears his throat and speaks, softly but firmly. "Annie. Leave the girl in peace. Let her enjoy her good fortunes for one day."

Ama glares at Gung, and then her gaze settles on me. "You lucky I listen to Gung."

Gung snorts and waves her over to watch *Wheel of Fortune.*

I know I'm lucky.

BREAKER

13

"Breaker. You've got to stop flicking your cigarette butts all over the porch," Mom scolds as soon as I walk in the door. "It looks like the front of a biker bar out there."

I sigh, shrugging, and give her an unpleasant look. Little Red smashes into my knees, and I curse. It makes Red giggle and Mom's voice raise another octave.

"Don't curse like that in the house!" she snaps

"So, what, it's okay to curse outside the house?" I ask. Stepping outside the front door, I shout, "Damn it all to hell," and then step back inside.

Mom's tanned face has gone all red, and she stands up from the couch. "You know what I mean. What's the matter with you?" Her expression drops down to pain and exasperation.

I shake my head, staring down at the floor, not really sure myself. When I lift my eyes, her face is full of pity, which I hate even more than the anger. "What's for dinner?" I ask, knowing full well that's going to light a match to the fuse.

Her fists clench as she looks at Red. "Red, honey, go to your room and play for a while."

Red's head snaps up, and he grins lopsidedly. "You're gonna fight, aren't ya?"

She nods. I step back.

The bedroom door closes, and she turns back to me. "I know you've found it hard to assimilate back into civilian life."

"Assimilate?" I snarl. "That's a big word for you. Did you overhear that from one of your clients while you were scrubbing their toilet?"

She sweeps her dyed blonde hair behind her ear and growls at me. "At least I'm working. I'm doing something to support this family. While you, you..." Her pointer finger hangs in the air, shaking.

Guilt. Guilt splaying open to anger.

She can't possibly understand.

I throw my hands up in the air and storm into my room, grabbing a flashlight. When I come out, I shake it in the air. She steps away from me like she's worried I'm going to hit her with it. It hurts me more than I could imagine. I lower the flashlight and barely whisper, "I'm outta here."

She yells after me. "If you're not going to college, you need to start pulling your weight, Breaker. That money should be used for something other than smokes and gas."

I shiver and my heart drops down an inch or two at the way she says my name, like she hates it, like it's not my name anymore. The shine of green on a palm leaf is like the inside of my eyelids.

Breaker. Breaker of the iceberg. The titanic. Sinking. "We'll call you Iceman!" Sargent announces, slapping me on my shaking back. I shrink away from his touch. Hunched over, scared someone's going to single me out.

Sargent dips his head to catch my eyes and smiles.

"Don't worry, Iceman. No need to be so scared. You probably won't even see active duty."

I move down the street as if I'm fighting against the current of a river. I just need to keep my head above water. Need to find a way across. A way to fix it. Fix me.

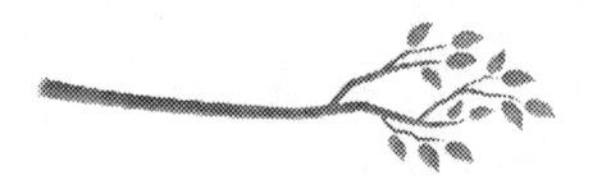

The tree finds me easily. It only takes a few minutes to get there this time, which is odd considering the hours it took me to get home last time. Almost like it has moved closer. I laugh sadly. I'm losing it. I must've just got turned around last night.

Night will close in soon, and I slam my back against the wide trunk. Closing my eyes, I wait. I listen. I hope the girl shows up.

The bark is warm, comfortable, and I'm so goddamned tired. It feels like arms wrapping around me, keeping me safe while I rest.

Dragging a hand across my face, I whisper to the dark, "Are you there?"

I get no answer, just an owl hooting and bugs that have no sense to hide underground in this weather chirping.

Looking up, I groan a deep, painful noise that sums up my frustration with the world and how I don't seem to fit into it anymore. The leaves catch my pain and hold it, seem to suspend it. As I stare up, the branches seem to part, make shapes before me, cutting the sky into segments. They creak and call to the stars, and I join them.

Help me. Make this life easier.

I scrunch my eyes and then relax, letting the numbness coursing through my body nurse me toward sleep. My heart still hoping, never learning.

I don't know what I was thinking would happen anyway.

BREAKER 14

The sun may never come. Those bright light spokes waving over the land like hope are distant to this place. If the sun rises, it rises sloth-like. Dirty and disgusted with the rest of us down here, scratching at the earth, searching in the wrong direction.

Opening my eyes, I find it hard to adjust to the light. Here against the tree, it's dark, sheltered, so time is hard to tell. But I feel that weird disorientation of being asleep for a few hours. Groggy and drugged. I yawn and jump up, my hands still pressed to the burly trunk. I ask again, "Are you there?" The dark answers with silence.

Shrugging, I step away from the tree, leaving its umbrella of darkness and hopping over the brook. The ground holds my feet like I'm walking through fresh tar, and I pull away forcefully.

Sound bursts open like I've been in a bubble. Birds sing to the setting sun, and I stare up at the pale bulb in confusion. It should be nighttime. I arrived here just as the sun was setting, and I've been sitting and sleeping against the tree for hours. I work to understand, but can't—a persistent, heavy fog clouds my lazy brain.

I walk out of the woods, the branches ushering me from their home almost urgently, spiked branches poking me in the back and dragging down my jacket.

As I stalk down the street, I hope Mom has calmed down after our fight. I hope she hasn't circled menial jobs in the wanted ads for me or, worse, phoned a college.

I crash up the crumbling stairs, and they whine under my weight. Inside, Mom stands exactly where I left her, hands on hips. "What?" she snaps. "Did you forget something? Or do you have another insult you'd like to throw at me?"

I pause in the doorway, the screen door smacking my back. Raising my eyebrows, I open my mouth to speak, but she cuts me off. "I thought you just *had* to get outta here, Breaker."

My foot presses into the welcome mat, brushing away dark mud and confusion. "What are you talking about? I've been gone for hours?" My voice is high and unsure. Because nothing makes sense right now. Mom laughs in a stilted, panicked way and Red comes from his room, arms swinging at his sides, staring with wide eyes.

My comment has thrown her. Mom's hands release their grip on her hips, and she stares wide-eyed at me too. She leans in and sniffs the air around me. "Have you been smoking pot?" she asks sternly. Red giggles, and her head snaps around to him like the twang of a rubber band.

I shake my head vehemently. "No!" I run my fingers through my hair, my hand coming to rest on my neck, pressing down on all the little hairs that are standing on end.

She's still gawking at me like I'm crazy and she wants an explanation. I don't have one. Maybe I'm just tired. Confused. I don't know. I sleep so badly that maybe a five-minute nap feels like hours to me.

I finally enter the living room and Red comes to stand between us, his hands out like he's breaking up a bar fight. Streams of orange-tinged light pour through the splits in the blinds, and my heart feels a little singed.

"Mom, I have a really important question to ask you," Red says, blinking up at us. Grateful, I step around the two of them and head for the fridge.

Mom sighs, exasperated by me. By the whole situation. "Sure, honey. What is it?"

He ties his hands behind his back and looks up at her, acting all innocent. "Can I have my friend Jacob over on the weekend? His parents said it would be fine. They said they could drop him off after church. Please." He says all this in one breath. I let out a strained laugh, quickly swallowing it when I remember Jacob is Jake, the Asian kid from school.

Hand on the fridge door, I say, "Uh, Red, I don't think that's such a great idea..."

Mom's eyes raze through me like lasers as she says to Red, while still glaring at me. "Of course you can, sweetie. I can't wait to meet him."

I want to pull the blinds closed on this scene. Shut out the light. She doesn't realize what she's agreed to. But I can't even bring myself to tell her.

Mom pats my head and gently pushes me into the group of children getting ready to board the bus. Leaning down, she whispers in my six-year-old ear, "Why don't you sit next to that kid there? He looks friendly." She points at the short, smiling kid with coppery skin, shiny dark hair, and almost black eyes. When he smiles, his teeth look as white as fresh paper and he's wearing a Mickey Mouse Club backpack. I like him already.

I point to him and ask, "That kid with the Mickey Mouse backpack? Okay, Mom." I start walking toward him.

Grabbing my arm, she yanks me back hard. She digs her nails into my shoulders and turns me toward another kid with pale skin and blond hair. "No, that kid there," she says, narrowing her eyes and lowering her voice. "The one with the blond hair and green backpack. Stay away from that other kid, Breaker. You hear me? You can't trust people like him."

Sunny

15

A blurry, cream-colored blob hovers over my face. As my eyes start to focus, I can pick out the details of a long, linen robe and a bearded face with a knowing, serene expression. Plastic Jesus is very disappointed in me, I can tell.

Ama taps his face to my forehead like he's kissing me and places the figure carefully down on my bedside table. Then she pokes my cheek in with her finger until it presses against my teeth. "You come to church today," she orders, tart perfume wafting from her neck.

I grip the covers and try to pull them over my head, but she's holding them tight in her uncannily strong hands. "Not today, Ama," I say quietly but firmly. *Not ever.*

She releases my covers and stamps her foot. Jesus wobbles on the table, looking a little concerned for his safety now. "Not today. Not ever!" she exclaims, exasperated with my lack of faith.

Groaning, I roll over. I would do almost anything for Ama and Gung, but I'm not going to church. Going to church makes me a liar. I don't believe what she believes, though I sometimes wish I did. It would be so much easier.

She huffs and marches from my room. This is one argument she won't win. She attributes my survival after the bombing to God. I attribute it to beams falling the right way, to me standing just south of the giant chandelier that hung in the middle of the lobby. When it came crashing down like cut icicles, it was just chance. Nothing more. And a lot less.

Her faint complaining drifts from the kitchen to my ears. Gung's response protects me, catches me like a net. "You can't force her. She decide for herself."

"We going!" she shouts angrily down the hallway. Then, hopefully, she croons, "We get Dairy Queen after..."

When she gets no response, she shouts a collection of rude words in Chinese and storms out the door.

I don't get out of bed until I hear the Cortina backing out of the driveway.

Wiping my eyes, I yawn. I'm still a little on edge. It wouldn't be the first time Ama has hidden and jumped out to surprise me with a cross in one hand and a rosary in the other.

"It's my dying wish for you to become Catholic," she'd lamented once.

"Um. You can't have a dying wish. You're not dying," I'd replied.

She pursed her lips and grimaced. "I want it now. Why wait until I'm dying? How I know you fulfill my wish?"

I snorted. This was Ama-Logic. I didn't say what I wanted to say, which was, *Wouldn't God tell you, you know, up in Heaven?* That would set her temper on raging fire, so I just ended the conversation.

Now, as I peek around the wall lined with old family photos, my shoulder rattles the one of my mother and father on their wedding day. They both look so serious when neither of them were serious at all. My mom's hair is pulled and rolled tight in a classic Chinese hairdo. My dad looks stiff in his military uniform. They stare blankly just left of the lens. Maybe looking at Ama gesticulating behind the photographer... I touch my finger to the faded black-and-white photo, wishing I believed they were watching over me right now, that they were happy and together somewhere nice where everyone gets free Dairy Queen for eternity. Not rotting in a French graveyard in Vietnam that's most likely been desecrated several times by now.

I picture bad things and gulp, turning my thoughts to the outside. The window is bordered in condensation.

The frost draws prickly patterns on the forest floor, preparing for winter. I walk to the kitchen and put the kettle on to boil, warming my hands around the outside.

This place couldn't be more different to where we came from. But then, I guess that's the point.

There are few reminders of my old life here in the Catskills. What was white is brown. What was open to the humid air is closed and cozy in the cold. What was grand is now modest. I like it this way. I need it this way.

I shudder, grabbing Gung's coat from the back of his chair and pulling it over my narrow shoulders. It smells of sweet tobacco and sawdust. I wrap it tight and pull the French toast wrapped in tinfoil Ama left for me from the fridge.

I usually study on Sundays, but now that college

offers have come, I don't feel very motivated.

Sitting at the kitchen bench, picking at the soft toast, I flip through the newspaper and wonder what I should do. My mind ticks back to the tree. The feeling of time not moving the way it should, the bathwater swishing at the base of the tub. I tap my chin with a pencil. I've been to that tree hundreds of times since we moved here, and it's never happened before. The only factor that was different was the man with the cigarettes.

I drink the rest of my lukewarm tea and stalk to my room to change.

If anything, it will provide me with a distraction until Ama and Gung get home.

As I'm pulling on a sweater, I grimace at the thought of another lecture about church from Ama. That spurs me on. I layer my clothes, pack some food in my backpack, and head out into the blasting cold, determined to be wrong.

16

After our argument, Mom won't even look at me. She talks, but through the side of her face, her eyes distant, her fluffy hair hiding her expression. Brushing blue eyeshadow over her lids as she stares at herself in the mirror, she says, "So I guess *you're* not coming to church?"

I shake my head.

Through puckered lips, she hisses, "I'm thinking of changing congregations anyway. Since those new families moved to the neighborhood, it just doesn't feel..." She coats her mouth with cheap lipstick and presses her lips together to even it out; it's the color of cheese wax. "The same."

Red strolls in wearing his church clothes and grins at me. His buttons are done up all wrong, and I bend down to fix them. I pat the top of his head, noticing it feels rather crunchy. "I think you've overdone it with the hair gel, kid." I smirk, and he frowns. Smoothing his shirt, he blinks up at me. I force a smile. He returns it with his crooked, giant front teeth. Poor kid. I hope he grows into that mouth of his. "Nah, forget what I said. It makes you looks older." I wink.

Red hits Mom on the butt, and she jumps. "Don't forget about Jacob coming over after church, kay?" She smoothes out her church skirt and blouse. All powder blue and polyester. Her cheeks are already bright red from overheating.

She turns and smiles, patting his bird's nest hair. "Of course not, honey! I even bought cherry popsicles for the occasion."

This turns grown-up Red back into a little kid, and he hyperactively zooms around our small living room in excitement.

I should tell her Jacob is not who she thinks he is, but I don't. Maybe it's revenge. Or maybe it's because, unlike me, she has no reason to feel the way she does. Before the war, I tried so hard to unlearn her lessons. To see people clearly. But atrocity can't be unseen. The memories are racked up inside me, playing like records on an endless loop. They mar my view.

I don't want Red to be like me. Hooked together with hate and fear.

I don't want to be like me either.

The coward in me jumps forward though, and I opt for absence. "Have a great time with your friend, Red," I say. "I probably won't be here when you get back from church. I've got some things to do."

Red groans, and Mom rolls her eyes. "Aw. Can we play in your room?" he asks hopefully.

Both Mom and I say, "No!" at the same time.

My feet lead me back there. It's like marching in line. Troops following an imaginary thread, believing they are safer in numbers. My heart twists, and I thump it with my fist. Numbers scatter just the same as any living thing when threatened. They fall flat to the ground when shot at; they bleed and seep slowly into the wet ground.

My hands shake as I walk down the deserted Sunday street. The layers of gray and brown of the timber buildings are like uncreative paintings. There is little color to break it up, but I kind of like the predictability of it.

I take a long drag of my cigarette, hands still vibrating.

I want to be like Red, I tell myself as I climb over a sagging fence and enter the edge of the woods.

Padding over dead leaves that make reminiscent squelching noises, I search for the ugly tree, retracing my footsteps. I arrive at where I think it will be, but it's not there. Thin birches cover this part of the forest, knitted together like prison bars. I squat down and smack the frozen earth. It should be right here.

Raking a hand through my hair, I exhale smoke and frustration.

It was right here. I point at the ground like I expect it to sprout up between the squashed weeds at my feet.

Weary, I think about giving up and heading home, but my want to avoid Jacob and Mom overpowers my laziness so I trek on, listening for sounds of water and hoping they will lead me to the tree.

The sun burns down between the leafless trees and pounds my forehead. I duck my head. It's not the heat that bothers me. It's the light. In the shadows, I can hide. The sun tries to break me open. I pull my collar up in a weak attempt to shield myself. *You can't lie to the light.*

I move faster, my head swinging back and forth, my ears listening for those tears over rocks. It can't be far now.

Pausing in the comfortable shadow of a large pine, I take a drink. My head feels hot, but the rest of me shivers with icy cold. I curse and kick the ground. *What am I doing here?*

I turn around, thinking this was a stupid idea. A voice can't fix what's inside me. There are pieces I left behind. Missing pieces I can't recover.

"Goddamn it!" I shout, scaring the birds scratching in the undergrowth.

"Sh! *Silence*. Quiet. The Christians might hear you." Her voice pierces the shaggy forest, and I walk toward it. Following tiny laughter, bleeding through the trees like liquid silver.

Peering around a spiky bush, I see one thin leg wearing blue flares stretched out over a knobbly root. Red-and-white striped socks stand out against her buckled shoes. I creep closer, careful to approach the tree from the opposite side so she can't see my face. My hand reaches for one of the tumorous growths as I step over the brook, and it feels abnormally warm, like skin. I sit down between two roots pouring like lava into the water.

I don't hear her leave.

Waves of silence float through branches and pull at the last remaining leaves. I watch them skate through the air in front of me. Wishing I was that light.

"Are you dangerous?" she asks. "Not that you'd tell me if you were, I guess…" she mumbles to herself. "Murderers probably don't introduce themselves like,

'Hey, nice to meet you. What do you do for a living? Accountant? *C'est bien*. That's nice. Me? Oh, I'm a murderer…'"

An unfamiliar chuckle softly echoes in my chest. It's solitary. Lonely. "I'm not dangerous," I answer, and the chuckle squeezes between my ribs and gets away from me as I realize I cannot say, *'I'm not a murderer.'*

She shuffles in the cushion of dead leaves and sighs. "Why are you here?"

I prop my arms up on the roots like they're the arms of a chair, letting them support me. "I'm not really sure. Why are you here?"

"To test a theory." I sense that she's stood and is about to come around to my side of the tree. My heart pounds. The water rushing past suddenly seems like it will flood and wash me away.

She pokes her head around the trunk and says, "Hi. I'm Sunny."

I lift my jacket to my face and turn away from her before she can see me. Into the thick canvas, I say, "If it's okay with you, I'd rather you didn't see my face."

My smoky breath suffocates me.

"*Quoi*? What? Why? Are you a wanted man?" she asks. "Am I going to see your face on a poster?" Her voice is musing but slightly on edge.

Think of something quick. "I'm, uh…I'm badly scarred. My face is, um, all messed up. And truth be told, it scares most people away."

I am a bad, bad person. *The worst.*

I can feel her hovering over me as I'm buried in my jacket. "Oh, I don't care about that kind of thing," she trills.

Still hiding my face, I whisper tersely, "But I do, Sunny." This part is true. I truly do care if she sees my face right now. If she recognizes me from the store, it will all be over.

Sounding disappointed, she mutters, "Okay. I'll go back to the other side now."

She moves away. I wait until she sits back down before I say, "My name's Breaker. And thanks."

Her soft accent rolls over the knobbly bark and nestles in my ears. "So what happened to your face, er, Breaker? Surely that can't be your real name."

I pull my knees to my chest and let my head collapse between them. "Sadly, it is. Um. My face…" I close my eyes. A flash of a bad memory crosses my lids, and I clench my teeth. *A bullet tearing through his cheek, shattering his teeth. Ragged skin dripping like red ivy from his jaw.* I shudder and the tree softens behind me, warming my back, making me feel…relaxed.

Sunny speaks, her words like warm steam from a cup. Comforting. Inviting. "It's okay. You don't have to tell me."

It makes me want to tell her something even if it's not my story. "I was shot in the face…in Vietnam," I tell her.

"I'm sorry." And she sounds like she genuinely means it.

I don't say *'it's okay'* or *'thank you'*. I'm so tired of saying things like that. "Sunny is a pretty strange name too."

She sighs, and it sounds like something light and free. "Yeah, my name is Soleil, which is French for the sun," she says in a flawless French accent. "Sunny is just easier for people to spell and pronounce."

So, is she French? French Asian?

Dipping my fingers into the leafy debris, I watch bugs flee from the soil in my hands. "What's this theory you're testing?" I ask.

I can almost see her tapping her chin. Thinking whether to trust me. She decides not to. "Hypotheses are very personal things, Mr. Breaker… Er, what's your last name?"

I roll my eyes and groan, giving her the truth. "Van Winkle."

She snorts delicately. "And you said my name was funny! Are you kidding?"

If only.

"Breaker Van Winkle," she says, testing my name out. I like the way it sounds coming out of her mouth, softened by her accent like it could come from someplace else. "It has a strange ring to it. Like it's the name of a character in a book or a villain in a movie." She laughs, mostly talking to herself. "Wa-ha-ha, you've not seen the last of Breaker Van Winkle!" She puts on a Russian accent, and I roll my eyes.

"Anyway… Okay. If you don't want to talk about your theory, why don't we talk about something else?" I ask, wanting to skip over my stupid name and the questions that follow. I look up at the sky. The steely clouds seem to hover right over the branches. Wind tickles my skin, but the clouds don't move. It's like they're listening in on our conversation.

But she's stuck on my name. "Is it a family name? Breaker, I mean?"

I rub my chin and sigh. "No. My dad's name was

Rush." Might as well get it over with since she won't let it go.

"Rush? Like in a rush? Wow. Oh, I am sorry," she says laughing, but then it stops like a shut-off tap. "What do you mean *was*?"

"He took off. A long time ago."

"Oh."

"Yeah, so, I think that's enough about me for now. Can I ask you a question?"

"Sure," Sunny says brightly.

Trepidation bites at my tongue. "Where are you from?"

"That's a complicated question with a complicated answer," she says.

"I'm twenty-one. An adult according to the government. Apparently, I can handle abstract concepts and complicated answers," I say, enjoying how easy this has become in such a short time. She laughs, and I swear the remaining leaves around me shake.

Sunny

17

I'm fascinated by someone whose scars are on the outside of their body. Having only dealt with internal ones, this is something new, something I'd like to explore. The fact that he's a soldier also makes me wonder. I was on the civilian side of the war. The innocent bystander who got caught up in the violence.

I've seen the way some of the vets have been treated since they returned home. What must it be like to be on the losing side of a war a lot of people think they shouldn't be fighting in the first place? I shudder when I think about the things he must have seen.

Breaker clears his throat, reminding me that I haven't answered his question.

"Oh, right... Where am I from?" I start my spiel. "I was born in England. My mother *was* Malaysian-Chinese-Irish and my father *was* French. We traveled a lot because he was a diplomat. His last post was in Vietnam, which, up until the war, had very strong ties with France... So, um, that's where I came from before I moved here."

"Well, that certainly explains your accent," he says in a quiet, thinking kind of tone. "Why did you say 'was' about your parents?"

I grin, which is a strange reaction to his question. Because, obviously, he's asking whether my parents are still alive. There's a little of Ama in me after all as I do enjoy shocking people. "My parents were killed when the French embassy was bombed. I live with my Malaysian-Chinese-Irish grandparents now. We immigrated here after the bombing."

Leaves shuffle and his boot taps the edge of one of the roots. It sounds solid and hollow at the same time. My grin has slipped from my face as dust threatens to clog my lungs. Clouds gather around my body, pushing, pushing, but I put my hands up, trying to keep it at bay. I lean hard against the trunk, a small, warm pulse seeming to flow through the bark and into my skin. It's soothing. I blink slowly and yawn.

My eyes pop open when he says, "Malaysian-Chinese-Irish-French. Interesting mix..." There's a tightness to his voice that wasn't there before. It's like a vine is slowly choking him. "What's your last name? Can't be as bad as Van Winkle."

That name. The leaves above tremble gently.

The sky is still and hazy. A bluish light settling over the branches. I breathe in. The smell of damp, decaying things is everywhere. My eyes droop, sleepy. "La Chance," I answer with a yawn.

He yawns too. "I like that. La Chance." He butchers the name with his American accent. "Sounds like Last Chance."

I pull my legs up and roll my arms over the blackish branches, scarred but still growing, like me. The morning seems murky. When I peer out toward the rest of the forest, it feels like I'm staring at one tree repeated a thousand times in a mirror. I blink in confusion.

"Do you feel...?" I start. I stretch my arms, which

feel leadenly hard to lift.

But then he says, "So Last Chance, are your grandparents at church with the rest of the town?"

His voice brings me back to alertness. "Yes."

"My mom's there too with my little brother," he rambles. "Church isn't really my thing, I mean, I believe in God, but…I don't know. There's something about it that doesn't sit well with me after everything I've seen…"

A crow squawks close by, although it sounds like its being smothered by a blanket. My fingers dig deep into the trunk of the tree, spongy pieces crumbling in my fingers, rotted through. The rushing water sounds quieter than before, humming like a struggling Hoover in the background.

Breaker speaks again, and his voice is stronger than before. Louder. "Seems like maybe we've both seen some pretty horrible things."

My head snaps to the side, my ear pressing into the trunk, a whispering snore coming from beneath the bark. "I never *said* I'd seen horrible things." The roots around me close in, hold me like a mother's arms.

A huge sigh that almost sounds like a whistle at the end. "This may sound strange, but I can tell by your voice that you were with them, your parents, when it happened."

"Oh." I squirm uncomfortably. The conversation is turning on me.

"Sorry," he says.

"Sorry is such a pointless word. Anyway, don't be. It wasn't your fault." Breaker is quiet for a moment. He then proceeds to ask me lots of personal, but not too personal, questions.

How old are you?

Eighteen.

Where do you go to school?

Tri-Valley

Do you speak French?

Yes, fluently.

Are you going to college?

Yes

It's like he's trying to peel the first superficial layer from my body. I can feel the air of him trying to get to know me pushing under my jacket. Thing is—I don't really mind it.

In turn, I ask him questions too. We talk like this, back and forth, for maybe about an hour. I'm not sure. Time seems unimportant. An afterthought.

I pat my stomach. I don't know how long it's been, but it gurgles. I start thinking about Ama and Gung getting home and wondering where I am. Lifting my wrist to my eyes, I check for the time, forgetting I'm not wearing a watch. Small pieces of bark are stuck to my skin like dragon scales, and I scratch them off. They leave a tea-colored stain.

"I think I better get going," I say, starting to get up. My hands hold the tree trunk like they need it to stand, like they don't want to let go.

"Oh, okay. Yeah, it must be nearly lunchtime," Breaker says, voice sounding disappointed.

"Maybe I'll see you back here again sometime?" I say, high pitched and nervous.

It's like this was a blind date. Quite literally since I never got to see his face.

His darkened voice replies, "I'd like that." And I feel a blush creeping over my tanned cheeks.

I step away from the tree and into the sun, breaking through its shadow like I'm pushing through a thin skin. The warm air turns sourly cold the minute I come out from beneath the branches. I don't look back, trying to respect his wishes.

I squint up at the sky. The way the sun sits high over the land as if pasted on the end of a flagpole, I know it must be around midday. I stroll through the gaps in the trees, swinging between them, feeling somewhat lighter. Like he took something from me, something I didn't need nor want, then crushed it in his hands and made it disappear. *Like magic.*

BREAKER

18

I wait until I'm sure she's gone before I get up. It feels hard to move, my body stiff and drawn to the ground like a magnet. Gripping the trunk, I pull up. I release my grasp on the trunk, stretching, and almost fall forward.

Bars of sunlight poke through the branches, trying to stab at me, and I move into the shadow of a large bush.

I touch my heart, and my hand gets snagged in my clothes. I turn it over and inspect the tips of my fingers. They are caked with broken bits of bark. I scratch at my skin, finding the bark hard to remove. Sticky sap glues the pieces to me. I stare wide-eyed at them, wondering how they came to be there without me noticing. But then, I was so caught up in our conversation I didn't notice much of anything except her voice.

Her voice. I like how her voice doesn't fit with her face. It makes this easier. Easier is better.

She didn't recognize me—that much is sure. I sigh with relief and shame for how I acted in the store. Cursing myself for not making an actual time to meet her again. Whatever she's making me feel, I want to feel it again. Somewhere between healing and forgetting.

I reach for my cigarettes, realizing I haven't touched them the whole time we were talking. My fingers tremble as I pull one from the carton. A breeze blows my match out, and I curse. My words whisper back to me, echoing against nothing but air. I cringe. Without her here, this place gives me the creeps. I take another step away from the tree, feeling a pull backward like I left something behind. I turn to the tree, a weird heat crawling up my neck.

The wind tickles the branches and pokes into the hollows, creating an almost human sound. Like the woods are talking with volume turned way down.

I frown. Stare at it for a moment, waiting for something strange to happen. But the woods quiet down. Normal noises like creaking wood and tiny paws scurrying through leaves are all my ears can catch now.

Yawning, I pat my open mouth. It's just an ugly tree, nothing more.

I pick a path littered with gray leaves that leads upward and walk away from it, energized with new strength. I need to kill some time before heading back home. I don't want to be there when Red has his friend over.

Sunny

19

I'm still scratching my hands of sticky bits of bark when I enter the dirty gray field that sits behind our house. The sun is high. I lick my lips, parched and hungry and kind of hoping Ama and Gung got me Dairy Queen even though I didn't come to church with them.

I walk fast, staring at my feet to avoid the various rocks and decaying logs that litter this backyard. The house is dark with shadows; the wooden shingles hang over each other in a wobbly pattern like pulse lines. I don't notice the red lights bouncing off the glass of the kitchen window until I'm up on the back porch and kicking off my shoes.

Footsteps thunder toward the back door. It swings open, and Ama's stricken face appears. I don't recognize her at first. She's without makeup, dark freckles color her cheeks, and she looks like she hasn't slept in days. My first thought is—*Gung*.

I open my mouth to speak, but it's gone all dry and cracked. That cough, that cough of his, it didn't sound right. He's been wheezing and groaning for weeks now. He's old, but not that old. It could be his lungs or his heart or, or, or…

Ama's cold hands grab my face and squeeze as hard they can. My jaw aches from the pressure. "Sunny," she exhales like a prayer. "Sunny." She squeezes my cheeks together still harder, making it impossible to speak. "Where you been all this time?"

She pulls my face inside and my body drags with it, one of her feet still on top of my foot.

Inside, a police officer in his socks leans against the kitchen counter with a steaming bowl of soup at his elbow. I search for Gung. Usually when they get home from church, he takes a nap in his chair. He's not there.

Finally, she releases my face, so I can talk. "What do you mean by *all this time*? Where's Gung? Why are the police here?" I gulp, air not coming in. I'm a fish on land. *Throw me back. Throw me back.* "Did something happen to Gung? Ama?" My eyes dart from her to the policeman and back again.

Ama cracks. Her knees buckle, and she grabs at a bar stool to steady herself. "Why you run away? You nearly kill me. And Gung, his heart, it's broken." She claps her hands together violently and pulls them apart to demonstrate broken. "We so worried for you, Sunny. We call police, but they say you not missing long enough. Gung search the woods..." She comes at me then, grabbing both my shoulders and shaking me violently. "Why you do this to us?"

I stumble back, my foot catching on the burgundy rug. "*Quoi*? What?" I smile, thinking this is some prank of Ama's. I look to the policeman for confirmation, but his eyes are so serious. He lifts the soup bowl to his mouth and sips directly from it without a spoon before carefully placing it back down on the bench.

Finally, the policeman speaks. "Miss La Chance," he begins. "Your grandmother called us this morning to file a missing person's report. But since you have returned, I see no point in investigating further." Ama's nails are biting into my shoulders. "As long as you promise next time you decide to go on a trip for a few days, you inform your grandparents. They were very worried about you, young lady."

I step back from Ama, shaking out of her grip and glancing out the window at the police car, the red lights circling, circling with no siren. Nausea begins to take over. I manage a nod.

A few days. The words make no sense.

A few days? How could I have been gone for days? It's a mistake. It has to be.

The officer still hovers, waiting for me to say something. I can feel Ama's temper building behind me, growing like a cloud of black smoke, filling the room.

"I'm sorry, Officer. It will never happen again," I say quietly and nod, blood draining from my face.

Gung appears, shuffling from the hallway, looking pained and pale. "Thank you, Officer," he says. "Sorry for the trouble."

I still don't understand what's going on. As I watch the police car pull out from the driveway, I have this horrible feeling. This gray, oppressive feeling I can't quite name.

Gung collapses in his chair. He looks exhausted, and I kneel on the rug beside him. Ama hovers in the background with her hands on her hips, scowling.

"Have I really been gone for days?" I ask, scared of the answer.

He nods solemnly. "Gone two days." He holds up two devastating fingers.

"I...I..." I need to explain, but I don't have an answer. He looks so hurt, so disappointed, and it kills me. "I'm sorry," I say weakly.

He waves me away, avoiding my eyes.

I get up, tears starting to well. This isn't my fault. It can't be. I turn to face Ama. Her teeth are clenched, her eyes popping with rage.

"You tell me where you been? Is it boy? Is it drinking?" She stands so close I can smell the Imperial Leather soap on her skin. I shake my head, swallowing down the theories. The intense shame at disappointing them.

"No, Ama. This has to be, ah, *l'erreur,* a mistake. What day is it?" She stares at me like I'm crazy, tilting her head and coming closer, trying to smell alcohol on my breath.

"Tuesday! It Tuesday. You miss school. You miss work." She turns her head to Gung. "George, she been drinking. Must be!" Her arms flap around like an out-of-control windmill.

Tuesday.

How can it be Tuesday?

BREAKER

20

I walk a trail up the mountain for a couple of hours and then head home, figuring Red's playdate will be over.

When I hit the town, I'm surprised by how much traffic there is. A school bus rolls past, loaded with little faces, and I stop.

Nervously, I fumble for a smoke and then give up. My eyes follow the bus around the corner until it disappears.

It's Sunday, I say to myself. *It's Sunday,* I try to convince myself.

I pick up the pace, almost jogging to my neighborhood, watching the houses become more dilapidated as I go. I thunder up the stairs, tension in my chest and fear in my heart. I open the screen door to find Mom straightening the lounge. She looks up from rearranging the cushions and stares at me, hard and cold. "Where the hell have you been?" she asks. If there's concern in her voice, it's buried under months of disappointment.

I step over the threshold and smile awkwardly. It feels slapped on my face, fake and plastic. "You shouldn't curse on a Sunday."

She looks at me like I'm nuts, a look I'm very used to, and then bites her lip, her eyes darting around the room. "Are you high right now?" she whispers. Then she comes closer, shaking her finger at me. "Don't bring that shit into my house, Breaker. I'm warning you. Seriously, after everything we went through with your dad, how could you?" She is agitated but sadly unsurprised.

"What are you talking about, Mom? You always tell me off for cursing, especially on the Lord's day."

She quirks an eyebrow and says, low and frightened, "Breaker, it's Tuesday."

I think I already knew, but hearing her say it forces a hard shudder through me. I look to her and say through my teeth, "I'm not high, Mom. I'm sorry I didn't call, but I crashed at a friend's place for a couple of days. I should have called."

She shrugs, and I can feel her distancing herself from me more and more. "Yes, you should have."

Something like excitement rushes through me. A wavy line of electricity. I feel that pull again. Back to the woods. *It must be the tree, right?* I stare at my feet, desperate to turn them around and walk out again. Whatever it is, I wonder if it happened to Sunny too. My fingers itch with sap and the last little shreds of bark. I wipe them on my pants.

The screen door creaks and Red crashes through the entryway, throwing his school bag on the floor and colliding into me. "Where've you been, Break?" he asks, worry in his tone as he wraps his arms around my middle and squeezes. I pause. I can't run out on him. Even if Mom doesn't care where I've been, he does.

"I'm sorry, bro," I say, patting his head and pulling his arms away from me before I start to feel caged and want to fight my way out of his grasp. "I didn't mean to scare you."

Red shrugs unconvincingly. "Yeah, well, you missed my playdate. You didn't get to meet Jake."

Mom snorts in the kitchen. "Go put your things away and wash up, hon."

Tuesday. Two days. Two days gone. Two days I didn't have to think about *them* or the past or wherever the hell I'm heading. Two days without nightmares. A few hours with Sunny took two days I don't need or want back.

As soon as Red exits the room, the atmosphere changes. Mom slams a cup on the bench like a summons, and I go to talk to her in the kitchen.

I pull up one of the frayed vinyl barstools and sit facing her. "I'm really sorry."

She frowns, cranes her neck to check if Red's still in the bathroom, and whispers tersely, "So you should be. You didn't warn me about his *friend* Jacob." She says the word friend like it's dirty. Like it should be scrubbed raw and clean.

Oh.

"It was so embarrassing. His mom came right up to the door and knocked, calling out to me in that accent. Meesus. Van Weeenkeell." She does a horrible impersonation of the mother's accent. "God!" She slaps a palm over her forehead and drags it down her face. "The neighbors probably saw her. They probably think I'm friends with one of *them* now."

I narrow my eyes. "What do you mean by one of *them*?" I challenge.

She shakes her head, wisps of blonde hair floating around her face. "You know…them. Them! Yeesh,

Breaker, I thought you of *all* people would know what I'm getting at."

Thankfully, Red comes back in the room, so I'm saved from trying to work out and explain my very complicated feelings on *them*.

"Jake really wants to meet you," he says, climbing up on the stool next to me, his pale hands barely a contrast to the white tile counter. I nod, eyeing Mom curiously. Her back stiffens as she pretends to wash dishes.

"Sure," I say, surprising myself.

Two days, two days, two days, echoes in my mind. The pull so easy to grab a hold of. The need to go back so strong. I'd agree to anything if it meant I could get out of here quicker.

He leans his head on my shoulder and I tense, but I don't jerk away like I normally do. "Yes!" he shouts. "So cool!" Mom squeezes the water out of the sponge in her hands until it's bone dry.

I decide to save Red from her bullshit. "How about we meet in the park? Play some ball or something?"

Red seems so excited by this, which makes me feel instantly guilty. "Really? Really, really? That would be so great, Breaker."

I pat his head and ease myself from the stool. My weariness is starting to return. Whatever energy I had is slowly being sapped after that encounter with Mom. I grimace.

Mom makes a small gesture. An almost grudging one. "Will you be staying for dinner?" she calls after me in a weakened voice.

Red pleads. "We're having hot dog casserole."

My stomach gurgles. If I've been gone for two

days, I haven't eaten in two days either. I feel hungry but not starving. I did my survival training. Two days without food. More importantly, without water, should have a much more significant effect on me than it has. I scratch my head, still standing in the short hall while Mom awaits an answer. "Okay. Sure. Dinner," I grunt.

Red runs to me and gives me another squeeze, and I try not to squirm. "I'm glad you're home." Then he steps back and gives me a toothy, chipmunk grin. "Don't you go disappearin' like that again, ya hear?" He waggles his finger at me, and I laugh. Just one short little laugh, but enough to push some light into an otherwise dark and dusty cavity.

"I promise," I say, half-intending to keep it.

Finally alone, I collapse on my generally untouched bed. My head sags into my hands. I wonder how Sunny is feeling. I can't find out since I don't even have her phone number.

I want to come up with a rational explanation for what just happened, but I've got nothing. I want to run back there, but I don't want to upset Red again.

Two days.

Two. Days.

21

Two days?

It's impossible. Maybe he drugged me. Kidnapped me. How could I have no memory of any of it? I tap my chin while Ama stares at me, through me, burrowing a needle-sized hole through my chest. The phone rings, startling us both from separate introspections.

Gung stands up to answer, but then collapses back in his chair. He seems weak. And it's my fault.

I run to the phone, winding around Ama as she stands deathly still. A clay soldier biding its time.

I want it to be Breaker, and I mentally cross my fingers. "Hello?"

"Oh my God! Sunny. It's you. Where the hell have you been? We've been worried sick. I've been so scared. I thought maybe some woodland hacker had dragged you into the forest and chopped you into pieces. Jesus! You gave me a fright, girl!" Cara says all in one breath.

"It's okay. I'm okay," I whisper into the phone, my hand sheltering my mouth.

Cara picks up on my tone and whispers too, "Are they listening?"

"Uh-huh," I say with Ama's piercing eyes on me.

"So you can't talk right now?" she says, seeming to enjoy the intrigue.

"Yes."

"Talk at school?" she asks.

"*D'accord*. Sure thing, Cara. That would be great if you could give me a ride to school. Thanks!"

"Gotcha," she says, and I can almost see her winking exaggeratedly through the receiver.

I hang up the phone.

Ama moves slowly and quietly like a cat about to pounce. I decide it's best to cut her off before she starts. "I'm going to my room," I announce. "I'm grounded."

I start toward the hallway and she grabs my arm, swinging me to face her. "Eat first," she orders, pointing to the counter and the rendang curry she's prepared for dinner.

My head falls. "Yes, Ama." I slink back to the counter to eat my dinner in terrifying silence. I know I have to go back there. I also know that if they catch me, nothing will save me from Ama's wrath. It'll be like the tornado that sucked up Dorothy and her house from Kansas. Only I'll land in fire and brimstone, not Oz.

I feel a pull like a string through my chest. Tugging me back to the woods. I need to know for sure. I need proof.

The Mickey Mouse in my clock smiles at me with his black, soulless eyes. His arms twist and tick, tick, tick. It's eleven o'clock. Ama approves of Mickey, but she has a huge problem with Donald Duck. I grin as I think about what she said, "That duck has bad temper. He should be plucked and roasted. That what duck is good for. Not spitting and screaming like drunk man on Chinese New Year."

Turning slowly like a pig on a spit, I ease out of the bed, trying not to make any noise. The floorboards creak and I stop, barely breathing.

Carefully, I pull on my boots and a coat. Then I take my knapsack and lift the clock from the wall, tucking it in between a notebook and a bottle of water. To carry out my test, I need another clock.

The only other clock in the house is a brass desk clock that sits on top of the TV. I close my eyes, praying that Gung is not asleep on the couch, and then tread softly toward the living room.

Soft snoring followed by a wheeze makes my heart sink. Gung's slipper clad feet poke out from the green armchair he always sits in. Lives in. I creep up behind him, hovering over his head like one of Ama's spirits. He breathes uneasily. The air enters in a thin stream. The strain, even when sleeping, is upsetting to watch.

His hands are clasped over his round belly, controlled and neat. I understand why he often sleeps out here. I imagine Ama sleeps curled in a whirling ball, arms whipping out to slice like a spinning saw blade.

I take a silent breath in and hold it, tiptoeing in front of Gung to lift the clock from the TV. Guilt pulls at my ankles. If he wakes and finds me gone, it will hurt him. *He won't wake,* I tell myself as I shake the guilt free. It leaves a stain on the patterned red carpet. But I *need* to know.

Clutching the clock to my chest, I pad to the kitchen and scrawl out a note. I put it inside the tea canister so it will only be discovered if I'm not back by morning.

I place the brass clock in my bag and exit through the back door, fighting against myself the whole way across the field. Because this is not me. I don't sneak out in the middle of the night. I don't even think about disobeying my grandparents.

The minute my toes touch the edge of the woods though, a stronger feeling takes over. The cord tugging me to the tree pulls harder. Dragging me faster. I bend and stumble over logs, my face getting scratched by branches as I struggle to keep up with my feet.

My heart beats like the flutter of the birds that scatter in my wake. I'm frightened and excited at the same time. A cloud of warm calm pulls me closer and closer.

The stars are clear tonight, the moon cut into slices like a pie by the straight black branches over my head. I close my eyes and walk a few paces. I'm being guided. I could be blindfolded, and I'd still find my way here.

I say it to myself, *I don't believe in spells and magic trees. It's not plausible. It's not possible.* At the same time, I'm being blindly pulled through this warm tunnel of air straight to the tree. I touch my heart. It jumps around in my rib cage, disagreeing with me.

The sound of water rushing over rocks. I'm near and the pull gets stronger. I resist, locking my legs and winding my arm around a narrow tree trunk. The shadow of the ugly tree is imposing before me, sprawling branches, the tips like pointed fingers beckoning me to come closer. I bite my lip and dig my heels into the dirt. Fighting against my body. Fighting against that sense of peace this strange place offers.

With one arm still hooked around the tree trunk, I drop my knapsack, bending down to find a flashlight.

A stream of light falls across my face.

"How long were you gone for?" he asks.

"Two days," I reply shakily.

"Me too," he says, a hint of happiness to his voice.

My feet struggle in the dirt. "*Je ne vois pas*... I don't see...how this could possibly be a good thing, Breaker. I lost two days of my life. My grandparents called the police. I'll be lucky if I'm not grounded til' graduation."

Something like a snort comes from across the clearing. "It's not. I'm not. Ugh!" he says in frustration. "I'm just glad I'm not going through this alone, you know?"

I grunt, feeling like I'm not in control, scared to let go.

"You feel it too, don't you?" he asks, standing a few yards away from me in the shadow of a pine tree. "The pull."

I squint into the dark, but I can't make out features with his flashlight on my face. I gaze just left of the light and see his arm is also wrapped around a tree.

My head drops. "This is crazy. I must be crazy," I whisper. "I shouldn't have come here. Is it you? Did you do something to me?"

He sighs and steps forward, then steps back. "Of course not. I'm as confused as you are." His voice is high, slightly panicked. "I would never... Sunny... I didn't do this."

I shake my head. I don't believe him. I've been to this tree hundreds of times, and this never happened before. It has to be him. My foot drags across the dirt, and I pull it back sharply. Excitement is fast turning into fear.

"It has to be you. Unless I have finally lost my

mind," I say. He drops his torch to his side, but I don't feel like I have any energy to pick mine up and use it. I yawn.

It would be nice just to rest for a minute. Stop worrying. Just…stop.

Breaker talks mid-yawn, "If it is me, I didn't do it on purpose. I don't know or understand what's happening any more than you do. I'm sorry, Sunny."

I rub my eyes with my spare hand. So sleepy.

I came here for a reason. I just can't recall…

The forest is quiet, dreamlike. The air warmer and sweeter. I release my arm from the tree and my knee knocks my pack, the brass clock rolling onto the dirt. Slowly, lazily, I grip back onto the trunk.

"Oh. Right," I say, my mouth as wide as a lion's.

"Sunny… Sunny, right what?" Breaker's voice sounds soothing, softly floating across the air, though I think a bear growling would sound soothing to me right now. Ama's twanging voice pulls at the edges of my stupor. *I knew a man who was eaten by a bear…*

"We need to test it," I announce slowly, my brain filled with syrupy sap. "I need solid proof."

Breaker's voice struggles to pierce the soft clouds surrounding my brain. "How?"

BREAKER

22

I want to believe in magic. So bad. I want to believe that time can be changed. That things can be undone. But the idea is buried. Hope is there too, pressing against a thin layer of dirt. But how can magic exist side by side with horror?

"Sunny, how?" I ask again, fighting against my drooping eyelids. There's a weight to them. They're lead.

She said it wasn't a good thing. This is where we differ. While I was happy to lose a couple of days, she was upset. Bitterness swirls in my mouth. That's because she has a life, a family who cares if she's missing.

It would be easier. It would be simple to just…to just sleep.

"I have two clocks, *deux*," she announces, as if I should know what that means. I'm so sleepy, but I cling to the sound of her voice. To the melody of it. An unwanted image of her face flashes through my brain, and that ruins the small moment of peace. Fear and distrust resume their play of trying to bust me open. "*Allez*. Come over here to me and I'll explain."

"But my face," I manage.

She groans. "Okay, all right," she concedes. "What I'm proposing is that you take one clock and sit against the tree. I'll hold the other one here. We'll wait say half an hour, and then we'll see if the times on each clock are different. Does that make sense?"

"Sort of." My forehead creases with effort.

She yawns loudly. "If time actually slows down when you're in contact with the tree, then the times on the clock will be different."

"What if I can't get away from the tree?" I ask doubtfully.

"I'll call to you. If that doesn't work…I'll come get you," she says.

My heart shrinks and shimmies, dropping low. I close my eyes, and a green haze clears to…

I never know what Sarge is doing with his hands. I know I'm supposed to understand all the signals, but I get confused. I usually watch the others for cues, but they're up ahead in a place that makes me want to curl into a ball and screw my eyes shut forever. He pulls a palm leaf down over his head, signals to me.

I shake my head. I don't understand. My breath is coming in too fast, and I can feel myself getting dizzy.

"Wait here," he whispers, dirt and other people's blood staining his cheek like a slap. "I'll come get you when it's over."

I reach out. "Wait…" I whisper.

His eyes are hard and focused. A glaze of distance over them as he prepares to do what he needs to. Jaw tight, he says it again, "I'll come get you."

He springs from his hiding place, and I crawl backward. I can't listen to this anymore. I can't be afraid anymore.

I slide in the mud on my stomach for what feels like a mile before pulling myself against a tree. "Come get me, come get me, come get me," I say over and over again, my hands over my ears, my leg bleeding everywhere, dark, dark blood that's almost black.

"Breaker, did you hear me?" she says, her voice singing to me from above like it's nestled in the fork of the tree. "I'll come get you."

I nod. "Yes, sir," I blurt before I can stop myself.

Thankfully, she ignores it.

"Catch!" She throws a white plastic disc at me. It hits my stomach and falls at my feet. I pick it up and dust the dirt from Mickey Mouse's face. "You ready?" she asks.

My hand gradually releases its grip on the tree I've been holding onto and I walk forward, the clock tucked tightly under my arm.

It's the easiest, dreamiest walk to the tree. It feels like this is where I'm supposed to be. Every step I take is a footprint to home. I want to turn back to check where Sunny is, that she's watching me, but then she might see me. She'd see the liar. It would be all she sees. The ground feels soft and springy. As I get closer, the noise calms. And once I climb over lumpy roots and nestle into the trunk, I forget why I was fighting it. I forget to care.

It would be easier…

The hard plastic edge of the clock pokes into my underarm and I pull free of the haze, placing it on my lap as my eyes droop. Without Sunny with me, sleep is all my body, my heart, wants. I fight sluggishly, jerking my head back and forth but feeling bound. I watch the second hand move slowly, twisting Mickey's arms in what would be quite an uncomfortable pose.

My eyelids shutter like they're ready for a storm, but then I hear a voice, softly calling through the sludge of my consciousness. I can't see, though I'm not sure if it's because my eyes are closed or the dark. It's just so hard to care. "Wake up," the voice urges. Tick goes the second hand, Mickey points out and away. "Breaker, Breaker," Sunny whispers. Something pads up my leg and fumbles in the dark, grabs the corner of my jacket, tugging it hard. "Breaker!"

I lurch forward, feeling like I'm attached to the trunk with Velcro and she's just torn me violently from the bark. Pieces of it crumble around me, and my fingers are sticky with sap again. My face is pointed down at the ground and I stay that way, afraid she will recognize me.

She takes my collar and pulls me forward another foot. "Take my hand," she says, her voice clearer as I disconnect from the roots. "I promise I'm not looking at your face."

I take it. It's like a door slamming shut on my dreams. The moment I touch her skin, I awake. The peace is gone. The caring about stuff starts right back up, and I hate her for it.

She pulls me across the stream, stomping through the water. Her breath huffing in excitement or panic, I'm not sure. We walk for about ten minutes in silence. Hand in hand. I want to let go, but I don't want to either. As we get further away, I feel more alert, more like myself, which is not a good thing.

Once she's satisfied we're a safe distance from the tree, she releases my hand and throws my pack at my feet. "Here," she says, handing me my torch. Hers clicks on. She has turned away from me. She leans against my back like we're about to have a duel, and I fight with myself. I want to lean into her, feel the warmth of her skin, the expansion of her ribs as she breathes, but I can't. I shuffle forward so there's a small slice of space between us.

She sighs, holds her breath, and then sighs again. "What does your clock say?"

I click on my torch. I don't need to read it really, because I know it's only been a few minutes since I left her. I pat my pocket, searching for my smokes. "Um, my clock says it's 12:46 AM." I feel her shudder, her feet scratching around in the undergrowth in an agitated way. Then she lets out a nervous laugh. "What?" I ask. "What does yours say?"

"*Promets-moi*. Promise me you didn't mess with the time, Breaker. I know it'd be a great burn, but still…" she whispers. "Promise me you didn't."

I shake my head and curse, which makes her giggle. "I promise," I say, this dark shadowy feeling creeping up my arms. "I didn't touch it." This feels like a bad thing. A sacred thing I'm not supposed to know about.

"My clock says 1:23 AM," she says quietly.

Now I laugh. "Yeah, good burn…" My words are met with silence. "Hang on. Seriously?"

She pushes the clock to my hand. "Seriously."

I pick it up and read the numbers. She wasn't lying. What felt like a few minutes to me was more like half an hour to her. "Shit!"

This time, I do lean back. And so does she. I need to feel something real, something to assure me that I'm not dreaming. We look up at the sky at the same time, and our skulls knock together. "*Merde!* Shit is right, Breaker." Her voice is small, tiny thoughts bouncing around as she tries and I try to put this together. We sink to the ground. "I think we need to test again," she says, tapping her foot on the ground.

"What? Why?" I'm super-creeped out right now. I don't want to go back there.

"Have you also experienced time, uh, *où le temps est comme ralenti*? Slowing down?" she asks. "The first time this happened, I came home and it was like no time had passed at all."

I think of that argument with Mom. How she was still standing in the exact same spot, even though to me, I'd been gone hours. "Yeah, I guess I have."

She sounds like a scientist when she proclaims, "We need a consistent result."

I stand up as she does. "All right," I reply reluctantly. This all sounds too hard. I'd rather accept what we know and leave it at that. But she's insistent.

We take turns, sitting in different positions around the tree, Sunny always careful to avoid my face. She writes in a notebook the directions we're facing, makes me mark north, south, east, and west into the tree.

As I cut the last marker, dark sap bleeding from the trunk, I feel it sigh. Not exactly a human sigh. A breath of wind that seems to come from the earth and the trunk and the branches. It's warm like exhaled air from a mouth.

We retreat with her notes. Again sitting back to back.

"Ready?" she asks before leaning against me. I force myself not to lean away. I am a pillar of salt. I could crumble at any moment.

"Ready," I say, not really ready at all.

"Hm…" She hums, the tap of her pencil on the paper kind of annoying because it's not rhythmic. It's completely random. "So the length of time seems to be around one minute to thirty minutes. And vice versa, thirty minutes to one."

She pauses, awaiting a what—a *huh* kind of response?—but I get what she's saying. One minute at the tree is thirty minutes on the outside. Or it's thirty minutes at the tree is one minute on the outside. "We only tested pretty short periods of time though. It may grow exponentially…" she ponders.

"And it's dependent on the axis you're sitting on, right?"

Her back straightens, surprised. "*Absolument*! Exactly! East-west speeds up time and north-south slows it down."

I watch the stars. The trees trying endlessly to block my view like hands getting in the way of a photo. "It's impossible," I breathe, even though I know it is possible. More than possible… *Fact*.

The hair at the back of our heads rubs together, and it makes a weird scratchy sound. Her skull leaning on mine is uncomfortable, but I don't move away. "There's more too," she says, her hands planted by my sides as she stares up at the sky with me.

I don't think I want to know.

I think I already know.

"Breaker. This is your fault," Sunny states, with no blame in her voice.

Sunny
23

Breaker's back flinches, and I feel him shift away from me. I hear the flare of a match and smell the foul smoke of a cigarette circling us. "I know," he mumbles.

"Did you know before?" I ask, still not believing that we're having this conversation. That what just happened, happened. How could a few minutes against the tree be over thirty minutes where I stood only a few yards away?

"No," Breaker says. "But I think I'm starting to get it now."

I shake my head. "I mean, this seems impossible. It *is* impossible. I've been coming here for a year, and this has never ever happened before. But then you show up and like that..." I snap my fingers. "Instant time warp."

"Why me though?" he asks sadly. Like either he doesn't think he's worthy or he doesn't want to be part of this.

I'm jittery. My legs shaking. My heart somewhere in my shoes. "I don't know."

"This is far-out!" he exclaims. "Man, Red would get a kick outta this."

"Red?" I ask.

He stands, a shower of bark and debris falling from his jacket and into my eyes. "My little brother.

He's ten, and he would love this kind of thing. Anyway," he says, trying to jump off the personal platform. "What do we do now?"

My brain does that thing, splicing and sorting and trying to make sense of the world in parts. "I wonder if your brother would have the same effect, whether it's a family thing or it's just about you," I muse as I stand, still with my back to him, though both of us have switched off our flashlights.

He chuckles, stops, and then chuckles again. "Could have. But Sunny, you're not listening to me. What do we do?"

Facts spin like pointed shapes in my brain. "What about your dad? You said he took off years ago. Do you…" I start, but then find it hard to finish. Missing parents are not really something I want to get into, but…

"Do I what?" he asks with a hint of curiosity mixed with irritation.

"Do you actually know what happened to your dad?" I ask.

Breaker steps away from me. "He's not in the tree if that's what you're getting at. We get a phone call a couple of times a year when he remembers that he's got two sons."

"Oh, okay." I sigh. "Sorry."

He snorts. "What are *you* sorry for?"

I don't answer, and silence floats between us.

He rambles around awkwardly, his hand accidentally hitting my arm. "So again, I ask, what do we do now?" he asks.

"I don't know," I say quietly. "We could report it to the police, although I'm sure they'll think we're crazy. We could test it again just to make sure, but I think that's too dangerous. I mean, what if we lose even more time?"

I turn toward him, and he turns away. "I meant what do we do *right* now?" he asks, and I can tell he's smiling though I can't see his face. "Do you want to hang here or do you need to get back?"

I look down at the clock he slid back to me. The gold balls at the base twirl around at a disturbing pace. The clock reads 2:01 AM. I swallow. Ama is going to kill me now anyway.

I try to sound careless, but it comes out more squeaky. "I could hang."

We find another tree that's wide enough for both of us to sit against without touching each other and settle against its trunk. It feels cold and hard and not at all like our tree.

Our tree?

I try to get comfortable. "Do you still feel it?" I ask.

Breaker's feet kick around as he tries to nest himself more comfortably too. "The pull? A little… It's not too bad right here…with you."

I can feel it too, but it's faint, like blackberry thorns that cling to skirts when walked by. They catch for a second, but then fall away. Berries make me think of bears, which makes me think of Ama, which makes me shudder.

It's colder away from the sleepy warm air of the tree, and I hug my legs to keep from shivering. "This is a real trip, right?" I say, pressing my back against the tree and huffing cold air into the inky sky.

"Uh-huh," he mumbles.

I picture his face, deep angry red scar slashed across his cheek. Sundown is such a tiny town; I'm surprised I haven't seen him around. Haven't noticed a guy with a horribly scarred face. "Are you scared?" I ask.

His voice is gravelly, deep, something I want to run my fingers through. "Nah, I'm not scared. I'm a bit surprised… A bit unsure whether this is actually happening, but no, not scared. Are you?"

I shake my head. "I'm scared what Ama's going to do to me when I get home." I laugh nervously, and he joins me but his peters out into a dark sigh.

"I doubt my mom will even care that I've been out all night," he mutters.

"I wish that were the case for me," I say stupidly.

"Don't wish that." His words are an armful of kindling dropped to the floor.

I know I should go home. I know that the longer I wait, the worse it's going to be, but it feels as if standing up and walking away from him breaks a spell. Snow White stays in her glass coffin; Rapunzel gets a haircut. I feel, I don't know, responsible for him.

The strike of a match and the smell of smoke. I take small breaths to try to avoid taking too much in. "Are you going to tell anyone about this—your brother Red or a friend or something?" I ask.

A breath in. A cough out. "No one would believe me except Red, and I don't want him wandering out here."

I touch my chin to my chest. Ama would believe me too. But she can't know about this. It opens a basket of snakes, slithering in all directions. "Okay, well, then maybe we keep it a secret for now. You know. Until we know more…" I send feelers out into the dark. Hope they land on sympathetic ears.

"Good idea."

I look up to find my peace. My diamond of sky. There's one in every tree. Splintered branches brace themselves just for me. The air stills and ripples with warmth I can almost wind my hand around. "Hey… Breaker?"

"Hmm?"

"I know you started this. But don't you wonder where it might end?"

BREAKER

24

Where does it end? With me showing Sunny my face? With me being able to look in her eyes without my gut twisting in disgust? It will end, that's for sure. But I feel like I need to keep it going a while longer. However long I've got.

I know she meant the whole time-warp thing. But that's a question I have no answer to. It's new and unbelievable and I lied when I said I wasn't scared. I'm terrified, but I felt like this was a way to keep her. For a little while longer.

Holding to the shadows as the pink and orange glow of sunrise starts to pour over the soggy ground, I think about telling her the truth.

Maybe she'd find it fascinating, a case study. A guy who's falling for someone's voice but can't stand to look in her face. I snort, and then smash my boot through an icy puddle. This isn't going to work. Funnily enough, I will eventually run out of time.

Sunny

25

I thought I'd be ready next time it came. I've seen it so many times before that I thought I'd be prepared...

My feet are feather light despite the bizarre experience of last night. I skip over the loose stones and broken branches as if I'm a ballerina. Twirling when I come to an open spot of dirt on my way home. I reach up and part the branches to get a better look at the sunrise. The glow behind the trees makes the forest look like it's on fire.

I have a secret, but it doesn't feel dangerous. It's feels precious, special. Like I'm one of only a very few to find out there is magic in this world. It's a privilege and I scrunch it in my hand, feel it heat my palm like a hot coal.

Standing at the edge of the woods, ready to step into the field behind our house, I freeze. Ama will know something's up. She's going to pry my eyelids apart, inspect me with those dark eyes, and just know.

The grass rolls like a Spanish tongue, pinkish under the rising sun, and I stall. A small pull backward like I'm one of those talking dolls with a string in its back. I take a deep breath and approach the house, but instead of going in the back door, I walk down the side and around to the workshop, following the sound of sandpaper on timber and the smell of furniture oil.

Gung's workshop is a safe place, a warm haven from the craziness awaiting me inside. The garage door is open a crack and I lift it enough to slip inside, closing it behind me. It makes a loud groaning noise, but Gung doesn't react.

His back is to me as he carefully sands a long length of a timber that must be part of my bed. I lean against the long-dead motor of the door and watch him. This is his peace. His diamond of sky. This is where he gathers his strength for Ama.

I cross the floor, my feet dragging through drifts of sawdust to reach him, and gently tap him on the shoulder. He doesn't react again, because, as I suspected, he already knew I was here.

"Gung. *Je suis désolée*. I'm sorry I upset you." I clasp my hands together and bow my head. "I promise, I'm not doing anything bad, anything you would disapprove of," I plead.

He grunts, nods, and picks up a long, heavy piece of Oregon, handing it to me. "Turn over and sand other side," he orders, slapping a piece of sandpaper onto my already overburdened arms.

"Yes, Gung," I answer, staggering to the neighboring workbench and putting it down with a clunk.

He reaches up high and pulls down another length of timber, measuring it carefully and marking it with the pencil behind his ear. He hums a familiar song, one that breaks my heart. It's a wish for me to stay a child, not grow up, outgrow, and leave. Sadly, I hum along, trying to find my peace in the rough grain of the timber, tiredness starting to play catch up with me now the excitement has ebbed.

Ama is above, faintly, clattering around in the kitchen. She hasn't come down to scream at me, which hopefully means she didn't notice I was missing.

After about half an hour, Gung speaks, "If it a boy, I no want to know."

I giggle. Touch my mouth. "No, it's not like that. It's..."

I sidle up to him as he saws the timber. "Ai ya, Sun," he grumbles, shaking his jowly head. "I said I no want to know." He chuckles, and I laugh.

"Can I help you with this?" I ask after I've finished sanding, leaning my chin on his rounded shoulder.

He nods. "Coffee."

I gulp. I don't want to go upstairs yet. I'm enjoying the quiet and the rich smell of tobacco and sawdust. Sensing my apprehension, Gung looks up, stops sawing, and sort of smiles, sort of grimaces, his hooded eyes crinkling in the corner. "She not know you sneak out. I found your note. And I no want her to know, okay?" His lips are thinly spread; he's displeased with me, but his fear of one of Ama's storms outweighs it.

"Okay."

I lift the garage door and leave it open, padding out of the workshop, yawning wide as I go. From the kitchen window, Ama stares down at me, a scowl pulling her mouth down. She points at me and indicates for me to cover my mouth when I yawn. I take a deep breath and climb the stairs.

"You up early," she states, pushing a bowl of oats toward me, a blob of brown sugar floating in the center. "Eat!"

I yawn, this time covering my mouth. "I wanted to help Gung with my bed," I say, lifting my spoon to my mouth slowly. Ama turns away from me, gazing at the mist-blanketed morning. She sighs sadly. Guilt spears between my ribs for lying to her. "He asked me to bring him some coffee." She nods, still not making eye contact, and busies herself making a pot. I watch her old but nimble hand squeeze a blob of condensed milk into the bottom of a glass, and then pour the steaming black liquid over the top. Like night and day swirling together.

Quickly, I shovel the rest of the oats into my mouth and move to the sink to wash my bowl. We have a dishwasher, but Ama refuses to put anything in it that isn't already sparkling clean.

I bump Ama's hip with my own and she laughs, bumping me back. I press my cheek to hers, which is soft and dusty with powder. "Love you," I whisper as I scoop up the coffee and try to leave.

She clamps her hand down on my wrist and points out the window. "Cara here for school."

I'd kind of forgotten all about school. Cara pulls into the driveway and exits the car. With my hand wrapped around the hot coffee mug, I walk swiftly to the front door.

Cara's scream presses like a cold wind through the cracks in the door. Night and day collide and shatter as I drop the coffee and rush outside.

Sunny

26

"Oh my God! Oh, my God! Jesus H. Christ!" she screams through pushed-together cheeks that make her look like a chipmunk. I stop running and approach her slowly, following her gaze that's beaming a line into the workshop. She turns to me, her eyes wide and full of tears. "Sunny," she says like a gasp, like an apology, shaking her head over and over.

I force myself to look inside, picturing blood and torn skin, but there's no gaping wound, no ripped limbs. All I see is Gung. Whole and in one piece. My heart beats every other second, slowing to a honey drip. Gung lies on the floor, his eyes closed, his hand still tightly gripping the saw, sawdust fanning around him like he was midway through making a snow angel.

"Gung," I say softly, my fingers pressed to my lips. I stall for half a second before running to his side.

Skidding to my knees, I check his pulse. It's weak, but it's there. He's breathing so shallow it's like toes deep in the ocean. I place a hand on either side of his face and shake him gently. "Gung. Wake up," I urge, my voice split like a log. I turn to Cara, who's frozen in the driveway, shaking gently like a washing machine on its last spin cycle. "Call an ambulance." She stands dumbly, hands at her sides. "Cara," I bark. "Call an ambulance now!"

She races upstairs and into the house, brushing past Ama, who's huddling in the doorway, too afraid to cross the threshold. "What is it, Sun?" she squeals from the house. The word *it* sounding like *eat*. "Sun?" she screeches, her voice getting higher and higher with every second I don't answer. "Sunny? *Apa?* What is it? What wrong?"

This is bad. This is more than I can cope with. This is… Fear rains from the sky, sharp, icy hail trying to shred my flesh and pull away at my sanity.

I turn back to Gung. His face looks as gray as the floor, his skin sagging and loose around his neck. "Gung, please, I can't lose you. Wake up. Wake up." I pat his cheeks gently, terrified at how cold they are.

"George!" Ama screams so loud the workshop shudders. "What happening? What you done?"

I find Gung's puffer jacket and roll it up, placing it under his head. "It's going to be okay," I say to him and to myself. *It has to be okay.*

His chest wheezes, the last breaths of an accordion that's been stepped on by a crowd. I take his hand in mine and squeeze, getting nothing in return.

I can hear Ama stomping down the path, crushing dead and living things under her feet. When she reaches the door, she grips the frame and wails, mouth open like a train tunnel.

"*Ama, aidez-moi.* Help me move him," I order, but she just shakes her head. Tears and a dry choking are all I can get out of her. Cara appears in the doorway, stepping over the threshold, white except for her reddened cheeks. "Cara, come here," I beg. "Help me sit him up." She obliges, though frightened. Ama squats down on the ground and starts praying.

Together, Cara and I drag Gung up to sitting and lean him against the leg of the workbench. He groans a little, but he doesn't open his eyes. "The ambulance is on its way," Cara whispers, her eyes darting to Ama. I know what she's thinking, because I'm thinking it too. Ama's a storm brewing. The beginning of a tidal wave way out in the ocean. It's building and building and, soon, it could sweep us away.

I don't know what I'm doing, but I press my ear to his heart. I think I just want to assure myself it really is still beating in there. Then he coughs once, and Ama jerks up from her muttered prayers. "George!"

His eyes sway to me and show strain. They show so much pain, but when he looks back at Ama, he manages to smile. *"Baik,"* he manages. Which means, *I'm okay*.

He's not okay.

She shakes her head as acid tears hit the sawdust. Shuffling over to him, she takes his other hand. "George, you can't go," she whispers, pressing his limp hand to her cheek. "Not your time. Not your time." She sways on her haunches and I stare at them both, real fear clattering in my ears like hammers on nails and chisels scraping at my skin.

This family won't work without him.

Ama won't work without him.

"What you do with him?" Ama asks desperately as

they wheel Gung's gray and weakened body into the back of the ambulance.

He tries to lift his hand to wave her away, to tell her to calm down, but it's too much effort. I put my arm around her and pull her back so the men can do their job. The paramedics ignore her questions; they're tired of her constant interruptions already. I watch Gung disappear, shouting at him before they shut the doors, "We're right behind you."

Ama shakes, confused and furious and frightened. I keep her pinned back to stop her from banging on the ambulance doors. "Hospital bad place," she almost hiccups. "Too many ghosts looking for new bodies, Sun."

I nod and pretend I believe her.

Cara puts a hand on my shoulder, and I lean into it. "I'll drive you."

Whatever belief I had in magic spreads out and blows away like the sawdust in the ambulance's wake.

"Soleil La Chance?" is called out from behind a rickety card table. Names scribbled on stacks of paper rise like a paper city.

A warm hand on my shoulder gently pushes me forward. I look up, bending my neck back as far as it will go. The man with the crew cut and the dark green jacket winks at me. "I'm right behind ya, kid."

I step forward.

The woman at the desk scans her list with a pencil, names of people who have died or have been reported missing. "Soleil La Chance, the embassy recovered your pare..." She glances up, sees that I'm just a gangly teenage girl wearing an army shirt and no shoes. "Oh, honey," she whispers, pity dripping from her eyes. "You're Pierre and Siew's kid. Right, okay, um, I don't know why they brought you here." She looks up at the soldier behind me, and he leans down so she can whisper something in his ear.

I strain to hear them. I know my parents are dead. And I'm "unclaimed". That they don't know what to do with me. The woman touches the back of her bun like the answer is there, staring down at her page. They don't think I belong here with the rest of the straggly, torn-to-shreds children and mothers and fathers searching for their hearts. But I do.

Calmly, woodenly, I ask, "Have my grandparents been called, George and Annie Douglas? They are my next of kin."

She again taps her page. I imagine if she ruffled those pages, the names within would scream in pain. There are too many, way too many, names.

I wipe the dust from my brow. "Here." I take the pen from her hand and write down the number. "Call them, please."

A man comes up behind her and talks over the top of her head. "Miss La Chance. Your school has offered you accommodation in their boarding house while we sort out…"

While you sort out a dead French ambassador and his wife? And the child they left behind?

"Sort out the next move."

I shake my head. The man behind me holds still, and I find myself leaning into him for support. "No. I'll stay here, in the camp." These lost and desperate souls are my people now.

"Thatta girl," he says in the twang that I'm starting to find comforting. He addresses the two volunteers in front of us, "She's brave, this one! Yanked her out of the rubble three days after the blast. Collected rain water in a broken coffee

cup."

There are concrete-colored clouds growing behind me; they chase me down. They want to bury me again. Cara prattles nervously as we follow behind the ambulance. Ama sits in the back, her hand gripping her seatbelt, pulling at it uncomfortably like it's strangling her.

I glance at her in the mirror. *Stay calm.* "Ama. It's going to be okay. *Baik?*"

She nods, but it seems like she's not here. Her eyes roll around, never landing on anything.

"Bike?" Cara repeats, not understanding, but she's used to us switching languages like we do clothes. "Sure thing, Mrs. Douglas. Sunny is right. Your husband is in the best hands. I know one of the doctors there. We live on the same street as his daughter, Betsy. Anyway, Betsy is smart, so her dad must be really smart. And, well, yeah, I know. All doctors are smart. Like Sunny is going to be a doctor. Ha! Then you won't even need to go to the hospital when stuff happens…"

I place my hand on Cara's arm, and she stops talking.

Ama stares at me in the mirror. "This your fault." Then she turns her gaze out the window with eyes dark and boiling as burning oil.

Cara takes a sharp breath in and holds it, her fingers whitening around the steering wheel. She starts to protest, to defend me, but I put my hand up to stop her.

"I'm sorry, Ama," I say, trying to catch her eyes and getting a disbelieving look from my friend. But Cara doesn't understand. Whether it's my fault or not, I must apologize.

Ama harrumphs and crosses her arms, her face cracking into a million anxious pieces before me. I know she's scared. Whatever I can do to ease her pain, I'll do it.

Something drips over my neck and pulls tight. I lay my hand on my throat, touching the rosary beads Ama has slung over my head. "I don't know. It probably too late for you, but maybe this stop spirit jumping down your throat." I stifle a laugh at Cara's wider-than-saucer eyes.

"*Merci.* Thank you, Ama," I say, bowing my head. "You always take care of me."

I hold onto the rosary tightly. I'll take any good luck I can right now.

BREAKER

27

By the time I get home, everyone has already left for work and school. There are signs of life. Dirty bowls in the sink with dried, milk-soaked cereal stuck to it. Red's forgotten drink bottle on the counter. I was supposed to take Red to school today, and I sigh with relief that I don't have to, plodding to my bedroom. My eyes feel burned and red and I actually feel like sleeping for once.

I shed clothes like snakeskin and try to crawl under the covers, giving them a sharp tug so I can get the blanket out.

There are so many things to think about. Magic. Sunny. Sunny and me. Her voice. Her face. My heart starting to thaw and dry out. But for now, I feel at peace. I need sleep, and I'm not afraid to take it.

The window is open just a crack and the sounds of this small-town filter through. Someone's chopping wood. Birds scratching in the undergrowth sound like snakes wiggling across the leaves. Our neighbors talk to each other over their fences, but then are drowned out as a siren sounds, building and then disappearing down the street. They pick their conversation back up, and I close my eyes.

The jungle that usually hangs in front of my eyes recedes, and all I can think about is our backs touching.

How it didn't feel like home and how that was a really good thing.

Sunny

28

I shouldn't feel so uncomfortable. This is where I want to be. I want to wear the white coat and stethoscope around my neck. That will be my rosary. I run the beads through my fingers at my throat, counting.

We park the car, and Ama springs from her seat. "Ama, wait for me," I plead, but she's already crossed the parking lot and is pushing on the door that says 'pull'. I look to Cara. Her dear expression is so worried for me, for Gung. "I'll come in with you," she states. I shake my head.

"Ah, *non*. No. You should go to school. If you could let them know what has happened, I'd really appreciate it. Tell them I won't be in for a day or so." Truth is that I don't want her in there with me. I know Ama is going to make a scene and the less witnesses, the better. "Thanks so much for the ride. I'll call you later, okay?"

She sighs and leans in to hug me. I squeeze my thin arms around her ample waist. "I'll pray for you." When she pulls back, she gives me a strange look and reaches out her hand to brush my forehead. "And yes, you *need* to call me. We've got a lot to talk about." She shows me her finger, sticky with sap and bark.

I gulp. I don't know what to say to her, how much to say. "I need to get inside," I mumble and turn away from her station wagon, listening to it roar away from me as the door eases shut.

The hospital looks more like a residence. Its low roof and pale brick seem to invite me to a dinner party—not a crisis. Ama's voice greets me, her temper washing over the staff and spilling into patient rooms. She waves a clipboard in a nurse's face. "I don't know about insurance. George know. Ask him!"

The nurse purses her lips and glances at me. "Mrs. Douglas, please calm down. In this country, *we* do things a little differently to what you might be used to."

I almost pity the nurse. At the same time, I relish in Ama's next words. She stands on her tiptoes, leaning over the counter, eyes black as coal. She tilts her head and studies the nurse. "And what about your native country, Yugoslavia? They do things different there?"

The nurse's eyebrows rise as she chokes on a cough. Ama looks suitably triumphant and she digs the knife in a little deeper, twisting it for extra effect. "We all come from somewhere different, unless you telling me you Native American?" She points a hard finger at the nurse, who leans away.

I grin at Ama's uncanny ability to pin down where anyone comes from and take the clipboard from her. "*Allez*. Let go. Let me fill this out for you." Ama releases the clipboard and steps back from the counter, still pointing her finger at the flabbergasted nurse as she walks backward.

Looking up, I ask the nurse, "Can you get me an update on George Douglas, please?" The nurse jumps up, eager to get away from us.

We sit down in hard plastic chairs, and I start filling out the forms.

Fishing around in Ama's purse for her insurance details, my hands brush over candy wrappers and at least four different rolls of Lifesavers. I know Gung is very organized about this kind of thing, and sure enough, all the things we need are in the zip-up compartment of her handbag.

Ama takes a loud breath in through her nose and clutches her heart, scrunching the maroon, perfume-soaked cardigan she's wearing. I touch my cheek to hers. "Don't worry, it will be okay."

Her eyes dart to the corner where the fire sprinkler hangs down. "Breathe through nose. Don't open mouth," she hisses through a slit of her lips. "Spirits."

I suck in my lips and nod. Better to be safe than sorry, I guess.

On the top of the insurance form, she writes in perfect English script.

It's not your fault, Sunny. I am sorry for blaming you.

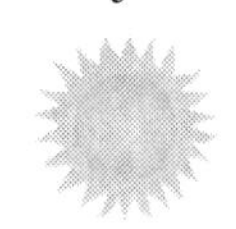

An hour later, a doctor emerges from behind glass doors. I try to read his expression, but I can't tell if he is regretful or hungry.

"Mrs. Douglas," he calls out. When Ama stands, he does well to hide his surprise at a Chinese woman with an Irish surname. "Your husband is awake and can see you now. He had a mild heart attack, but he is stable." He puts his hand on her shoulder. "He's going to need to make some lifestyle changes."

She looks so tiny, staring up at the tall doctor, his bristled black moustache moving when he talks. "What his eyes like?" she asks him, walking by his side with her purse clutched to her chest. She doesn't acknowledge the words *heart attack*. But I understand. I know how serious this could be. The doctor looks to me, and I nod.

"Er... His eyes are fine, clear and responsive," he answers in a wary tone.

She frowns. "Maybe cunning hider."

She doesn't explain her comment, but I know what she's talking about. She thinks if Gung has been taken over by a spirit, his eyes will change color.

We follow the doctor to a patient room, and he opens the door for us. "Your husband will have to stay here under observation for a few nights, but then he can come home."

Ama groans. To her, Gung staying here is worse than the heart attack.

I step into the room quickly, desperate to get a look at him. Saddened by what I see.

Gung looks half his normal size. His arms arranged neatly at his sides, an oxygen mask over his mouth. His eyes are mostly closed, but his head moves to follow me.

Ama comes to his other side and kisses his forehead. "You scare me, George."

He tries to talk with the mask on, but then pulls it down. "*Maaf.*" Sorry.

I pull the mask back up. "Gung, you need this."

He nods.

Ama fusses around with his blankets, tucking them in at his toes. I take his hand and squeeze. His eyes are watery, and it spreads to my own. I keep my fear inside, but I can feel it clawing at my ribs, looking for a way out. I don't. I can't. Won't think of what might happen if he doesn't pull through. Seeing him like this, so weak and gray, is turning my insides to jelly. It's raking sharp things over my chest. I try to take deep breaths, but they get stuck halfway down my trachea. Maybe I've swallowed a spirit like Ama said. My hand goes to my throat. That's what it feels like.

Not now. Later. Panic later.

I watch Ama sweep a silk scarf that must have come out of her magic purse into the corners of the room to scare away any dead ones that might be hanging around looking for a way in.

I will fall apart later.

29

It's about eight PM before I can convince Ama to leave the hospital. She's only satisfied to go once she's seen what Gung's had for dinner and personally and professionally attacked all the kitchen staff. I call Cara to pick us up.

The stiff wind smacks us when we exit the hospital. Cara's in the ambulance drop-off with the motor running, and we jump inside. "You good girl," Ama says, patting Cara's wavy blonde hair.

"How's Mr. Douglas?" she asks all too brightly.

"His heart mildly attack him."

I twist my nose and clench my teeth to stop a laugh at her rearrangement of the words.

"But he be okay." Ama yawns. "And now I need to cook."

Cara looks to me as Ama buckles her seatbelt. "He had a mild heart attack," I tell her, feeling little things breaking inside me. I stumble over my words. "He's p-pretty sick."

Cara's expression falls. "Oh man, I'm so sorry."

She pulls out of the hospital, driving down murky highways toward home.

Ama's soft snoring starts about two minutes after we leave the hospital, her chin tucked under and resting on her chest.

Cara checks her in the rearview mirror and then says, "So, are you gonna tell me what happened before? Where the H-E-L-L have you been?" She spells the word even though Ama's fast asleep. I pull the rosary from my neck and let it drop down slowly, pooling in my palm. I'm scared to tell her. With everything that's happened, it's just too much. And it feels, well, unreal.

Dust clouds gather in my peripheral vision. I feel that crushing feeling, that trapped-under-concrete sensation. "I, um, I…went to NYU for this open-day thing, and I stayed with a friend from Chinatown," I lie. "And I…um, I forgot to tell Ama how long I'd be gone for. You know, she just overreacted like she always does."

Cara can't look at me for very long, but the glances she shoots my way are doubtful and disappointed. "Oh, okay, right. Yeah, that makes sense, I guess."

My breath is getting tighter. Like someone's winding a string round and round my middle. Gung looked like someone had stolen his color, like he was living in a sepia-toned film. I close my fingers tightly around the rosary, wondering why I can't talk to Cara about the tree. Is it because I don't want to or because I don't want to make it real? It all seems so impossible now, like a bad dream.

"You know you can tell me anything, right? You're my friend. You can trust me. I tell *you* everything," she says, trying to push something out of me. But it won't budge. It's clutching the doorframe, unwilling to be admitted.

"I haven't got some juicy gossip, Cara," I snap. "*Zut!* Damn!"

Cara's lip quivers, and she focuses her attention on the road. "Uh-huh."

"Thank you for the ride, though. Seriously, I really appreciate it," I say, trying to wipe away the hurt feelings, sweep them under the chassis.

"No problem," she says curtly.

We get home, and the house looks the same and so empty. There's some evidence of what happened scattered across the ground, and the fear I felt this morning picks up right where it left off like a bookmark. Ama jolts awake and exits the car. "You stay for dinner?" she asks Cara, who shakes her head. She's upset with me.

"Raincheck?" she says to Ama, who looks up at the sky. This makes Cara and I giggle as we exchange knowing looks. We'll be okay. I just need some time to work through this. Work out exactly what to say. "I mean, maybe some other time, Mrs. D, okay?"

Ama turns and hobbles up to the front door, feet turned out, always looking like she just jumped off a horse. "*Baik baik,*" she says, waving behind her. "You good girl to help us today."

I walk past the garage and start to see those spirits Ama's always talking about. Black shadowy shapes that lurk in the corners, waiting for an opportunity. I stop, peer into the dark space.

"See you at school?" Cara shouts from her window as she backs out of the driveway.

I nod. "Sure."

She drives away with a hurt expression. I know all

sorts of theories are gathering in her head as to why I'm not telling her anything and what has really happened over the last few days.

Ama hovers in the doorway. "You coming?"

I stand there, arms at my sides, feeling lost. Feeling like I can't go in when Gung is not there. He's part of the home. Without him, it's just a timber shack harboring a tornado.

"I'm going to go for a walk. I need to clear my head," I say, hoping there won't be follow-up questions.

She's too distracted to be angry and simply yells, "Bears!" Waving a warning finger, she then slams the door.

Something calls. Warm, sweet air and comfort. A chance to forget.

BREAKER

30

A sudden weight on my middle wakes me, and I gasp. Quickly, I flip onto my stomach, throwing whatever it was from the bed. A fleshy "oomph" as Red's body hits the drywall brings me back to time and place.

I jump from the bed and rush to his side. "You okay, Red?" I ask, patting him down for broken bones and blood.

He shrugs, a split of sunlight cutting his expression in half like a black-and-white cookie. "I'm okay." He stands up and casts his eyes over my unmade bed. "You slept in your bed," he states with a grin.

I nod and get up, sitting on the edge. Red comes to sit next to me. "What time is it?" I ask.

Red collapses back on my bed, much to my irritation. He tugs at one end of the cover and rolls himself into it like a pig in a blanket. "It's about five," he answers, staring up at the ceiling.

"You're so weird, kid," I say, watching him roll back and forth like a coke bottle on its side.

He stops rolling and turns to glare at me, but it just looks cute. "No, you're weird! You're the weirdest guy in Weirdtown."

I chuckle. The hard edges feeling a little sanded down and rounded. I grab the sheet, pick up my sausage-shaped brother, and double wrap him. He squirms and wriggles, his pale face going bright red.

"Weird kids need to be restrained," I say, throwing him over my shoulder while he shouts for Mom.

"I'm gonna kill you," he screams as I toss him on the sofa. He starts unraveling himself while Mom watches from the kitchen with a soft smile on her lips. When we make brief eye contact, she looks away, afraid to pierce this normal moment. This *family* moment.

We wrestle for a second until Red is so out of breath that I stop, worried he's going to hyperventilate. I smile briefly, then wipe it from my face. These moments are so temporary. The feeling that prevails is how much I've let him down. How one encounter like this leaves me exhausted and ready to hide in my room again.

"You here for dinner, Break?" Mom asks, lightness forced into a cautious tone.

I pause, scratch my chin, and Red catches my eyes, a plea reflected at me. "Sure, Mom. Dinner sounds good."

I flick the TV on and collapse on the couch. It's the news, and my eyelids close like a blind. Whatever they've got to show me, I've seen worse.

"So, honey, what did you learn at school today?" Mom asks as she dollops mashed potatoes on my plate. "We all know what Breaker did…slept all day." She rolls her eyes, but then laughs weakly to cover her dig at me.

I concentrate on chewing the meatloaf that tastes more like rubber made into the shape of a meatloaf. Mom used to be a good cook, but since she started working more, everything's rushed. I swallow and try not to grimace. It's not her fault.

"We learned about greater than and less than. I sat next to Jake, and then, well, we got separated 'coz we were talkin' too much. Now I have to sit next to Sissy Smells a Lot."

I snort, and Mom sighs with relief disguised as irritation. "If that, er, Jake kid was distracting you from your work, then I'm glad they separated you. And you shouldn't say that about Sissy. She's a good kid; I know her parents. They live up on Golden Elm, in one of the nice houses."

Because, apparently, where Sissy lives determines how nice she is, just like the color of her skin. Old wheels start creaking and turning in my brain, Mom's comments oiling the joints.

I want to say something, but I don't. Something like, 'Red should be allowed to choose who he wants to be friends with'. That maybe Sissy does smell a lot, and that's why she had an empty seat next to her. That Jake is probably a very nice kid with a nice family and good hygiene and that she shouldn't judge him so harshly.

But I don't say any of those things because saying them means meaning them and not feeling like a hypocrite.

My legs jitter under the table. *It would be nice right there by the tree...* My brain and my heart could stop fighting with each other. I could escape.

Red's incessant clicking fingers snap me out of my

trance. A waft of sweet warm air passes under my nose. *It calls.* And if it's calling me, maybe it's calling Sunny too.

"Breaker's dreaming again." Red sighs dramatically. "Anyway, Mom, it's just for the rest of the week. If I'm good, I can pick who I want to sit with next week. And I'm gonna pick Jake."

I take a second helping of mash and look directly at Mom. "Sounds reasonable to me," I say with a warning in my eyes.

She bites her tongue.

Red chatters, and I try to respond. I lift the subject of Jacob and keep it off the table, feeling like I'm holding it over my head like a football and someone's going to tackle me soon.

After dinner, I clear the plates, wipe the table, and thank Mom for dinner. Her eyebrows arch in surprise, but she doesn't say anything smart.

"I'm going for a walk," I announce, grabbing my jacket. I check my face in the mirror and my hair is a disaster. I try to tuck it back and smooth it down, but it's messed up.

"Can I come too?" Red asks, standing on his tiptoes.

Mom saves me. "No, Red, it's a school night." But then she digs the knife in and twists by saying, "Breaker doesn't have anything going on in his life, so he has the luxury of being able to go out whenever he wants."

Pausing, I think about arguing with her, but then think better of it. I swing out the door and then turn around. "Tell you what, kid. On Saturday, I'll take you for a hike. How does that sound?"

His hopeful smile breaks my heart into jagged little pieces I'll use to torture myself later.

As I leave, I swear to myself that I'll follow through this time.

31

The embers on the end of my cigarette guide me down the street. An orange firefly floating in the dark. The smoke pulls me away. Warm air thick as fingers takes hold of my shirt and drags me between the houses and into the woods.

I head in the familiar direction, my brain like a compass pointing to where I was last, but it's like I'm pushing against something. The *something* keeps butting me right when I want to veer left.

Walking for a good forty-five, I become increasingly anxious that I'm not going to find the tree. I come to a small clearing, hear the babble of water tickling the rocks, and pick up the pace, sloshing through the freezing water and stopping dead in a large, scarred piece of earth. Water seeps into my boots, icy and uncomfortable. I shift from foot to foot, listening to the squelch and feeling the weight of a phantom pack on my back and the ghost of a rifle in my hands. Color flashes before my eyes, dark green and sharp like pine needles. I breathe, but my heart refuses to beat normally.

"What the fuck will we do if they come at us now?" Grimsby mutters as we follow Sargent into the water.

"Depends on how long you can hold your breath for, man," someone murmurs up ahead. His joke falls flat and

sinks to the riverbed.

We look ridiculous, guns over our heads, arms reaching high like we're all puppets on strings. Grimsby is right. We are sitting ducks as we wade through the river. A mosquito settles on my nose. I watch, crossed-eyed, as it sucks my blood.

My arms shake embarrassingly, even though the rifle is not that heavy. I look left to right, searching for signs of fear in the other men, but if they're afraid, they're hiding it well. And even though my head is above the water, I hold my breath until we reach the shore.

Ten men climb out of the water, squelching in their boots. Tired, wet, and miserable.

I groan. And Grimsby collapses beside me. "You know what I miss the most right now?"

"Cuddling up to your mama?" someone jokes.

Grimsby reaches out and punches him in the arm. "Close. My mama's damn dryer."

We laugh, but then the laughter turns into sighs as thoughts of home enter our minds. Everyone's expressions turn inward. Eyes distant, mouths pulled down.

But we can't stay like this for long.

We squeeze the water from our socks as best we can and keep moving.

My lip stings. I realize I've bitten down on it so hard it's bleeding. My mouth tastes metallic and rusty. I could stop and squeeze out the water, but I can't slot myself back into that memory. I don't want to stay frozen in this wrong place. Warm air lassos my waist and drags me away. And this time, I stop fighting and follow by instinct.

The light is spare when I finally stumble onto sandy soil. I raise an eyebrow, my head sweeping back and forth. Because this is the ugly tree, but it's not in the same location. *How could it move?* I approach it slowly, my eyes casting over the swollen lumps and bumps of the trunk. Its roots sprawl outward, sitting on top of the ground rather than sinking into it. The ground is not soft and spongy; it's dry, like I'm standing in the desert. A desert in the middle of the Catskills.

"Weird, huh?" Sunny's voice parts the branches. She's behind me.

I freeze, still staring at the tree. Listening to it buzz, watching it almost sigh.

Without turning, I reply, "Very."

I step toward it, and Sunny's tone is sharp with warning. "Don't touch it. Remember? It's not safe."

My hand falls to my side. "Yeah, sorry, it's just…"

"It's hard to resist," she finishes. There's something hiding in her words. An added sadness that wasn't there before. "I'll close my eyes if you want me to, Breaker, then you can come sit." I hear her pat the ground. *I should just tell her the truth.* "Okay, they're closed. Let me know when I can open them."

Turning around warily, I see the tip of her sneakers poking out from beneath a long skirt with little daisies on it. I pad quietly over, taking a minute to gaze into her twilight-lit face. Her eyes scrunched shut. Her heart-shaped mouth relaxed. Wisps of dark hair dance around her face, and I almost reach out to sweep one behind her ear.

"You settled?" she asks, eyes still tightly closed.

Quickly, I shuffle around to the other side of the tree she's leaning against and plant myself in the sandy soil. "Yes," I reply, the image of her petite features floating like a low moon before my eyes. I lift my hand, staring at my fingers that still ache to touch her, and tilt my head. Hate didn't overflow like lava and scorch everything good in front of me. I had a simple, unattached-to-the-past thought. She was just a pretty girl. When I looked at her face, it was just a girl's face. I curl my fingers into a light fist and rest it on my knee. *Don't think about it too much.*

Glancing down, I watch her dig her fingers into the sand, lifting it up and letting it drain from her hand. "It moved," she states. "But I still knew where to find it."

I stare down at my dirty jeans, the edges of my jacket crusted with grime. "Yeah, me too."

She sighs like dust blowing across the desert floor. "I almost went to it. I so wanted to. It's like it wants something from me. You know?" She sounds distressed. Her voice edgy. Higher pitched."Oh. *Je ne sais pas*. I don't know. I'm so tired. I'm so, so tired." Her hand scrunches into a fist, and she thumps the ground. It makes no sound. "I can't go through this again. I can't. But I guess I knew it could happen. They're old. He's old and he smokes this pipe and he coughs all the time and I upset him. I-I should be better than this. I should have been a better granddaughter."

I move my hand close to hers, my pinky just brushing the edge of her fist. I want to take it away. Whatever happened, I want to take it for her. "Sunny. What happened?"

She breathes in deeply, holds it, and then, silence. Her hand relaxes, and I stare down at her five dark fingers for one heartbeat before I wind my own in hers. A blast of air surges toward us, blowing my hair back, and then the buzzing recedes. The normal sounds of the forest return, the only out-of-place noise is the sniffing and soft moaning of Sunny. She's crying.

I squeeze her hand, and she squeezes back. "Sunny?"

She starts to speak. "He… I…." Tears seem to be shutting down her mouth. She's in pain.

I don't think; I pull her hand and her body follows. She's a hard ball of sadness, pressed neatly into my chest, and her heaving cries soak my shirt. She hasn't looked up, her face buried in my jacket, and I wrap my arms around her, letting her weep. Feeling too warm and too happy to be sharing the pain of this girl in my arms.

"He could die," she whispers. "He could die, and it'll be my fault."

I rub her back slowly, soothingly. Golden light pokes through the branches and splashes onto her back and my eyes.

I sigh. The sun doesn't want to set tonight, and I need it to.

Sunny

32

He smells of cigarettes, bitter and unpleasant. I press my forehead against his Jack Daniels t-shirt and try to calm down. But my heart hurts, and it keeps pushing water into my eyes. Darwin said, "Tears are purposeless," and I tend to agree, but it happens anyway because I'm so scared I'll be left alone with Ama. And I don't want to lose the only person who understands me.

I think of him, lying weak and gray against the white sheets of the hospital bed, his face pained, brave but pained. A new lump of fear rolls up my esophagus. I can't stand the idea of Gung suffering. I shiver, and Breaker holds me tighter.

He rubs my back, small spirals across my ribs, and I try to slow my breathing to their rhythm. "What happened?" Breaker asks again softly, keeping me caged in his arms.

"My grandfather had a heart attack," I murmur against his chest, moving my head to the side so I can hear his heartbeat. I bring my palms up to his chest and listen as it picks up. He stops rubbing my back for a moment.

"Oh, wow. I'm really sorry. Will he be all right?" He sounds genuinely concerned, and I feel genuinely comfortable in his arms.

"I don't know," I answer, trying to picture Breaker's scarred face. Perhaps his cheek is misshapen, one eye pulled down like he has palsy. I shrug minutely, knowing I don't care what he looks like. Right now, he's being a good friend.

"That blows," he says, his warm breath disturbing my hair.

I try to lift my head, my chin dragging up the center of his chest. Initially, he tries to stop me, keeping his large arms resting on my shoulders to weigh me down. "Breaker," I whisper, feeling smothered. "I can't breathe."

He releases his hold on me suddenly. "Shit! Sorry!" and I slide my face up to his, bracing myself for a shock.

I breathe in sharply, completely taken aback by what I see—a perfectly unscarred face. A strong jaw, dark scruffy hair, and dark eyes that bored into mine with such hate less than a week ago. So much so that I'd stumbled backward in my checkout.

His entire body tenses as I stare into his wary expression, tracing all the ways in which he's perfect, smooth, and un-torn. Sunlight cuts streaks across his face, scarring him temporarily with orange.

I gasp, scrambling backward out of his lap, sitting back on my heels and just staring while he just stares right back at me. "It's you." My lips pool on the *ooh,* not sure where to go. What to think…

His gaze falls to the sandy floor, eyes dropping like there's lead weight in his vision. "I was hoping you'd forgotten all about that day."

I shake my head, unable to believe that this is the same guy. The one who wouldn't let me serve him.

How can it be the same guy? "You're the jerk from the supermarket?" I ask, though I know the answer.

"I'm the jerk," he says in shame, still unable to meet my eyes.

I swallow, cross my arms, feel the dust moving in like a door slowly closing, and cough.

"*Mon Dieu*! My God!" I cover my mouth. "Is this some sick joke? Did you do this to mess with me?"

He looks up slowly, his eyes showing fear and then, strangely, relief when they meet my eyes. "No. It was a coincidence that I met you out here. I promise."

I stand up, staring down at him, and he seems to shrink beneath me. It makes me feel bad for him. It shouldn't, but it does. He seems so…so conflicted.

Anger is hard to hold onto when grief is warring with your heart. I shake my head. "I don't understand this at all, Breaker. Are you even a vet?"

He stands too, leaning against the trunk, his eyes darting to the ugly tree, which feels like it's pulsing electric with energy. "I am. I swear. Look, I'm sorry I acted like such an asshole. I'd had a really crappy morning, the worst, and you just caught me at a bad time." He steps toward me. "That's why when I heard your voice in the forest, I didn't want you to know who I was. Not until you'd had a chance to get to know me better."

I retreat from his advance, hand up. "No. *Arrêtez*. Stop. I know that look you gave me. I've seen it before. It wasn't about a crappy morning." I gesture at my face. "It was this. What I am, where I come from. The color of my skin."

His jaw clenches, and his hand flies to his face like

he's trying to work it through. "No. It's not like that. I mean, maybe at first, but not anymore." He runs a frustrated hand through his hair and swears. "Please. Please don't look at me like that."

"Like what?" I challenge as I grasp my skirt in my fist.

His anger pulses out from his body, mixing with the warm air of the tree and increasing the temperature. "Like you don't want to. Like you can't stand to look at me."

Why does his voice slice at me like a scalpel?

My cheeks flush, sweat glands starting to tingle under my arms. "Isn't that what you did to me?" I mumble, wanting to pull back the words as soon as I say them because they only hurt. *Why do I care that he's in pain?*

Turning his back to me, he pulls back his arm and punches the trunk in front of him. It bounces off, providing complete resistance, and he winces. I think that will stop him, but it only pushes him forward. I gasp as he starts punching the tree. Over and over.

I catch small words with big meaning. *Hate. Hurt. Stupid. Not. Good. Enough.*

The sun is slipping, but I catch the dark stain growing across his knuckles. I should be scared. Terrified. But as I watch him punish himself, the sap dripping down, the mash of bark and broken flesh, I feel compassion. I understand trauma, violence, and what it takes from a person. It can take so much that people lose themselves, lose who they used to be. I inch forward and place my hand on his shoulder. He swings around, eyes wild for a moment, and then instantly embarrassed. "Breaker, stop," I whisper.

I touch his fist, wet with blood, and place a steady palm over it, sheltering it from further harm. Our eyes meet across acres of pain. The dust recedes like a morning fog.

"I don't want to be like this," he breathes. "I hate that I'm like this."

He took some of my suffering, so now I will do the same for him. "I know."

I wrap his knuckles in a handkerchief, laughing awkwardly at the fact that it has a little kitten printed on it. The air temperature sinks lower and lower as he calms.

We sit in the sand, a small fire glowing beside us. Neither of us knowing what to say without making things worse. Though I don't know how it could get any worse.

"I'm scared to look at you," he whispers.

And that's how it can get worse.

He sits next to me, resting his elbow on his knee and holding his injured hand up. I breathe in and hold it. I don't know what to say to that, so I stare into the fire, watching the flames curve around the air that pushes out from the tree. It bends like it's burning around a bubble.

"I want to…but I can't," he begins. "It could change… I don't want it to change."

I push the tip of my sneakers into the sand. It's as dry as a sack of rice. "What are you scared of? What do you think's going happen?" I ask, although I'm not sure I want to hear the answer.

"I'm scared I will start to hate you," he mutters, leaning toward me just slightly so that our clothes touch, but not our skin. I pull the sleeve of my cardigan down over my wrists. "I listen to your voice, and I'm okay. I saw your face for an instant and it was okay, but it could change. I don't trust it. Usually when I see a face like yours things come up. Things I don't want to feel, they just come up." He gestures with his hands, fingers fluttering like moths rising from a field.

He's like me, but different. "You know that's crazy, right?" I say, even though it's not crazy at all. I know that those bad memories sometimes push through the cracks. Sometimes, it's subtle. Small, clawing fingers that scratch away at the sane edges. But other times, it's like lightning. The view in front changes so suddenly, so forcefully, that the old pain drowns the soul. It can be a sound, a smell, a face…

He exhales, straightens. Then he says something that cuts through the smoke, the banter stacked like kindling next to us. "I know *you* know it's not crazy at all."

I edge away, uncomfortable. "Hmm. Guess you got my number, huh?"

Something like a flattened chuckle emits from his chest. "Maybe, or at least one of the digits."

I snort. "I hope it's eight."

"Eight?"

I imitate Ama's voice, "Eight is lucky number." He doesn't respond. "Breaker, you should look at me," I say.

He shakes his head. "It's not a good idea."

I hold my hand under his nose. "Does this scare you?"

He gazes at my hand, then takes it in his own, running his thumb over my fingers. My stomach churns at his touch like I've swallowed my twelve stars. They fizz and twinkle, creating light inside me. "No, it doesn't. But it's different."

Maybe I should leave. Ama's probably worried about me. There might be an update on Gung... I try to stand. "I should go," I say with surprising regret. "I don't even know why I'm still here." He grips my hand, and I give very little resistance as he pulls me back down beside him.

"Please. Don't go," he pleads. He brings his hand to the side of my face and brushes it shakily. "I don't want to be like this," he says again. "I'm trying." He's quiet for a moment, eyes searching the dark. "Tell me about your grandfather."

A spike of sadness hits me just above my heart like I'm being pinned to a corkboard as I remember him lying in the sawdust, weak, helpless, Ama screaming in the background. I bite down on the feelings. "*D'accord.* Okay. Gung is strong. He'll be okay. He is the sweetest, kindest man you'll ever meet. He has a temper, but he rarely uses it. Only when it's truly warranted. He puts up with a lot living with me and especially Ama. He's been through a lot too. War, beatings, losing his daughter... So, you know, a heart attack, that's nothing!" I say with false lightness. "Besides, Ama would never let him die."

Breaker shifts in his sandy seat. "Is he your dad's

dad or your mom's dad?" he asks, ticking off an imaginary list of mundane questions.

"My mom's."

"My grandparents live on the other side of the country, in San Jose. I've only met them once," he volunteers. "I don't know anything about my dad's parents. He never spoke of them..."

I throw another stick on our meager fire. Breaker pats his pocket and pulls out a pack of cigarettes, offering me one. I shake my head, holding the back of my hand to my nose. "Those things'll kill you, you know?"

He strikes a match and mumbles, "I know," through mostly closed lips. He inhales and exhales a puff of smoke. I turn away from the smell.

"So when did you come to America, Sunny?" he asks.

"About a year ago," I answer.

He coughs tarry, stale air into the night. "Your English is great. You must be a quick learner."

I groan, pulling my cardigan close. "You know it's only in an English-speaking country where someone would assume that. For your information, I already spoke English, French, Chinese, and a little Vietnamese before I even came to America. And over there, that's not uncommon."

He puts his hands up in defense. "Sorry!"

I look at my watch. It's after eight o'clock. "I should go," I say. "I have school tomorrow."

"You're in high school," he states, reminding himself.

I jump up. "Only for a few more months, then college." The thought of choosing drags me under. I stare up at the sky, looking for my diamond. My sign of comfort.

"That's cool," he manages, which makes me giggle. As does the weird casual direction this conversation has taken. From drama to school and college. I get the sense he's just trying to keep me talking.

"Anyway," I say, edging away from him. "I really should get going."

"Wait!" He grabs my wrist.

His eyes meet mine, turning from gold to steel and then back again. "I don't know what you want from me, Breaker," I groan, exasperated.

His sigh is relief and agony, a mask he must keep changing. "I want to *see* you again."

I search his face. His eyes are like dragonflies, beautiful and impossible to catch. "Why?" I ask, incredulous.

He dips his head and chuckles. "Why do you think?" Then he pats his chest like he's surprised that noise just came out of him.

I roll my eyes. "Um. You know how confusing you're being right now?"

He chuckles again. "I do."

Problem is that I do want to see him again. I want to understand him better. Understand the layers of trauma that can veil a person's heart to only see fear and hate when they look in my eyes. And to be truthful, I want to help him shatter them. Then maybe I'll know where to start on myself.

"Do you go to Tri-Valley?" he asks.

I nod.

"How about I pick you up after school?" he asks

warily, wincing like he's not really sure he wants to do it.

"I have to go straight to the hospital to visit Gung," I say, trying to press my voice into a less flustered shape.

He runs a hand through his dark hair and says, "I'll drive you."

"Fine." I cross my arms and stare down at the smoking figure. Wondering why on earth I would say yes to this. He doesn't look up, continuing to stare into the flames. "Don't touch the tree," I warn, swaying in the warm air wrapping around us.

"Not without you," he says quietly, and it's like the flames have reached up and slapped my cheeks for how much they're blushing.

I turn, skidding in the sand, and walk away. I know he's smiling at my back. I don't know how I know. I just do.

33

The dry grass of the barren field scratches at my ankles and burrs burrow into my socks. A strange smell wafts from the golden windows ahead.

Walking faster, I reach the stairs of the back porch, pause and listen. The familiar sound of Ama crashing around in the kitchen is interrupted by something I've never heard before. Ama cursing in English.

"Aiya! Damn it!" she shouts as I pull open the screen door and slip out of my shoes. My puffy eyes sweep the room, somehow still hoping that Gung will be sitting in his chair, puffing away and watching Ama from the corner of his eye to make sure she doesn't burn down the house.

I move past his chair, imagining his strong hands gripped over the arms, ready to pull up if needed. But it's empty, dented with his ghost, and I shudder.

The rest of the house is dark save a halo of light around the kitchen and dining area. I sniff the air again, my stomach starting to growl and then retreating to a purr. Because on the countertop is a casserole dish filled with a white, gluggy substance that emits a smell like cheesy vomit. I pick up a spoon and poke it gently, watching it wobble under a burnt crust.

"Ama," I whisper and she jumps, spinning around with a fork in her hand.

"Sunny, why you scare me like that!" she exclaims. Her eyes are round and rimmed in red, her expression frustrated. Darwin was wrong. Humans cry because it produces a response in other humans—a need to protect, envelope, and fix the problem.

"What is this?" I ask, pointing at the charcoal-crusted goo.

She looks at me like I've said the dumbest thing ever and frowns. "Mac-an-cheezz," she answers, buzzing her zees like a honeybee.

Now it's my turn to look at her like she's just said the dumbest thing ever. I don't think I've ever seen cheese in this house, and definitely not pasta. I laugh, cover my mouth, and dodge the fork that comes at my face. "Um, what on earth for?"

"Don't you laugh at me," she snaps, pointing the fork at me accusingly. "I don't know what happen. I put elbows in milk. I put in cheese. Put in oven. Should work, no?"

I giggle, and she pokes me sharply with the fork. I jump back, lifting my shirt to reveal three prong wounds, a lucky snakebite. "Ouch! Oh, *je suis désolé*. I'm sorry. But I have to ask again, why?" Ama is an amazing cook. Her noodles are full of flavor and never too greasy. Her rendang can strip layers from a tongue, but in a good way. But looking at this glob of what was once cheese, pasta, and milk, I can tell mac'n'cheese is way out of her field of expertise.

Her lips quiver a little, and my giggle gets sucked from the air. I stare down at a pamphlet she must have grabbed from the hospital about heart attacks. "I try make American dish for doctor. I want him take good care of Gung."

She wraps her arms tightly around herself, rocking on her heels. Her thin body shakes, and it splinters my heart. I walk around the island and stand in front of her. "You don't need to do that, Ama. The doctor will take good care of Gung whether you feed him or not. I promise. It's his job."

She shakes her head and squeaks. "I don't know what else to do, Sun. I cook. Cooking what I do." She brings her hands up in front of her before wrapping them back around herself like she needs to contain them. "I will die if he dies!" she exclaims dramatically, her face to the ceiling.

This is where Gung would interject and tell her she's being ridiculous. I step into his worn slippers and say, "*Non.* No. You won't die. You will be sad. I will be sad. We will both be horribly sad for a long time, but we won't die. We'll still have each other." Gung's slippers feel made for me and uncomfortable at the same time because I'm not ready to wear them.

She grunts then and looks at the floor, rubbing at a splash of milk with her toe. "Not if you go to Stanford."

Anger rises, but I shouldn't expect any less from her. She's nothing if not opportunistic. I take the tray of cheesy milk and head toward the front door. "I'm not doing this with you right now."

I hear her praying for a better behaved, more obedient granddaughter as the door closes behind me.

BREAKER

34

I wonder how dumb this will turn out to be. How long before she realizes I'm so not worth the trouble? I know I'm asking a lot—for her to bear with me as I try to make eye contact and struggle…and fail.

Staring into the flames, I feel raked over the burned wood and charred earth. And I feel pulled to the tree. The flames lean that way too. The force of whatever it is coaxing everything with energy into its arms. I yawn loudly, pushing my toes into the sand and burying my hands up to my wrists.

It would be nice…to rest for just a minute. I blink slowly seeing Sunny's almond eyes behind my lids. Her soft brown hair, straight as spaghetti. My eyes fly open, and I spring up. I promised I wouldn't touch it. And I want my promises to start meaning something.

I back away from the tree, pushing against the air like it's a plastic sheet I must break through. It's powerful. Sunny is right—it wants something from me.

As scary as that is, it's not as scary as what I have to do tomorrow.

I'm trapped, my arms and legs wearing bark and sticky with sap. My shirt is disappearing under a layer of brown. I

try to speak, but the only noise I can make sounds like leaves rustling in the wind. I'm exposed, my head craning to the shadows. My fear creeping toward me, warming the earth as it goes.

Suddenly blinded, I try to scream. But it has grown right over me. Consumed me. The wind howls through my mouth.

It's the sun. I'm blinded and exposed by the sun, and I can't move to the shadows. I can't move at all.

Red shakes me awake. "Dude, wake up," he says, his eyes unnaturally close to mine. The dark blue in them reminds me of the heavy skies we only ever caught a glimpse of when the rain clouds parted and the palm leaves shifted.

I sit up and he shuffles back, sitting on the end of my bed. "You know it's pretty boring to dream about the weather. I dream about robots and apes talking like people, and ooh, flying." He stretches his arms out wide, pretending to be a plane.

"Huh?" I say, wiping the sleep from my eyes and squinting at my strange little brother.

"You were all like, sunny, sunny!" he says, clasping his hands together and calling to the ceiling.

I groan and throw a pillow at him, which he catches and throws back at me. "Get out!" I grunt, pretending to be annoyed.

He grins and jumps to the curtains, throwing them open with a flourish. "Looks like you're right." The sun blinds me, spreading light over the dust bunnies and piles of unwashed clothes. "Looks like it's gonna be a bright, bright, sunshiny day!" he sings, darting out of the way as I throw my jacket at him.

Ugh! I'm gonna have that song in my head all day now.

Sunny

35

Cara slaps my hand. "Ouch!"

"What's up with you? You're gonna mess up your nails!" she scolds as she drives.

I roll my eyes but stop biting my fingernails. "Shouldn't you be paying attention to the road?"

She purses her lips. "I'm a woman. We can multi-task," she snaps, and we both giggle.

I crack the window, letting some of the cold air slap me awake. Breathing in, I smell wood smoke, water melting into soil. Nothing sweet and warm on the air here, but I yawn all the same.

"So..." Cara starts. "Late night?"

I nod, pulling down the shade to check my face in the mirror. "Ama tried to make mac'n'cheese," I say, pulling my hair into a ponytail.

Cara snorts and jumps in her seat. "How'd that go?"

I smile, but it's forced in lopsided. Because it's funny, but at the same time, Gung's lying in a hospital bed with a bad heart... "Disaster!"

Cara switches on the radio and we sing, tapping our hands on the dash and steering wheel. For a few minutes, everything is normal between us.

When we pull up to the school, she takes forever to park, in, out, in, out, trying to line herself up perfectly.

Finally, we get out.

As we separate toward our different lockers, she calls out, "See you after school."

My eyes dart left and right, looking suspicious like I think someone's listening. Swiftly, I run after her, clutching her shoulder. "Um, actually, I'm getting a ride from someone else after school," I whisper as she spins around.

I hurry back to my locker but hear her grunting and following behind me, sounding like a mummy in one of those old horror movies. Before I can fight back, she's grabbed my arm and pulled me into an empty classroom. I can't even feign surprise. I knew this was coming, and I don't know why I was avoiding it. "Sit!" she orders pointing at a desk.

I sit down and she stands over me, her round, usually cheery, face trying to contort into a serious expression. "Sunny. Tell me what's going on. Now!"

Looking to the window, I stall, thinking of my diamond of sky. Thinking of being trapped. When I come back to Cara's face, I fade and buckle. But not all the way. There are some things she doesn't need to know, and there's one thing that will keep her sufficiently distracted. Staring down at my desk, my eyes grazing the curse words and 'history blows chunks' carved into the wood, I mumble, "I met a boy."

She squeals. Coughs. Tries to cover her squeal. Squeals again and slaps a hand over her mouth. Cara likes to think of herself as a feminist. Squealing over a boy doesn't fit her idea of that. "Okay," she says, her hands smoothing the air. "Okay. Who? Do I know him? What's his name? When did you meet? How long have you been dating? Oh, I just knew there was something more going on with you." She congratulates herself and squats down to catch my eyes, waiting for her answers.

I sort through her questions and answer, "His name is Breaker Van Winkle. Yes, you do know him. He was the guy at the store who didn't want me to serve him." Cara's eyebrows rise at that, and she bites her cheek to stop herself from interrupting. "We're not dating. We're just friends." *I think.*

She crosses her arms. "The homeless guy from the store? Sunny, you can do so much better than that. And Van Winkle? That's a really weird name. Sounds like the name of a wizard or an elf or something." I stiffen at her words, but also take in these little details I've not had time to ponder before now. "And even if you're not dating, something *more than friends* is happening whether you want it to or not," she says, touching my cheeks. "'Coz your cheeks are as red as apples."

"He's not homeless," I snap defensively. "He's just… He's just got some problems. I think I can help him, Cara. I'm kind of fascinated by him."

She groans in frustration and slings an arm around my shoulders, pulling me in for a hug, which I lean into. "You would choose the strange guy with the bizarre name, with all the problems, wouldn't you?"

I squirm in her arms, and she releases me. She knows I don't like to be contained for long. "We're not dating," I state firmly.

The bell rings as she pulls me from my seat. "Sure, sure," she says between grinning teeth.

School passes with a nervous twang like that Chinese mandolin music Ama listens to, mostly to punish me. I hop from class to class, going through the motions. I think that's what most of us are doing now. Waiting out the end of the semester for summer to start.

I drift off in French, my mind cast out like a fishing line and getting hooked into thoughts of the forest. I wonder what the tree will look like in the spring. Will it flower? Does it dry out as the streams lose their water or does it stay in a timeless bubble? I also think about what Cara said about Breaker's name, and as soon as the bell rings, I head for the library.

Instead of searching through the cards, I go straight to the desk. Mrs. Bernard smiles at me as I approach until her glasses are lifted to her eyes, then she frowns. "Miss La Chance," she says, still having trouble putting my French last name with my Asian-looking face. I ignore her sneer.

"I'm looking for any books on magic in the twentieth century," I say, leaning my hands on her desk, accidentally brushing the corner of the magazine she's reading. She pulls it away sharply. The fact that she wipes it on her knee to rub off my touch doesn't go unnoticed, but I try to keep it light. "I'm doing a paper on American myths and legends, and I need to fill in some blanks."

Mrs. Bernard's face screws up like she's bitten into a sour ball, but she does direct me to where I can find a collection of North American fables and folktales and one other book on mysteries and unexplained phenomena. I check out the books and exit the library, which is eyeball high with hatred and misunderstanding. I wonder if she even knows why she hates me. I pause. Suck in a breath. *Does Breaker?*

I shove the books in my bag as I meet Cara at the door. She's gripping her bag so tightly I think she might break her fingers, a look of excitement pulsing from her eyes. "You ready to meet your man?" she teases.

I swallow and push the door open, spilling out into the parking lot swept with ice and teenagers.

36

"Is that her?" Red points to a girl with blonde Samantha-from-*Bewitched* hair and flares that swallow her boots. I shake my head. Man, it would be easier if it were… "Is *that* her?" he asks again, pointing to another white girl. This time with light brown curls tied into pigtails. It's been ten minutes of him aiming his finger at different girls like a sniper and asking the same question over and over again. I'm about ready to either drive off or throw him out the window.

The truck is getting fogged up. I reach to the windshield and wipe away the condensation, stopping halfway when I see her. Droplets of water add silver highlights to her flushed, high-boned cheeks.

Sunny stands at the entrance, scanning the parking lot. From this distance, her features are blurred and her face starts edging toward *their* faces. Fear spiked with anger cuts across my chest. I run a palm down my face slowly, trying to regain my composure. Get back to *before* me. One breath. She's not them. Two breaths. I'm safe. I'm home. Three breaths. It's Sunny. It's *Sunny. It's Sunny.*

Instead of doing what I would normally do, which is run and avoid, I force myself to watch her. Accrue the details that make her Sunny and hang onto them like hooks for a rock climber.

"Does *she* know what your truck looks like?" my shrewd little brother asks. I curse, and Red snorts. She doesn't know my what I drive. I have to get out.

"No. But I can see her now. Wait here," I snarl at Red, whose excitability is reaching astronomical levels as he bounces up and down on the seat.

"She's here! She's here!" he shouts, ducking when I try to clip the top of his head.

The rusty door creaks as I open it and high schoolers stare at me as they pass. And I don't know if it's because I'm too old to be standing in the high school parking lot or if it's my army gear that does it. I smooth my hair down and button my jacket, feeling ready to bolt. Feeling like there's a gun trained on me and I'm a sitting target.

Sunny finds me and smiles carefully. A blonde girl squeezes her arm, and Sunny gives her a warning look. She starts walking toward me, and I'm horrified to see the other girl continues beside her.

Get back in the truck, I tell myself. This is an ambush.

They reach me and the horn blows, making us all jump, and the last few stragglers turn and point. I turn around to see Red grinning sheepishly in the window, and then he retreats from climbing over the steering wheel. He disappears behind the fogged-up windows, murky like jungle mist.

"Hi," Sunny says shyly, looking up into my face.

And now that she's closer, now that I can really see her, I start to relax. It makes me wonder. If I took the time to really look at every face, would I start seeing *them* differently? I realize *Sunny* is making me see things differently.

"Breaker, this is Cara, my nosy best friend," she says, sweeping her arm out and gently elbowing the blonde girl in the side.

Cara narrows her eyes and gives me the once over. I can't even pretend to smile. So, I just try to look less surly. "Sunny is like…the best. Like the best person I know," she says, her voice warmer and silkier than I expected. "Don't mess her around." She waggles a finger at me before leaning in to kiss Sunny on the cheek. Sunny leans right into it. A thing I would never do.

I look to Sunny, nervous, while Cara stares at me with fiercely transparent eyes. "She won't leave until you promise not to mess me around," Sunny says deadpan, her lips twisting to one side.

Red has written in the window condensation. It says—*Hurry up!*—but backward.

Laughing awkwardly, I try to sound sincere, when really I have no idea, "Um, sure, I promise. I won't mess her around."

Cara's round face breaks into a smile, and she slaps my back. I stumble forward, not from the force but from being touched. "Good! You kids have fun now!" she quips with a wink. "Call me later?" she says to Sunny as she holds her thumb and pinky out and to her ear. Sunny nods.

Sunny stands there in blue jeans and a checked shirt, a velvet jacket over her shoulders, her hair tied into a loose ponytail. With the books in her arms and backpack on her back, she looks young, sweet, and not meant for someone like me. But then she talks in that unusual accent of hers, and I can tell she's got more written on her pages than I can possibly understand.

She's seen a lot... Like me.

"*Allez*. Let's go," she says, walking to the passenger door.

I rush to open it for her, but Red beats me to it. "Welcome to the crappiest truck in the universe!" he says, demonstrating very clearly that he's ten.

Sunny giggles and bows. "Why, thank you."

I love that Red doesn't react to the fact that she's Asian at all. What took me days to even start to understand, he understands in an instant. Sunny is just Sunny.

Red insisted on the window seat, so Sunny and I are squashed next to each other as we drive. Her leg touches mine, and the air in the cab gets warmer with every turn that pushes us closer.

The truck rattles, held together by rust and duct tape. I lean across her and put on fresh air.

"So what grade are you in?" Red asks.

Sunny grins at him with neat white teeth, her dark pink lips spread wide. "I'm a senior."

Red looks her up and down and says, "You're pretty small for a senior."

I stiffen, waiting for him to say something inappropriate. Her face goes all serious, and she leans down to Red's level. "Well, I am part Irish. You know what that means?"

Red's eyes widen, totally caught up in her. I don't blame him. "What?" he asks eagerly.

"I'm part leprechaun, of course!" she announces

with a grin and a wink.

Red gulps, gasps, and then it registers. He slaps his knee. "Ha! Good one!"

A small laugh escapes my mouth and I bite my lip, trying to keep it with me. "Well, Red, this is your stop," I say loudly as we pull to the curb. Sunny smears the window to gaze at our crappy condo. The stubbly grass poking up between hard-pressed dirt. Red groans but drags his stuff from the floorboard after he gets out. "Tell Mom I'll be home later."

Red just raises his hand, pushes the door closed, and gives me a thumbs-up as he walks away. He's getting a little too cool for my liking. He stops on the path just as I'm about to do a U-turn and comes tearing toward the truck, banging on the window. Sunny winds it down, and Red's head comes at her like a bear trying to get at chip crumbs. "You should come with us on Saturday! On our hike. Remember, Break, you promised."

Sneaky little devil.

"Sunny. Sunny. Promise you'll come too?" He squints and tries to look cute, looking more like a wrinkly peach. "It'll be more fun with you there. Break actually smiles when you're around."

My cheeks get smashed with red.

Sunny glances at me for an answer. I nod, so she continues, "Um, sure, Red, I'll come with you if it's okay with your brother."

I lick my lips and mumble, "Yeah. You should come. It would be…uh, nice."

Red snatches this and runs with it. "Right, then, no backing out. It's a deal. It's solid. Hey, Sunny! You know he dreams about you. He…"

Quickly, I lean over Sunny's legs, my arms brushing her thighs as I roll up the window. Shutting out Red's commendable attempts to embarrass me beyond belief.

Sunny is as still as stone until I'm back on my side of the truck.

"You don't have to…" I start.

She gives me a no-teeth smile. "No. I want to. It'll be, uh, *amusant*, fun." That last bit sounded like a question.

Seconds bounce around the cab—one, two, three…

Now, without Red's constant chatter and our legs bumping into each other, the atmosphere in the truck has changed. It's filled with nervousness. Embarrassment. Pressure.

Glancing at my bandaged hand, Sunny asks, "How's your hand?"

I do a quick U-turn and head back toward the highway. "It's okay," I mumble, fumbling for my smokes. I fish one out and go to light it, but she stops me.

"If it's okay with you, I'd really rather you didn't smoke with me in here," she says, screwing up my nose. "Secondhand smoke, you know?"

My hands are bewildered, my brain scattered. "Sure. Um, sorry." I tuck them away.

Silence streams across the windshield as we pick up speed. She keeps playing with the spine of a book she has clutched to her chest. Staring at her hands, she says, "Breaker, why did you want to do this?"

I run my hands across the steering wheel, trying to give a good answer. One that won't scare her away. "I… um, I feel…" I sigh. I put on my blinker and pull to the side, the truck getting swallowed by the overhanging shadows of the forest.

"'Coz, you know, you seem like maybe you've got some problems and well, I have problems too. I'm happy to be your friend, but you know..." she starts.

The truck hums. I turn toward her and make myself stare into her almond eyes. I let the features frighten and then fold over me. The wave of anger rises, but there's a cap on it. It's contained.

"I know. It's just, I feel like maybe you'd be good for me," I manage.

She gazes down at her fingers and sighs. "Oh."

And I worry I've said the wrong thing. "I'm not saying this right. It's just...when I look at you, the anger I've felt since I got home, the fear, it's starting to melt away. Does that make sense?"

I reach out and put my hand over hers. Her skin is cool, soft. I wait for her to withdraw, but she doesn't. "It does, I guess, in a way. But you know I'm not the mascot for Asians in the greater New York area. I'm just one girl. I mean, it's definitely fascinating. Vietnam vet traumatized by his war experiences finds solace in talking to Asian girl with unlikely accent..." She says it like it's the title of an article. "I like the idea of helping you, Breaker. But what if I can't?"

The conversation has taken a real serious turn, and I feel like I'm surrounded by all the versions of me. I stare forward. "I think you already have."

She shakes her head and pulls out the book she's been playing with. "I borrowed these for you."

I shuffle closer. Each compression of air between us giving me hope.

37

Breaker taps the fuel gauge and turns off the engine. The heat doesn't seep from the cab—it's ripped from it, leaving any icy block of air in its place. I wrap my arms around myself and shiver.

"Sorry," he says. "I don't want to run out of gas." He starts to shrug out of his jacket, ready to offer it to me, but I stop him. His jacket stinks. But I try not to wrinkle my nose. Diving into my backpack, I pull out a cardigan. He takes it from me and drapes it over my shoulders. The action is intimate. Strange.

His hand lingers at my thin shoulders for a moment before it goes to his pocket, patting the pack of cigarettes I've asked him not to light up. He remembers, coughs, and runs a hand through his dirty hair.

The books sit in my lap, and we stare at them for a moment.

We flip through stories of men turning in wolves and Big Foot before we come to *the* one. I hear him drag in a breath and hold it.

The tree is much prettier than our tree. But then, it's cartooned and romanticized.

The old man leaning against it, his muscles wasted. His long beard doesn't fit with what I was hoping for. I sigh, just as Breaker says quietly, "Done."

I turn my head, meeting his eyes, which are awfully close. His chin rests on my shoulder, his cheek nestled in my hair. "That was fast. I haven't even started reading yet."

He chuckles, inches closer, and runs a finger over the old man's face. "Am I meant to be related to this joker?" he asks the icy air.

I read the first page and flip over. This man is Rip, a bit of a layabout. Good fun but always avoiding work, responsibility. Every now and then, I glance up into Breaker's concentrated face. He worries his lip as he reads at a super-fast pace. When he's done, he tells me and waits for me to finish. With each page, he leans closer, his hand now in my lap, toying with the edge of the page while he waits for me to read.

The temperature in the cab rises and the windows fog. He breathes steadily next to my ear. Sometimes, I hear a muttered word as he reads aloud.

"I get it," he says as I close the book.

I turn and he sidles back, leaning against the door and away from me. "Get what?"

"Wanting to escape, skip through the hard parts of life..." He stares through the foggy view of the windshield. His eyes focused. "I mean, this guy Rip avoided the whole war. He got to wake up once all the hard stuff was over. I wish I'd had that option."

His demeanor changes, a sort of caging happening before my eyes. Bars are thrown up, his jaw locks. His eyes are on a point that's probably far in the past. "You can't skip through your life," I say, bringing his attention back to me. "He missed his children growing up. Many of his friends died. If you skip parts of your life, even the hard parts, you'll lose the good parts, and what's left loses its value. You're not really living."

He nods, but there's tenseness to it. "I need a smoke," he mutters.

His hands shake, his fingers jitter. I reach out and take them in my own hands, and he exhales slowly. His eyes grace mine for a moment and then look away. "It didn't really give us many answers, though, did it? It's just a fable. A lesson to learn."

He takes the book from my lap, flipping it open to a page. Again, he slides closer. Leans in to share his thoughts and heat with me. "I see some of myself in him. I see a lot of my dad. Always fun until things got hard."

I laugh and catch myself. "Um. Sorry, it's just *you* don't seem very, uh, what's the word…jovial."

Breaker shrugs. "I used to be."

I knock his knee with my own. "I'm sorry."

He huffs, keeps flicking the pages back and forth. "Whatever."

I tilt my head, stare at the pages. It's not the revelation I was hoping for. There are a lot of differences. Parts not adding up. But I guess that's what happens over time. Things get twisted and shaped into something easier to swallow. One thing I do notice is the difference in the earth around the tree in the pictures. Dry and barren at the beginning. Rich and fertile by the end. My brain ticks over theories. But gets distracted when Breaker leans his scratchy face closer to mine.

I clap the book shut. "What are you doing?" I ask, turning too quickly, his stubble sandpapering my face.

Suddenly nervous and awkward, Breaker blurts, "I was going to kiss you." When my eyes widen, he adds, "On the cheek." He touches my cheek lightly with the tip of his finger.

Straightening, I ask, "What? Why?"

To which he smiles, his dark eyes glassy with a small sparkle. "Because I felt like it. I wanted to see what it would feel like."

I stop and think about it. The impulse. What makes someone want to kiss another? Gratitude, closeness, shock. Any of these would fit. I narrow my eyes. When Breaker starts to speak, I put a finger up to silence him. "I'm thinking."

He looks confused but leans back, waits.

Is there any harm in it? *Probably not.*

Would Ama kill me? *Only if she finds out.*

"Okay," I say, nodding my head and offering my cheek.

He sucks in a breath, leaning back. "Are you serious?"

Crossing my arms, I nod. "Yes."

He shifts awkwardly in his seat. "Well, now it feels weird. Um…"

I close my eyes and tilt my head up. "*Allons*. Come on. Just do it."

I wait a full ten seconds before I feel his lips press to my cheek, warm, rough, dry. The stars I swallowed seem to spin and shoot around inside my chest.

Giggling, I open my eyes. He's smiling. He has a nice smile. Shy like a jackal.

"That was pretty strange, Sunny," he says, knocking my shoulder.

I smile back at him. "I thought it was nice."

He rolls his eyes and turns the key, the engine

fighting for life in the cold. He grits his teeth as it turns over. When he's not watching, I touch my fingers to my cheek.

Brief as the sun kissing my face under crowded foliage.

It *was* nice.

BREAKER

38

Mist speckles the windshield. The word *nice* melts into a green haze settling over my eyelids. My heart hiccups.

"She's not like the others. She's a nice girl. A good girl. I think I love her," Chuck says quietly, and then louder, "Yes! I'm head over heels in love with her." The others snigger, but I lean away from his proclamation like it might be catching.

"You're lonely," Grims says, slapping Chuck's arm with the back of his hand. "Sure, they're pretty, sometimes pretty willing too, but are you saying you would take her home to meet your family?"

Chuck taps his chin, his eyes warm and speckled with the mist that's fast becoming rain. "You don't get it. She understands something. Something inside me. My family will get it. Won't they?" There's doubt in his mouth that only two seconds ago was spouting eternal love.

I keep my mouth closed. My knees tucked close to my chest.

"Iceman knows what I'm talking about. The girls, they're good for some "company"." Grims uses air quotes. "But that's about all. Be careful, man." He directs his comment to Chuck and away from me, for which I'm grateful. "They're not all that nice. There's a reason they cozy up to you. Those nice girls just want out of this godforsaken country."

Chuck blinks. Tries to frown and look thoughtful, but his mouth turns up in a goofy, love-struck grin. "Can you blame her?"

And I can't.

I've watched Chuck around the girl. Watched her shy away from him for days before she even talked to him. Then it grew like smoke from a fire, wrapping around them, pushing them closer.

I've not truly seen love up close. Mom and Dad wasn't love; it was something else between giving up and fighting against the middle. But Chuck and this girl… What's ahead won't be easy. They will have to fight to stay together.

That's gotta be worth something, right? That's more than nice.

I wanted to know what it would do to me. Would it send me spiraling down a violent, splintered rabbit hole or would it be a sign or a smash or something? Turns out it was none of those things. My head didn't explode with bad memories. I wasn't magically cured of all my prejudices. It was just a small kiss. Maybe a promise of what's to come, but, mostly, I felt her skin under my lips and she was right. It was nice.

We drive to the hospital in easy quiet. Nice is a good feeling—a normal feeling—and I don't want to disrupt it.

When I pull into the hospital parking lot, I realize I don't want to lose it either.

Sunny slides over to the door since she's somehow ended up crammed right next to me on the drive over. She grabs her bag and then pauses, leaning into the cab to knock my shoulder. "Thanks for the ride. And the…"

She smiles, glows even.

She's about to slam the door when I shout out, louder than necessary. "Um, wait!" She grips the rusted edge, swinging it back and forth as she waits for me to speak. "Can I have your phone number? You know, so we can organize the hike?" I cover.

Her gaze drops to the dark asphalt and then back up, her eyes a blanket thrown open on a grassy field. "Sure." She scribbles her number on the corner of one of her notepads and hands it to me. "Um, Breaker?"

I've got the number in my hand and I scrunch it into my fist tightly, scared she's going to take it away from me. "Yeah," I answer defensively.

"When you ring," Sunny says, her face knotted up with seriousness. "Don't hang up when she answers. Wait for me to come to the phone."

Confused, I nod.

She leaves me, and bad feelings push up between my feet like the grass growing around Rip Van Winkle as he slept. I start to wonder what's going to happen. When will I turn on her, stop trusting her, feel like she's dragging me back to the jungle?

I can't believe it's just over. That's not my life.

Sunny

39

Gritting my teeth without meaning to, I think about Ama answering the phone when Breaker calls. They make a horrible squeaking noise, and I stop. I turn back to the truck, fading yellow crusted in blood-colored rust. Breaker watches me with thoughtful eyes. I wave, but he doesn't wave back. I know that look. That response. He's not watching me. He's looking right through me to the past, caught in a memory. At least I won't poke him in the side with a bamboo skewer to snap him out of it like Ama does to me.

When I go inside, I hear the chortle of the truck driving away.

I take a deep steeling breath. I like hospitals. The uniform predictability of them. The staff shuffling through the hallways with a healing purpose. I nod at a nurse as she passes me, running my hand along the plastic handrail. This is home to me.

I wander the halls of the makeshift hospital like a ghost. Unattached. An orphan. Beeps and compressions flow from every doorway. Drips from IV fluids and blood. Small noises of pain. People who don't want to make a fuss or be fussed over. People who are alone like me.

Floating into a room, I sit beside a middle-aged woman, touching her hand. Her eyes slide to me, and she smiles.

"Merci, merci," she whispers, and I squeeze gently. It means thank you, but the English word would fit just as well. Mercy.

Amity kills the loneliness.

"You so thin," Ama says, pinching the small amount of skin clinging to the bone of my elbow. She waves her hand in front my eyes, and I blink. Cough the dust from my lungs.

I lean my cheek to hers. "How's Gung?"

She hooks her arm through mine and leads us to his room, the smell of a Chinese omelet getting stronger. The scent of pork sausage and chives fills the hallway, and I lick my lips.

"Gung is good. He come home tomorrow," she says excitedly. She claps loud as a firecracker, unaware of the sick people sleeping. She claps again.

"Ama!" I exclaim.

She shrugs. "Spirits like snakes in grass. Loud noises scare them."

My heart pounds hopeful in my chest despite the sound of bone slapping against skin.

We round the corner and see Gung's doctor in the hallway. He nods to us. Ama grabs his arm too, pulling us both into Gung's room like we're *off to see the wizard*.

Gung's awake, sitting up with a cup of tea and an omelet before him. On the chair are stacks of containers full of food. Ama breaks away and collects the pile, plonking them in the surprised doctor's arms. "Rendang. Fish curry. Singapore noodle and mooncake," Ama lists. "For you…to eat," she adds when he gives her a confused look.

"Thank you, Mrs. Douglas, that's very kind," he manages. I glance at Gung's chart, aching to have a look.

Settling on the bed next to Gung, I note his color does look better but he's still hooked up to an IV. "Have you got out of bed yet?" I ask, watching him chew his food carefully and swallow.

"I go out to smoke but the nurse, she yell at me," he answers disgruntled.

Ama's eyebrows rise as she points at him accusingly. "That pipe is why you in here, George. What you think, ah? No pipe. No smoke!" she shouts, and Gung appeals to me and the doctor. We both shake our heads in unison, and she harrumphs triumphantly. "My Sunny will be doctor soon too," she says slyly. I roll my eyes. She has her knife poised, ready to strike. "She go to NYU so she be close to her sick, sick grandfather."

An oily well pools in my chest, swirling with guilt and irritation. "Ama, not now," I groan. My eyes land on Gung, mid-eye roll. He pats his chest, and it hurts mine.

She ignores me. "Where you go med school?" she asks, trying to look innocent but the word *ruse* comes to mind.

Clueless, the doctor answers proudly, "NYU like I said before, Mrs. Douglas. And your wife is right, Mr. Douglas. No more smoking. Your blood pressure is quite high. Your heart and lungs are under stress. If you want to live a long life, you're going to have to make some changes."

Gung looks like he'd rather die than give up his pipe, his lips pull down like there's weight tied to the corners. I picture the gleeful massacre I just know Ama's going to perform when we get home—tobacco smoke and ash from a stack of pipes will pour from the chimney.

I lean into Gung's shoulder, which feels bonier than it should. "What kind of changes, Doctor?" I ask, getting out a pen and paper from my bag.

"Gentle exercise. No smoking. No alcohol. And reduce stress." He looks at Ama. "Also no greasy or fatty foods," he says, glancing down at the stack of containers in his arms.

Ama's not stupid, and she glares at the doctor. "My food not greasy," she snaps, eyes flaming as she steps in front of him. She nearly pushes the man right in the center of his striped tie, but I jump up and catch her hand. "You try my food!" she pretty much threatens. "Then you tell me it greasy."

Gung coughs, and everyone stops and turns toward him. "Thank you, Doctor," he says quietly but in that voice that makes everyone, even Ama, listen. "You write that down, Sunny?"

I nod, looking at the list. There are two things I'm worried about. The smoking and the stress. How can we reduce his stress when the only thing that calms him after one of Ama's electrical storms is having a puff of his pipe on the back porch?

My shoulders sag, and Gung pats my hand. Fear climbs my ribs like a ladder.

This is going to be impossible.

Ama sings as she drives, releasing the wheel to chant and gesture with her hands. She loves Elvis songs, singing out of tune and along to the background music rather than the lyrics. I lean against the window, the late nights catching up with me. My nose pressed to the glass, I steam up the glass. Ama turns to me, and the car veers into the middle of the road. Luckily, there are only squirrels and chipmunks to see us.

"Sun need sleep," she announces, and then reaches over to pat my head gently. She can be gentle when it suits her. "I make you supper and then bed." She gives her orders and then starts to do the hula, taking both hands off the wheel. I tighten my seatbelt.

I jerk awake when she slams on the handbrake while we're still moving. Shaking my shoulder, she cackles. "You dribble on seatbelt." Throwing back her head, she laughs. It's good to see her happy. Hopeful.

Slapping my homework on the bench, I watch her cook fried rice with leftover sausage, frowning when she realizes she's out of sesame oil. Sundown's Asian grocery supplies are practically non-existent. She rattles the pantry, picks through her spices, and starts writing a list. We'll have to go to New York on the weekend.

I shovel the rice in my mouth while scratching out my homework, barely paying attention to what I'm writing. Small oil stains bloom on the page when I drop grains of rice.

I'm midway through a large gulp of soymilk when the phone rings. My heart strums like strings on a harp. I reach for it, but Ama snatches it away, suddenly having the reflexes of a cat. "Douglas rezeedeence," she says with a wicked smile. I swallow my milk and wait. "Van what? Who are you to call my Sunny? Eh? Ah?" She tsks and nods, and I pity Breaker with all my heart. "How old you? That's too old. You too old! What wrong with you to call a girl in high school? Hm." I slap a palm over my face and drag it down, pulling the rims of my eyes with it.

I hold out my hand for the phone and Ama arches an eyebrow, ignoring me.

She watches me with dark ink eyes studying my reactions, her mouth twisted in amusement. "What you do? Ah, good, good. But now? Mm." She's killing me and relishing every second of it. "Okay. You go to church?"

I wrench the phone from her hand, and she screams, "Ai ya!"

"Your pudding is burning," I say, covering the mouthpiece. And that's enough to distract her. She rushes to the oven. "*Bonjour.* Hello, Breaker, are you still there?"

His voice through the phone is different, deeper, calmer. He chuckles. "I am."

Ama's ears are pricked as she pretends to tend to her pudding with her face on a listening angle. I stretch the cord of the phone around the wall and giggle. "*Désolé*. I'm so sorry," I whisper.

"*Apa?* What?" Ama asks.

Breaker breathes steadily. A warm feeling spreads across my chest like a bird's wings in summer. "It's okay. I'm okay," he says, sounding shocked.

I twirl the cord around my finger. Thinking this is strange and sweet and kind of unreal. "So what's up?"

I ask.

He coughs. "Well, I'm calling to organize the hike, remember?"

"Sunny and Breaker sittin' in a tree, K-I-S-S… Ugh! Mom!" I hear Red shouting in the background.

"Shit. I mean, sorry," he says.

"Pudding!" Ama announces.

I groan. Always interrupted. "Just let me ask Ama," I say.

"Oh. Okay, sure," he says, surprised.

Ama's dark eyes are an inch from my face when I turn around. "What you want to ask?"

I try for sweet, pleading eyes when I say, "My friend wants to take me and his little brother on a hike in the Catskills on Saturday. It will just be for a couple of hours, I promise."

She taps her chin, leaving an olive streak in her white powder. "A soldier. Mm. Good to his family. Mm." She sums him up from her brief interrogation, believing completely in her first impression. I secretly breathe a sigh of relief that she only saw his back when he came to the store. "What he look like?"

I frown. *What's that got to do with anything?* "Um. He's handsome, I guess. Dark hair, dark eyes. Tall…"

She nods in agreement. "Tall is good. Okay. Yes. But we need meet him first."

We quickly make plans for him to pick me up Saturday morning at nine. Thankfully, Breaker doesn't mention the fact that I just called him handsome.

BREAKER

40

I get off the phone and scrunch my hand into a rock-like fist. That was hard. Talking to her grandmother, Ama, whatever. Her voice is more like the voices I remember, that broken English thrown at us roadside as we marched past. When she spoke, I could feel the drag, the edges of bloodstained postcards puncturing my sides and draining my body. But I held on. Looking forward to talking to Sunny made me hold on. I talked myself back from it, listening to the words rather than the sound. I shouldn't be so proud of myself—it's pathetic—but I am.

But now I have to meet them. I release the phone and catch my reflection in the mirror over the hallstand. My hair stands up on its own, unwashed for weeks. I trail my hands down the collar of my jacket, twelve months' worth of sweat and grime makes it seem more dirt than material.

When I meet them, I can't look like a bum.

I shrug off the jacket and stalk to the washer.

At some point, Red comes and sits next to me, crossed-legged, staring at the machine. "What're we doing?" he asks.

The water is close to black. Washing a year of jungle, blood, and sweat from my body. Not letting go just yet, but at least starting the process.

I shrug.

"At least you might smell a bit better after this," Red says, hypnotized by the tumble of the machine. Black water swirling like a rip in time.

I scruff his hair. "Maybe I should put you in there then?"

He hops a foot away. And I laugh. Genuinely laugh.

The washing machine shudders, and I watch the water spurt down the drain. Particles of memories I'd happily forget. Things I don't know why I was holding onto. Is it armor? Comfort? Habit?

A sudden panic grips my shoulders and shakes, because it's my skin. I just washed away my skin. I stand, reaching for the stop button, but it's too late now anyway. It's been washed out to sea.

Red smirks and punches my arm, bringing me back. "You'll probably still stink," he says, pinching his nose. "Did you know a wolf can smell prey that's 1.75 miles away?"

My mouth makes a grim line. *No, I didn't know that.*

I hold my jacket up, dripping water on the top of Red's head. It looks as green as the day it was given to me. I snap it, and water sprays everywhere. Red jumps up, calls me a name, and goes to stand in the doorway. I hang it on a coat hanger off the door handle. Red makes me squeeze between him and the doorway.

"Now whatcha doin'?" he asks, arms crossed, watching me like I've been body snatched or something.

Rolling my eyes, I say, "Shower," and he follows me mindlessly into the bathroom. I put my hand to his back and gently shove him through the door. "Out!"

"Is this a girl thing? Do you have to be clean 'coz of Sunny?" he yells through the door.

My eyes rise to the water-stained ceiling. Thank God Mom's still at work. I run the water, getting out all the various shop-bought luxury items we never had in the jungle. Shampoo, conditioner, liquid soap. Line them up.

No, it's not a *girl* thing. But it is a *Sunny* thing.

Sunny

41

School passes like the flutter of wings. Air moves around us, sounds butt against our ears, but I'm not really taking it in. Gung comes home today. I have a shift at the store. When I get home, he'll be there. Back in his chair. Where he's supposed to be.

Cara smiles warily at me as we drive to the store. I pop my head out of my shirt as I change, catching her full-on staring at me, mouth open, desperately wanting to ask me something.

"*Comment*? What?" I ask as I button my shirt and slip into my smock.

"Are you going to tell me about the boy?" she asks, her eyes finally back on the slick streets. The arches of water on the windscreen.

I shrug. "There's not a lot to say." She squishes her lips into a best she can do scowl, which looks more like she's trying to whistle. "I'm sorry. There's just not much to it. He drove me to the hospital, we talked, he kissed me on the cheek, and then I gave him my number. He called me when I got home, and Ama interrogated him. She found him to be acceptable because he's a soldier and he's tall. We're going on a hike with his little brother on Saturday morning."

Cara turns on the blinker and pulls over. "Are you serious?"

I turn toward her, confused. "What?"

"That's a lot. What you just said, that's *a lot* to say." Her blue eyes blink and I narrow mine, trying to work out if she's angry or not. I decide not.

"Is it? Okay. Sorry." I lean back in my seat and watch the rain collect and build into bigger droplets.

She puts a hand over mine and pats it condescendingly. "So you are dating."

I frown. "I am? *Non*. No. Am I?"

She laughs then, short and billowy. "'Fraid so!" Then, more seriously, "Just be careful, Sunny. He's a bit older than you. I'll admit he's cute, for a guy who looks like a bum, but he might be after something you're not ready to give."

"I'm going to be late." I look at the clock and she drives back onto the highway, turning up the radio and singing along while her finger dances along the steering wheel.

Just as we're pulling into the store parking lot, I say, "You mean sex." And she nearly drives right into a parked car.

"Sunny!" she whispers, flustered and embarrassed. She pats her large chest delicately like I've just insulted the pope.

Now it's my turn to laugh. "Ça va, Cara, it's okay. I promise. He's trustworthy. He will respect my choices."

She bites her lip like I've just cursed at her but nods. I lean in, giving her a hug and a peck on the cheek. "See. No big deal."

"Okay." She laughs in an awkward kind of way, and I grin at her prudishness.

We walk arm in arm into the store.

I stack the cream from closest due date to furthest away, mindlessly focused on the task at hand. In the background, flat-sounding music plays from the ailing speaker in the back corner. I pick up the next container. It's leaking, stripes of cream running down the side, and I put it with the busted ones.

Cara ambles past me, mopping the floor. She gives me the thumbs-up and repeats what I said to her earlier. "Ça va."

The mix of the slimy cream canister and Cara's words rattle the ground beneath my feet.

Maman scrunches her nose as she lifts the coffee jug, rolling it this way and that as she inspects its dubious quality. Her eyes roll to the ceiling and back down, talking to one of the other diplomats. "I miss Parisian coffee!"

She calls me over to introduce me to one of the men. I brace myself for all the kissing.

A peck on each cheek from the thin, suited man. "Bonjour!" he exclaims, clasping my hand in his. I look to Maman, and she nods. Something rumbles. The coffee cups rattle in their towers. No one pays it any attention. It's probably another bomb or maybe a tank passing by. We don't think much of it.

The ground shifts as she hands me a cup. I stumble, dropping it, dark liquid spreading over the floor like rot. "Ça va," she mouths. It's okay. I look away, chasing after the cup as it rolls under a chair.

Then the earth decides to swallow us.

The manager's rough wiping of my arm brings me back. Cream runs down my arm, and he's swearing and mopping at my shirt. "Oh, Kez, I'm sorry."

"Welcome back to planet earth," he says gruffly, his coppery moustache an awning to his frown.

I take the cloth and wipe the floor, giving him a sheepish grin. "At least it was expired."

Kez grumbles, stands up, and wipes the cream on his already dirty apron. He grumbles a lot, but he's what Ama calls a good egg. Understanding, patient. But I know that expired cream is coming out of my pay.

When I was trapped, I remember staring at that coffee cup for days, split neatly in half like my family.

I pat my chest, my scrappy heart. Tonight, Gung is coming home.

Cara drops me at the driveway. Apparently, I'm not the only one getting calls from boys. She has to get home so she can casually stare at the phone until it rings.

I rub my arm from where she slapped me after I suggested she should call him, since she's a feminist. Creeping quietly up the path, I feel a little like I'm walking across sacred ground. I'm nervous. The picture I have in my mind of Gung's return might not be the reality.

Pulling apart the living room, I reorganize it in my brain. Paper cutouts of Gung's chair. Ama and Gung. A pipe. I put the pipe on a shelf. Gung in the chair, watching TV. Ama stands, surveying the scene with her hands on her hips. Gung sits in the imprint he left, not quite filling it. Thinner but content.

I try other arrangements. Gung in bed. Ama in the kitchen. The pipe in the fireplace where Ama wants it. Each one seems acceptable, and I can move through into the real lounge.

Slipping out of my shoes at the door, I listen for the usual racket. My ears straining like palms cupped to catch water.

The door clicking open sounds lonely.

I follow slight, unassuming noises. Swish of water. Bubble of oil. Ama is in the kitchen.

"Where's Gung?" I whisper.

Ama turns around, expression placated. Pale with makeup, red with lipstick. "Sh! Gung in bed!" Her whisper is still like a shout across a gaping canyon.

She points to a meal, chicken rice and some sad-looking, wilted bok choy. The ginger opens my sinuses and makes me smile. "*Merci.* Thank you, Ama." I lean across the counter to touch my cheek to hers. "Can I go say hello?"

"Eat!" she orders in her bellowing whisper.

Ama makes me eat every grain of rice before I'm granted leave to see Gung. She warns me not to wake him as she shoves me down the hallway. I get to the door and stall. Scared of what I might see.

Warm air calls from outside. A press to forget. A warm blanket to throw over difficult feelings. I shake it off and walk into their room.

"Ah, Sunny," he says. Propped up with pillows, he beckons me with a frail arm. The plastic bracelet still clings to his wrist, and I grab Ama's sewing scissors from the dresser. "Come, sit." He pats the bed.

I hurry to his side. His eyes are still quick, darting to the large cross hanging to his left. He mumbles something, touches his chin to his chest, and then looks at me. "You studying hard?"

I nod. "Yes, Gung." I carefully clip the bracelet and place it on the bedside table.

He clasps his hands across his belly. The air smells sickly. The tobacco smell washed out and away. "Mm. Good. I don't want your studies to suffer because of me."

I lean my head on his shoulder. Listen to his wobbly breaths. "They won't, I promise."

My brain didn't come up with this arrangement. The paper cutouts lie toppled in a pile in the middle of the room. He pats my hair and hums a song while I wrap my hands around his soft middle. Stopping to cough, but sticking to it. I tell myself, *He's strong. He's lived through worse. And so have I.* But maybe there's only so much one body can take…

He finishes his song and sighs. "I need to smoke." His eyes crinkle and appeal to me. I shake my head. "Ama." Just one word, a thousand meanings.

"Mm. Yes. Ama." He closes his eyes. My heart breaks. My head hurts. My past and my future clang together and signal something is ending. But I will not accept it.

He's strong. He's lived through worse.

He will live through this too.

BREAKER

42

"What's her name?" Mom asks excitedly after Red sold me out for a Ding Dong and a tall glass of milk.

"Sunny La Chance," I reply. Kind of enjoying the secret of Sunny's background. Kind of relieved too.

She stacks the dishes in the sink. "And she's still in high school?" I glare at Red, who shrinks to one eighth his size on the stool beside me. "She's a senior."

Mom rolls this information around in her mouth and decides to swallow it. "Okay. So, she's eighteen. Will you be home for dinner?"

I'm already dragging Red by his jacket out the door. "Yes."

The door slams shut, and I try not to clip Red across the head. *Little Judas.*

When we climb into the truck, I turn, giving him my most menacing stare. "You better behave today. That mouth of yours is becoming a liability. We may need to staple it shut."

His eyes widen, and he clamps his lips tight.

He's so quiet on the drive to Sunny's that I'm worried he's storing it all up for the moment we step foot on their threshold.

Her house is modest. An old hunting shack converted into a home. But it fits here. It's typical of Sundown. Its occupants are not. Stepping out of the truck, I straighten my jacket. I wonder if lizards and snakes feel this way with their new skin? Too shiny. Too conspicuous. I roll my shoulders, take a deep breath, and walk up the stairs with Red snapping around my elbows. The zipper to his mouth broken.

"Aren't you gonna knock?" Red asks, blinking up and raising his fist, ready to do it for me. I grab his hand before he hits the wood. He stares curiously at the jade charm hanging from the center of the door.

Noise from within gathers volume and arrives on the other side of the door. I knock. Almost immediately, Sunny pulls open the door. Her voice is a relief. Her face is *almost* welcome.

She shakes her head. "*Désolé*. Sorry."

I don't know what she's apologizing for until a hand clamps down on mine and Red's forearms and drags us inside. "*Apa ini?* Two handsome boys!" Mrs. Douglas says loudly, positioning us directly under her living room light. She releases us and slaps us into a straight line with her bony palms. Red is completely fascinated by her. I stare past her thin, dark frame to the large painting of Jesus Christ hanging behind the couch. It's all oily browns and yellowing light.

Her voice. I try to change it. Think of it as music. Or the wind. Something else. I tell myself I'll get used to it. Hands reach up and take my cheeks, tipping my head from side to side, and I force myself to look into her dark eyes, narrowed to suspicious slits while she inspects me. "Break Ah strange name," she says, poking my jacket, which is still a little damp. "Why Break Ah? You, uh…" She does a sweep of the room and grins. "You no touch my china." She waggles a finger at me mockingly.

"Ama," Sunny groans. "This is not how you're supposed to introduce yourself."

Red giggles and Mrs. Douglas' eyes switch to him, ignoring Sunny. She runs her hands through his hair while he stands still as a sentinel. "You got hair like devil," she says with a quirk of her lip. She bends down so she's at eye level. "You naughty like devil?"

Red glances up at me, and I shrug. I have no idea what to do so I just stand there rigidly, allowing her to assess our worth like cows at market. Red shakes his head vehemently. "No, ma'am."

She releases Red's hair and steps back, clucking her tongue. "Shame, you know. Sometimes can be fun, to be a little devil." She winks and pats his head gently. She likes him. I'm suddenly awfully glad he came with me.

I realize I haven't spoken a word since we got here and I regain my manners, which have spilled onto the red-and-gold rug. "Good morning, Mrs. Douglas. I'm Breaker and this is my little brother, Red."

Mrs. Douglas laughs, slapping her knee. "Red not a name. Breaker not a name." Then she leans in, taking both of our hands. "You two christened?"

That's when Sunny steps in. "That's enough," she says, flapping her hands in Mrs. Douglas' direction. Shooing her away like she's an excitable puppy.

A cough from behind seems to silence the old

woman, and everyone waits for the person who made the noise to stand. Mr. Douglas eases out of his chair and walks toward us carefully, his serious eyes on me.

I meet him in the middle. "Nice to meet you, sir," I say, offering my hand.

He takes it, giving me a strong handshake with rough, sandpapery hands. "Nice to meet you too," he says, bowing his head slightly. He's small. I tower over him in height, but there's a presence to him, a strength that makes him taller than anyone in the room. When he looks up, I see a soldier in his eyes. I see an Asian man, which picks at the loose stitches of my psyche with a sharp point. But I also see a man with a story. A family…

Mrs. Douglas skittles around us in a circle. She pinches Red and he jumps, rubbing the sore spot. She tsks and grabs his hand. "Come, you help me make snack."

Sunny leans into her grandfather and touches her cheek to his. "Gung, you should sit down."

He nods and eases back into his chair. With a point and dip of his finger, he orders me to sit down too. Sunny looks at me, then to the kitchen, and decides I must be safer where I am than where Red is because she gives me an *I'm so sorry* look and deserts me.

I clasp my hands, tight as a clamshell, and wait.

"You served in Vietnam," he says. It's not really a question, but I nod.

He shakes his head. "Terrible, terrible war. Guerilla war."

Flashes of fire and skin burning. The oil of palms crackling. Dark eyes floating in the spaces between the cramped green leaves. Always watching and waiting for their time.

I connect with his eyes, allow his face into my memory. "War is always terrible," I say.

He nods, his hand going to the table next to him, huffing when he can't find whatever it is he's looking for. "Yes. It. Is."

He leans back in his chair, folds his arms across his chest, and glances sideways. "Annie no let you leave until you eat." There's a small smile on his lips and a dry chuckle in his chest. A twist of sweetness that belongs just to his wife.

I stand up. "Oh, okay. Sure."

I step out of what felt like the eye of the storm and into the tornado.

Red grins with glee, swinging a bag full of little snacks wrapped in tinfoil and a red envelope heavy with quarters. "Your Ama is so cool!" he says to Sunny as we plod through the field behind her house. I glance back at it, a warm light lonely in the mountains.

Sunny smiles. "*C'est bon*. Good. I'm glad you think so. I think she thought you were pretty cool too."

Red laughs, shaking his bag of goodies. "She said I was darling."

"That's old-person speak for cool," she says, patting his shoulder.

Red looks so happy it kills me. Spinning that bag around. Surging forward and then running back. Letting his fingertips nick the tops of the spiky grass. I'm so glad he's not like me. I run a hand through my hair shakily and then pat my shirt pocket, seeking out my smokes. Sunny watches me closely. "Just one," I say, pulling them out greedily. She nods, turning her attention back to Red. I light it up and drag in a breath. I feel the warm air curling around us as soon as we enter the woods.

We stand in an awkward line. I finish my smoke and look at Red. "Lead the way, Little Red."

He frowns at first, but then points down a scratchy path determinedly. "That way."

As he charges ahead, breaking the forest and jingling with coins, Sunny's hand finds mine. And although my instant reaction is to pull away, I let it roll over me like steam.

"I love the way the sun does that," Sunny says, pointing to the rays of misty light shooting straight through the trees. "Beautiful." She sighs and stares, always looking up, gravitating toward the light, while my eyes are always on the ground, looking for dark stretches to hide in.

And I think, *She is the light.* And me? I'm the dark spaces between. The absence of light that gives the sun its contrast.

We follow Red. The forest sucking us into a scene that looks straight out of a Grimm fairytale.

Sunny

43

"So that was Ama," I say as Breaker pulls back a branch for me to walk under. Red is about thirty feet away, and I keep my eyes pinned to him. Speed up my feet when he disappears around a corner.

I can tell he wants to take another cigarette from his pocket, and I hold his hand firmly. "She's something else," he mumbles as he squeezes my hand.

"Yeah. She is. Was it difficult for you? I mean, seeing them?"

His jaw tightens, and then relaxes. "At first, yeah, but I found I could push through. Find them, like the real them, not the scary them my brain sometimes imagines, on the other side. Uh. Sorry, that doesn't really make sense, does it?" He shakes his head, his dark hair shading his forehead.

"No, it does. You, um, pushed through your first impression of them. Ignored the superficial and focused on the real details of who they are."

I think his lips turned up. For a tiny, split-into-a-thousandth, second. "Yeah, something like that."

"Ama likes you. And she loved Red," I say, swinging our arms. We make a V, Red at the point. We fly in formation, three very different birds.

"Yeah?"

I smile. "I think she's hoping you might be a reason to stay."

His arm goes stiff, and he stops. "Where are you going?"

I tuck my hair behind my ear. Stare up at the clouds squashed between the branches. "Stanford. In California. Well, if I get my way, that is."

His eyes are on his large boots, caked in graying mud. He yawns. "Oh, yeah. Right. College." Then he lifts them for a moment to find his brother. "Red! Slow down!"

Sorry I brought it up, I quickly downplay it. "Anyway. It's still a long time away. I still have to graduate. And I did get into NYU as well."

He is quiet for a while, his attention seemingly on his brother. His little red head bobbing between bushes and boulders. And the conversation just fizzles and floats to the ground like a fall leaf.

My cheeks are flushed. The air warm to the point of suffocating. I take off my jacket and my sweater, folding them over my arm. Breaker leaves his jacket on despite the heat. I sneak a look at his face, noticing the softer curl of his hair, now looking more brown than black. The fact I can actually see his eyes, serious brows, and flattish nose.

He releases my hand and runs ahead. Red has disappeared.

I hear Red shout, "Whoa!"

And Breaker shouts, "Stop!"

And then I start running too.

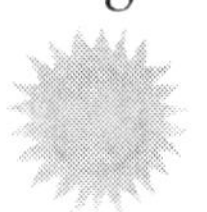

The ground isn't just dry; it's dead. Ash grey, the consistency of corn flour. Red's paused, midstride, his arms stretching toward the ugly tree. His footprints are inches deep in the troubled soil. He turns, a bewildered expression on his face. "But why?" he moans as Breaker catches up to him and grabs his sleeve.

Our eyes cast over the tree's now-brittle branches. A broken one lies to the side, and I feel pain. My arm twinges, like I'm being sawed apart.

Both Breaker and I suddenly rub our shoulders and then stare at each other, the ache feeling so real. "Break, let go," Red begs.

Breaker shakes his head, trying to clear it from the buzz, the warm, the *pull.* "It's dangerous," he warns. "Look." He points to the almost-desiccated branch on the ground. "It's dying. A branch might fall. Or it could snap while you're climbing it."

I take a step closer and so does Red, straining against his brother's grip. A weird sucking sound pulls our eyes to Red's feet. As he lifts his foot from the earth, water pools in the track. Concrete in color.

I gasp as a hot breeze sweeps past us and wraps around our bodies, pulling, pulling like an elastic band. I point to the wells in Red's footprints, and Breaker nods. "*Regardez.* Look."

Reaching forward, I take Red's hand, gently tugging him back. Red yawns, his hand burning hot in mine. "I'm gettin' tired," he says, patting his mouth. His eyes blink slowly. He drags his feet, sending puffs of ashy dust up around his legs. I push him in front of me, turning back to see a green bud appear and unfurl into a leaf at the tip of one the branches. *Amazing.*

Breaker yawns too. I snatch his jacket in my hands and pull him away from the tree. As we walk away, I give it one last look, watching as the budding leaf shrivels and dies.

I keep shoving them gently in the back, waiting for the air to change. When the icy breeze returns, when the light looks pale gold and the sounds of the forest return, I stop.

Red collapses on the ground, digging into his bag of snacks, and Breaker and I stare at each other for a long moment. Bridges are being built between our eyes. We will have to talk about it. But not now. Not here. He reaches out a hand and strokes my arm, a small smile on his lips. A reassurance.

It definitely confirmed my theory that it's something to do with Breaker's family. They are linked to it. Maybe it needs them to survive.

BREAKER

44

Sunny's eyes spark with curiosity. We look over Red's head as he plows through the strange collection of snacks Mrs. Douglas gave him. We've walked a long way from the tree, but when I look away from her, my heart strains for it.

Red glances up, mouth sticky with ginger candy. "I wanna go back to that tree," he announces, unaware of what it's done to him.

Sunny sits cross-legged on a log, picking at her sandwich and looking like a wood sprite. "Maybe another day. After lunch, I want to show you something else."

He gives her a doubtful look, and she smiles. It makes my lips want to curve upward too. "As cool as that tree?"

She moves to her feet but still in a squat, showing extraordinary balance. A cute frog wearing red sneakers. "Even cooler!"

The second hand of my watch ticks sadly and too fast. Time is starting to mean something different to me now. Where once I wanted it to disappear, race by to some far point in the future, now I want it to slow down. I want more time. Time to know her. Time to explore. Time to get used to her family…

Sunny touches my arm. "Do we have time?"

I want to give her all the time. I want to pile seconds in her lap until she can't hold anymore.

She rattles me. "Breaker?"

I nod. "Sure, if it's not too far."

We jump up, ready to follow Sunny through the woods.

Red has asked her so many embarrassing questions I've lost count. This one's a kicker. "Why does your voice sound like, *ooh la la,* but your face is more like..." Red's about to do his impersonation of Mickey Rooney in *Breakfast at Tiffany's,* reaching his fingers to the corners of his eyes, ready to pull, and I slam my hand over his face.

Sunny laughs. "It's okay," she says, giving me those eyes that have suffered through worse. "My father was French, and I went to a French school in Vietnam." She sighs. "Before the war, this was normal. By the end, well, let's just say... I was special."

I almost say, *You're still special,* but manage to stop myself.

She pulls back a branch to let us past. We're climbing up, the drizzly terrain getting looser and rockier.

"Why do you live with your Mama and Gong?" Red asks.

I correct him, earning a smirk from Sunny. "It's Ama and Gung, knucklehead." The ground flattens out and I hear water plummeting from a height, smell mossy rocks and damp dirt. She's brought us to the falls.

Puffing as she climbs, she says, "My parents died in Vietnam."

He doesn't ask how or why. He just mutters, "Well, that blows."

"Yes. It does," she says, far off. Thoughts flying out to the edges.

We follow a narrow path, curling around the edge of the falls, coming at it from a different angle than I usually would. She pulls back a leafy fern, revealing a flat rock that extends out over the top of the falls. We all shuffle to the edge and sit down.

The water streams around us and falls off the tip like it's the edge of world. Sitting here feels a little like we're floating.

Folding my hands behind my head, I lean back, staring up at the sky. Sighing a deep sigh, misty river water entering my lungs.

Before I have a chance to even touch my pocket, Sunny says, "No smoking here."

I raise an eyebrow but nod in concession.

She moves closer so we're sitting hip to hip, and Red sits beside her. I want her to lean her head on my shoulder.

"So now what?" Red asks, like he's expecting a laser light show or something.

She rests her head on my shoulder, and I try not move. "Now we listen to the river."

I close my eyes and listen.

The water cleans my thoughts, washing over my body like a clawing wave. Pulling parts of me away, letting me be the Breaker from before. Just for a moment.

I sneak a look at Sunny, her face serenely calm, her eyes open as she watches the water curl over a rock, the way it looks like a bubble. She dips her finger into the icy river until her finger goes blue. I reach in and take it between my palms, bringing it to my mouth to blow warm air on it.

She looks at me with hope that I'm not going to disappoint her. Or is that just what I see?

Red, previously entranced, glances at us and pulls a look of disgust. "Ew! You guys better not be about kiss or something."

I keep her hand between mine. Cold as ice.

"Shut up, you little nerd!"

And then Red splashes me with water once before I pick him up and hang him upside down by the ankles. I threaten to dunk him in the river to give his head frostbite, which will mean it goes green and falls off.

I don't hear another word about kissing or dating or love for the rest of the walk home.

Red waits in the truck while I say goodbye. I take her hand in mine again, rubbing the skin of her finger gently. "It still feels cold."

She bites her lip and stares up at me. Her face all types of confusion. Something has shifted. Somewhere between the tree and the falls, this became a date. I tilt my head and trace the shape of her face, her eyes. I wait for the punch. The fear and hate to return, but it's missing. It fell over the edge of the world. I just hope it doesn't float on back to me.

"I'd like to see you again," I say, the porch light suddenly flicking on and off like Morse code. "What are you doing tomorrow?"

Her eyes switch from me to the porch light too. "I, uh, I have to go to Chinatown with Ama and Gung, *après*, after church. To get supplies."

The door creaks open, and Mrs. Douglas' powdered white face peers through the gap. "Sun! It late! It cold!" She slips through the thin crack, proving how tiny she is, and bellows. "It not time for boys. It time for dinner." She claps her hands together like she's herding chickens.

Sunny pulls her hand from mine and presses her lips together, forming a thin line. When she opens her mouth to speak, the words are careful. Bracing. "You could come with us." She winces at her request.

Chinatown? My head's already shaking before I actually try to speak. "It might be... Um..." My hand goes to the back of my neck, almost like I'm trying to change the sway from up and down to side to side. Heart wants to say *yes*. Brain knows it will be tough. Body is confused but leans toward the least amount of effort.

"Too hard. Yeah, I know." She looks at her feet and then up at me. "Then again, it might be, er, *bon*, good..." She starts walking away. Mrs. Douglas shakes the collection of charms hanging from the door. "Think about it."

Thinking about it is hard too. I sigh clouds from across the sea, heavy with rain, always, always blocking the sun.

A hand up, weakly protesting. "I'll call you."

Sunny speeds up, taking the stairs two at a time as Mrs. Douglas yells, "No calls tonight! Tomorrow. You call tomorrow before church." She waves a thin, stern finger.

The single call, "Annie!" comes from inside, and she slinks back through the gap.

Sunny waves at me from under the light of the porch. Always bathed in light while I slink away under cover of shadows.

BREAKER

45

There are moments. Long, stretched-out moments that are getting longer and longer where I feel okay. Where I can be here, right here, and not back *there.* Knowing her, her family, is changing me. Back.

It makes me wonder—*Did I really bury him in the jungle?*

Sunny

46

The dust clouds are receding. I feel… I put my hand on my heart, feel it tapping my ribs, expanding like a balloon. I feel happy. I know things are complicated. That he's damaged in another way to me. But somehow, we're taping things back together. We're making a mess, connecting the wrong pieces, leftover screws rolling around on the table, but we're a step away from where we began. And that's a start.

My arm stings from a slap with the back of spoon. "Why you smiling?" Soy sauce rains down on my face. Ama narrows her eyes and directs her words to Gung. "It's that boy, ah?"

Gung nods in agreement, a small smile on his lips. "Mhm, the boy."

She leans in, our faces nose to nose, smelling like talcum powder and oil. "Isn't it?" She twists the handle into my side, trying to tickle me. They think this is funny.

I smoosh my lips together, but my teeth find a way out.

"Can he come to Chinatown with us?" I blurt.

They frown. Conspiratorial looks exchanged between them. "How much he can carry?" she asks the air, tapping her chin with that devilish smile threatening to flash across her face like a blaring advertisement.

Gung clears his throat and stands, shuffling over to the dining table. We watch with hearts that squeeze tears. He sits down with a disgruntled, "Oomph!"

"Um…" I start.

"He can come," Gung announces as Ama dishes up his dinner, a very plain soy noodle dish. He purses his mouth at the plate, unimpressed. "We need to buy many things!" He pokes at his dinner like it's a lump of roadkill.

I cover my mouth to smother my laugh.

Ama growls at Gung. "I like his uniform. You know, they save Sunny's life! When she buried under that building," she says, her voice like snapping teeth. Sharp. To the point. "Who pull you out? American soldier, that who!"

I roll my eyes. "I know, Ama."

I was there.

Ama changes her mind like the wind. After dinner, she pushes the phone at my chest. "Ask Break Ah to Chinatown."

Then she slinks down the hallway, walking backward as she tries to keep her eyes on me to make sure I dial. She does this perfectly, without bumping into anything, and I start to wonder whether she was telling the truth when she said she had eyes in the back of her head.

I pull out my notebook and find his number.

With each rotation of the dial, I feel more and more nervous. This could be a really bad idea. But if he wants to spend time with me, he's going to have to get used to this side of my life. I want to show him how not to be scared.

The phone rings twice, and then a woman with a tired voice answers, "Hello?"

I'm so nervous that I answer in French. "*Bonjour. Je m'appelle* Sunny."

"What?" The woman sounds like she's half asleep and kind of annoyed.

"Oh my gosh, I'm sorry. Um. My name is Sunny. Can I speak to Breaker, please?" My heart is ready to leave my body. It's had enough of this. I place my hand on my chest and threaten it to stay there.

"Oh, right, Sunny. Um, just a sec," the woman says, her confusion clearing. "Breaker, honey, phone."

I'm going to count to three. If he doesn't answer, I'm hanging up. One... "Hello? Sunny, is everything okay?" he asks, his tone edgy like mountain peaks. His voice calms me down. I breathe in, breathe out. Remind myself that I'm not a silly little girl. I'm a Douglas. I can handle this.

"Hi," I manage shyly, and then I pinch myself on the leg. *What's wrong with me?*

Breaker's tired breath presses through the holes of the receiver, streams of air tainted with smoke. "Um, hi. What's up?"

I don't want to ask him straight away. So, I start with Red and the tree. "That was an interesting development today, huh?"

"Huh?"

"You know, with Red and the tree. It's like, um, it's like it knew him or something."

Breaker is quiet for a moment. "Yeah. It was. I don't think I should take him back there. It could be dangerous."

My legs are jiggling nervously and I glare at them, like that would change things. "I don't know if it's dangerous. It's certainly fascinating. We just need to be careful, that's all."

I imagine him running a hand through his hair. Frowning and thinking. "Yeah, I guess."

We talk about the tree for a while. My theories, his lack of theories. Whether we should go back. Whether to tell Red anything at all. We talk about nothing too. School, college, Cara, work. Anything to keep the line open.

I glance at the clock. It's after ten. Ama and Gung have gone to sleep. I yawn, the time reminding me that I should be tired.

"I should go," I whisper, only now noticing that I'm sitting in the dark. The moon shines white light over the field so that the dead grass looks like sparklers sticking out of the dirt.

"I'll go," he says in small voice. Too small for Breaker.

I watch the grass stalks ripple with the breeze, a sea of felt-tipped light. "What?"

Then he says something so sweet I nearly fall off my chair. "If you hold my hand, I'll go to Chinatown with your family."

I grin, sure my smile can be seen from across the field, just a curve of white light floating in the dining room. "I promise. I won't let you go."

BREAKER

47

There was this life I was going have. It started with a dream, a future that I could almost touch. A way to get out of Sundown. Enlist. Fight for one tour and save enough money to pay for college. Then I could teach. Anywhere. But like a tidal wave, the reality of war swept my future out to sea.

I never thought it would return, but now, if I shield my face, squint my eyes and concentrate real hard, I can see it. Bobbing up and down on the waves like a message in a bottle, looking for me. Wondering if I'm still there. If I'm still that guy.

"Breaker! It's been so long. Why don't you ever call your old man?" my dad's deep, dark voice pummels my ears with all the missed birthdays, absent months, and disappointments.

I want to say, "How come you never call me or Red?" But I don't. Instead, I squirm on the other end of the line, my belly full of unspoken challenges, un-fought fights. Confrontation will only make him pull away more. It's what he does. If things get too hard, well…he just doesn't do 'hard'.

The papers sit on the counter, white rectangles sharp as any weapon. Black typed words that are going to change everything. Things I'm not sure I want changed.

"Dad, I've enlisted," I whisper.

"What did you say?" His voice is punched full of false enthusiasm.

Louder, tapping the typed words on the page with my finger. "I've enlisted!"

Silence—one, two, three. "Well, that's just... That's just great is what it is."

I'd laugh if I weren't so damn terrified. I want him to say, 'Oh, no'. Maybe something like, 'You're too young'. Or even, 'You must be scared'.

I knew he wouldn't say any of those things. I don't know why the hell I called.

"You really think so?" I ask, both hands gripping the phone. I'm trying to hang on. Not smash the phone to sharp, plastic, pieces. "It's really the only way I can afford to pay for college. Unless you've got some funds tucked away..."

Silence. Not even breathing.

"It's great that you're making your own way. I respect that. I served in Korea, for a while anyway. And it made me the man I am today." That's not a good thing, though he says it proudly. How can he not know that it's not a good thing?

I want to cry like a baby right now. I'm choking on it. And he's telling me it's a good thing. That going to war at nineteen is a good thing. "Dad, I'm scared I made a huge mistake," I admit, wishing he could be the man I want him to be. Strong. Wise. Here.

A sigh, deep and lazy. "Look, son, I don't know what you want me to say. Um. If you don't want to go, I have some friends in Canada..."

He doesn't get it.

I pull the phone from my ear. It's a struggle, like it's stuck to my skin with bubblegum. "I'm not doing that. I'm not a deserter. I just wanted some advice. I don't know. I thought maybe, for once, you might understand what I'm going through."

Holding the phone two inches from my ear, I hear him say, so softly, "Hey, man, no need to get so heavy. It's cool. You want some advice? Sure thing. Kill as many chinks as you..."

The sound of the phone hanging up marks the last time I will ever speak to that son of a bitch again.

Did I ever even have a chance?

Without my jacket, I feel naked. I keep running my hands over my shirt and vest, patting myself down like I'm scared my insides are showing. One charred heart and two tarry lungs. I cough. Search for my smokes where they'd usually be, in my breast pocket, and sigh with relief when I remember I put them in the back pocket of my cords.

After church, Red begged to come with me, screaming that he loved Sunny, that she was the best and he really wanted to see her again. I'd snapped, in a joking way, that she was mine and I didn't want to share her. And then Mom and Red looked at me like they didn't recognize me. It made me even more nervous.

As I'm about to climb the worn timber stairs, they open the door. First, Mrs. Douglas emerges with a trolley on wheels that overflows with paper bags. Then Mr. Douglas, looking solid, walking in a proud way, though I know it's difficult for him.

Mrs. Douglas yells, "The doctor say exercise!" as they wave and descend the stairs.

Then the sun comes through the door. She's a bright idea, a lightbulb switched on. Her hair is plaited and curls over her shoulder. Golden dragons sparkle on her red satin shirt. She smiles at me sweetly and catches Mr. Douglas' arm as he tackles the stairs, treading carefully and trying not to trip over her folded-up flares.

"Break Ah," Mrs. Douglas shouts, waving her arms. She hurries toward me with a red-lipstick smile. I nod, but my eyes are on Sunny, glowing red and gold. Could be the shirt, or maybe it's just that light she has within.

I shake Mr. Douglas' hand when they reach the bottom, and he bows his head. He gets in the driver's seat of their Cortina and starts the car.

My neck feels warm like a sunburn and I stand there, awkwardly staring at Sunny. "I, um, I like your shirt," I say, unwanted color creeping into my cheeks. I swear I used to be better at this kind of thing.

She smiles, no teeth, just a single dimple shaped like a star in the corner of her cheek. "Thanks, Breaker. I like your non-army-issue shirt," she says with a wink.

I shrug. Laugh like it's not a big deal, though both of us know it is.

I'm about to open the door for her when I feel a pinch. I jump. Feel my skin tightening, armor strengthening. "Ouch!" I swing around. "Mrs. Douglas?"

"Ah, yes. Strong arms," Mrs. Douglas says as she squeezes me like a plump pig she's about to slaughter. "You call me Annie, I think, yes, and call him George." She points to the back of Mr. Douglas' balding head.

I implore Sunny, but she just gives me a look that says, *Well, you knew what you were getting into.*

We get in the back, and the old couple sits up front. Sunny places her hand over mine, and we listen to Annie list one hundred and one reasons why Sundown needs its own Chinatown.

I find Annie hard to keep up with. In fact, I think they all do. She jumps from topic to topic, starting one conversation before leaving it dripping like wax from a candle, only to pick it up ten minutes later and expect everyone to know what she's talking about. But I'm trying. I'm really trying.

I never try…

I'm also smiling. Even if I can't follow Annie, I'm starting to like her. Although, I prefer George. He doesn't say much, but when he does, he makes it count. Like now.

"Annie, I'm parking. You be quiet. You make the boy's ears hurt. You make all our ears hurt!"

She stops for a few seconds while George tries to insert the Cortina into a very slim space. Sunny glances at me knowingly, one finger in the air. Once the handbrake is up, Annie starts talking again.

"I drive home," she announces as we climb out the car. "You too sick to drive."

George gives her a seriously frank look, but I see the amusement, the play, behind it. "Better to drive sick than drown when you drive in the Hudson."

I clench my teeth together, trying so hard not to laugh.

She toddles away. Over her shoulder, she shouts,

"I throw your pipe in Hudson!"

I lean against the car, watching them leave me behind, compressing my fear. Reminding myself that I chose to come. My eyes graze the drop-down signs with sharp characters. The lights aren't on, just the promise of red, gold, and green that will shine in the night.

Sunny stops midstride and turns around. A look of disappointment shines out from her eyes and I shrink down, wishing I had my jacket to hide under. She runs to me, light on her sneakered feet, and takes my hand. "I'm so sorry. I almost broke my promise." I realize then that she's not disappointed in me. That doesn't usually happen.

I breathe. Let her squeeze my hand. Peel myself from the car like an old sticker. *I chose this,* I remind myself again.

She walks slowly, allowing me to catch up, giving me time to absorb the clashing characters, the sea of foreign faces.

I think I'm okay because beyond any reason I can think of, Sunny has chosen me to be here with her.

Last time I was here, I rushed through the middle. Too scared and angry to look in or up or through. I kept my eyes on the Empire State Building and kept them off the people who make this place so alive.

With Sunny's hand in mine, I pry open my eyes, my mind, and let them show me their Chinatown.

Annie doesn't shop like we do. Like Mom does. This is an adventure, a challenge. She scales the mountain of every price tag and knocks the top off like a volcano.

The sign for Wen Fu's Discount Super Mart swings stoically in the cool wind. We follow Annie in and she heads straight for the noodle aisle, her flat feet slapping against the linoleum, pausing every now and then to straighten the woven mats that line the floor. I stand back, my hands planted on either side of a wooden box of okra. She runs her finger down the rows of dried noodles and snatches the pack she wants. "*Apa ini?* George, fifty cents dearer than last time we here." She flips open her notepad and writes down the brand and price, then toddles out of the store and across the road to Po Wing Food Market, searching out the same brand of noodles and writing down the price. Sunny squeezes my hand and shows me that star dimple before Annie even moves, then Sunny and George turn around and makes strides back toward Wen Fu's.

Annie overtakes them like a human racecar and pulls into the counter. "You trying to swindle me, Fu?" she asks, hands on the counter, pinching it with red polished nails. "I want to be loyal, but you make it hard."

He shakes his head, mutters something in Chinese, and flattens his hair behind his ears.

She returns the ball, bartering, "What you give Annie for loyalty, eh? I pay higher price for noodle, but you give me discount on…" She lists five other items. Succeeds in getting a discount for two. By the end, we have two large packets of noodles, the box of okra, and a carton of soymilk boxes. Wen Fu looks defeated.

And this is what we do. Zigzag across the street, trying to keep up with Annie.

It's a game. Fascinating to watch.

I think of Mom, mindlessly throwing items into her trolley, not even looking at the price. We always go to the same store, buy the same food.

Sunny brushes my hand with her fingers as we watch Annie snatch packets from the spice aisle, a rainbow of colors and smells. Annie has found life and joy in what I'd always thought was a pretty mundane task. I get the sense she does this with most things. Watching other patrons, I also get the sense this is not necessarily an Asian thing as much as it is an Annie thing.

And George's thing is saying *no* to some of her more outlandish requests and handing her small amounts of money. I'm guessing before I came along, he also got to be the pack mule.

As we leave our fourth store, Sunny pulls me to her face and whispers, "How's it going?" Her voice a sweet strand wrapping around my heart, holding all the slipping, stripped parts together.

I crack my neck and shrug. "Not too bad, actually." I've been so distracted watching Annie's performance that I've barely had time to feel anxious or angry. Thoughts roll around in my brain, ones I knew but needed to be reminded of. It's about knowing them as people. Individual people.

The trolley I'm dragging is half full, and my forearms are dented and marked from the bags Annie has hung over them like I'm a coatrack.

Annie announces, "Time to eat."

Sunny

48

I watch him closely. Waiting for an eruption. Something that sets the island of Breaker to sinking. But he seems okay. Well, sort of. When an Asian walks too close, he tenses, making a vast amount of space for them to pass by. In these tightly packed aisles, it means he keeps knocking food over. Gung catches packets of noodles and bright-colored jellies, carefully placing them back before Breaker notices.

He squeezes my hand so tight, unwilling to let go in even the tightest spaces.

But he's trying. So I will let him try, and I will let him make mistakes.

Ama pulls us into a noodle house we come to regularly. The owner, Zhang, a coiled spring of a man, welcomes us with fittingly noodle-like arms. "Ah, Annie, George. *Nǐ Hǎo*! Sit, sit," he says, bowing, sweeping his arms. "And howdy!" he addresses Breaker, who raises an unsteady eyebrow as Zhang tries to bridge that gap between East and West.

Pulling out a chair for Ama and me, he eyes Breaker with curiosity. A quick look around reveals he's one of only two white people in the restaurant. Breaker sweeps the room with his gaze—the eels in the fish tank, the intricate cork carvings on the wall. The smell is distinct, deep-fried shallots in peanut oil. It coats the walls. Breaker twists in his chair, parts of him fraying.

Gung and I have two pairs of eyes of equal understanding trained on him. This place stirs something uncomfortable in Breaker. Like a knife mixing rice. I can see his gaze turning inward. It's a look I know I have often.

Ama notices too.

"What wrong with Break Ah?" she asks, pointing at him with a black lacquered chopstick.

He looks so uneasy that my heart aches. He's a boy shoved in the girl's locker room. And I'm scared I've pushed him too hard, too soon. Hands clasped under the table, the high-buttoned neck of my shirt constricting my throat, I watch as he tries to say something. But the words dry up on his tongue. Sweat beads across his brow, and his color drips away slowly like water from a drying shirt.

I think Ama's going to make a fuss, draw attention by shouting and pointing at him with Chinese cutlery. But she doesn't. She tips her head, her dark eyes curling over him, reading his demeanor, his pained expression, and then she says, "We no have time for sit-down lunch."

She stands from her velvet-backed chair like a jack-in-a-box and shoos the three of us out of the restaurant. I smile when I think no one ever need wind her up. She's always ready to spring.

Breaker seems to crumple and restack his bones when he stands, walking out like each step gives him a reason to breathe. I take his hand at the threshold, and he glances down. So much sorry in his eyes. "I'm… I remember… It's not them. It's a…" He taps the side of his head.

"It's okay," I start, patting the rough cotton of his shirt. I wonder if it really is okay. If I'm making a huge mistake. He's as damaged as I am. Maybe our two broken halves don't make a whole. Maybe together, all we can make is a Frankenstein heart.

His grip on me loosens. His breath returns to a normal rhythm. It's over quickly like a flash flood, sweeping away debris and cleaning the streets.

Gungs pats his shirt and grunts, "I need tobacco," before ambling across the crowded street full of eyes shaped like mine, all on their own journey, collecting their own supplies.

Ama slams two paper bags against my chest, fresh pork buns, and asks, "Where Gung?"

My answer is drowned out by her shrieking war cry and she chases after Gung, determined to stop him before he buys himself a new pipe and tobacco to fill it.

I don't need to see the argument. I know how it goes. Nearby is the Kim Lau Memorial Arch, and I take Breaker to sit on a bench beside it. We can eat while Gung and Ama fight in the Chinese Medicine Shop.

Sweet and sour smells rise in the steam from the torn-open bun. I nudge Breaker. "You should eat, pack mule." He nods and takes a bite, his eyebrows rising as he chews. "*Oh, mon!* Oh, my! First pork bun?"

He swallows. "It's really good," he says in surprise, his eyes tracing the words on the arch. *Democracy and Freedom.* He bows his head. A secret prayer I cannot hear.

I bow my head also. We all fight for the same things.

"What's bothering you? Do you regret coming?" I

ask, pinching pieces of white-as-cloud bread together with my fingers. Puffs of dust encroach on my hunched shoulders. "I know she can be a lot. Ama, I mean. But she has a good heart."

"No," he says, an air of surprise hovering around his head like a halo. "Not at all. This was much, much easier than I thought it would be. And Annie is part of that. George too. She is something to watch. To know…"

I watch his mouth, listen to his words, his acceptance of my strange little family. Steam mixes from our breath and the pork buns in a spiced swirl. "Really?" I ask, disbelieving, holding a chunk of food to my mouth.

"Really," he says with a half smile. "Some things are hard. That restaurant, certain smells and words, but your family is not. I don't really understand why yet, but they make things easier. They…"

Heart beats side to side. Clogged with dust and straining for blood.

I drop my paper bag, clasp his face in my hands, and press my lips to his. Surprised at first, his lips feel fixed closed, but then they open. They soften. I taste salt, sweet, and Breaker letting go. And I start to think…

Maybe a Frankenstein heart is kind of beautiful.

"Ai ya!" Ama shouts, slapping us apart with her high, plaited-with-suspicion voice. Gung reaches for her sleeve, but his reflexes are slow. She rushes toward us like a bull charging the cape, her expression dogged like she might roll right over us.

Breaker stares at me. Breathless, disbelieving, his lips apart. Too scared to smile, although I know he wants to. Then he coughs. Gathers himself. I try to, but I'm a melting blob on the bench. I'm heat and sweetness. Love and Frankenstein stitches.

He scoops up the paper bag from the floor smoothly and collects the other shopping. "Mrs. Douglas, Annie, thank you very much for lunch," he says. "I've never had pork buns, and they were delicious."

She stops suddenly, a stake in the ground, and eyes him. She rattles her head like she's not sure if what she thinks she saw was what she saw. "You two." She points at us accusingly, her finger swinging back and forth like a metronome.

"Us two were waiting for you. Sunny told me this joke," he says, cheeks flushed, leading me into a story.

Hands behind my back, swinging like a school kid in trouble, I say, "Yes. A joke. And I whispered it. Because I was worried it wasn't very funny."

"What was joke?" she asks, narrowing her eyes to dark slits, searching for the liar between us.

Merde! Shit! My mouth opens and my tongue lags, useless.

Breaker saves me, and it makes me want to kiss him again.

"What's brown and sticky?" he asks.

Quickly, she answers, "A date. No. Coffee with condensed milk. Uh, *kecap manis,* sweet soy…"

Breaker laughs. "The answer is—a stick."

Darkly and very unimpressed, Ama says, "Oh, Sun." Her voice is packed with shame. "You right to whisper. That not funny. You not funny. You smart." She pokes me sharply in the ribs with her finger. "You pretty. You not funny."

Gung chuckles. "Ama right!" He shakes his head. "Terrible, terrible joke."

Snickering, I realize maybe I don't have much of a sense of humor because I thought the joke was pretty funny. Breaker nudges me gently with his elbow and winks. Ama has forgotten her rage and is rifling through the bags, checking them against her list.

I turn to Breaker in awe. He's unaware of the amazing feat he performed.

He just diffused Ama.

BREAKER

49

Like that, Sunny lets me go, both hands to her mouth as she tries to stifle her giggling. And I stand there, arms at my sides, waiting like a sentry on watch.

I'm waiting for my head to swirl with bad thoughts. Anger to flare. Anxiety to take over.

I wait.

I wait...

And then I laugh out loud.

Because I don't sink through the cracks into fire and fear. I don't shrink away, avoid, and shudder. It's not Sunny. I don't have to hold onto her like a life preserver. She's opened my mind, yes. She's exposed me to the real people. But now, the changes are coming from within me.

Maybe I'm actually winning the battle.

50

Monday after school, Breaker is waiting for me in the parking lot. I'm a sinking ship of books and intentions to study, but when I see him, it's like I've been bailed of water. He smiles carefully, and Cara slaps my back a little too hard. "Are you two steady?"

My face falls below my books, eyes coasting over the top like a toad. "Um. Shut up," I say rather unintelligently, my redder-than-apple cheeks betraying me. Then I shrug and almost lose my balance. Cara pins the pile of books down before I drop them.

"Maybe you should ask him to go steady," she says, winking in an exaggerated fashion, shaking her curled-back locks. She looks like one of the Partridge family, and I look more like a Chinese Cher. I sigh.

"*Peut-être.* Maybe." I know I won't. Not yet anyway.

I lean into her cheek, heating hers with my flaming one, and then break away.

Army greens stand out against the cracked gray asphalt. "You look strange when you smile like that," I blurt, nervous and caught off guard.

He crosses his arms across his chest and frowns, a nervous energy surrounding him like the string of a lit firework getting shorter and shorter. "Better?"

I laugh. He almost laughs. "No!"

He opens the door, and I jump in the passenger seat. A protruding spring digs into my butt.

"Where's Red?" I ask as Breaker climbs in next to me.

"He has soccer. I thought I could take you home, hang at your place until he's finished, and then go pick him up. Would that be okay?"

I tip my chin shyly. Blushing. "*Oui!* Yeah, that would be okay."

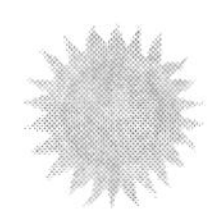

When the engine shuts off, the silence is as invasive as a tumor. Ama parts the curtains, and I run up to tell her I'm home before Breaker even gets out of truck.

Words spiraling out with nervousness, a warning tacked in there too, I say, "Breaker and I are going to hang out in the workshop for a while. I ate already. He ate already." I tilt my head to the side, trying to think of other reasons she may find to barge in on us. "Um. I'm going to study after he leaves, okay?"

She follows my words. Only listens to half of them. "What hang out? I bring you leftover mooncake for snack."

I'm jiggling around like I need to pee, trying not to get dragged into some long explanation and negotiation. "Hang out means we are going to *talk* and spend *time* together in the workshop. I want to show him Gung's pieces." I snatch the mooncakes from the counter so I can at least control that part.

She grunts, dissatisfied.

Pipe smoke swirls in under the back door, and her

nostrils flare. I take this opportunity to sneak out.

Breaker waits nervously by the garage door, looking dark and silty against the peeling brown paint. "Should I go up and say hello?" he asks, buttoning his jacket and straightening his collar.

I shake my head. "Nah. Maybe later."

I jerk open the door, and it shrieks a protest. It has been a while since it's been opened. *Not since Gung's heart…*

We step inside. It's as black as night. I step on his toes, colliding with his chest as I search for the light switch. The Chinatown kiss is a ghost haunting us right now. Dancing and weaving through the rafters.

I put my hands on his chest, and he puts his hands over them.

I try to look up, let my eyes adjust, and my nose hits his chin.

"Sunny," he whispers in the dark, chasing that ghost away as he finds my face with his hands and pulls my mouth to his.

Again, I'm melting. Pooling like wax at the base of a candle. It's less of a surprise this time so more care is taken. And we're closer, warmer, forgetting to breathe and smashing into the workbench. His hands don't wander. They stay on my face.

I'm a balloon trying to find the sky.

I'm lacking oxygen.

I'm forgetting something…

The light blinds us and pushes us apart. Swirls of sawdust creep along the floor as the cold breeze tries to find a way in. "Break Ah. Sunny. What you doing in the dark?"

Ama traipses in with three mugs and a teapot. She slams them down on the bench, pouring slowly while Breaker and I stare at each other and try to settle our chests into less frantic up and down motions.

She pours the tea from a height, showing off and doing it so slowly the water is probably cold by the time it splashes the cup. Once the tea is poured, she gestures to the dollhouses and the rocking horse, dragging Breaker to each one. She points out every minute detail and essentially wastes almost all our time.

"Why you always wear that jacket?" she asks, prodding him on one of his brass buttons. "You ever wash it?"

Breaker looks to me, shifts uncomfortably, and I step in. "Ama, that's personal." He breathes easier. I walk to the door and open it further.

She plays dumb as she follows us. "What personal?"

I huff. "It means you shouldn't ask him that question."

She makes a strange, dismissive noise. "Pfft!"

"Anyway, I'm going to show Breaker my room." Grabbing his hand, I drag him up the stairs, Ama right behind us. Warm air curls under my arms and entreats me to the forest. I squeeze his hand tighter and stride inside.

Gung is watching TV. I quickly kiss his cheek and give him a look. A make-Ama-back-off kind of look. He nods and catches Ama's arm. "Annie," he says, clearing his throat. "Sit down. Hollywood Square on." He pats the sofa and she teeters, watching me from the corner of her eye.

"Sunny! Look, Michael Landon!" Her butt finally sinks into the sofa, and her eyes go square as she stares at the box.

Dieu merci! Thank goodness!

I lead Breaker down the hallway. His eyes rest momentarily on the photographs of Chinese relatives dressed traditionally, and then to Ama and Gung on one of their many vacations before they became my guardians. Ama posed with giant sunglasses and a tailored jacket, her arm around Gung in front of the Eiffel Tower.

Sometimes it's easy to forget that they had a life before me. An exciting one.

I pull him into my small room and sit on the bed.

He looks too big for the crowded space. The towers of books lean in. Photos clutter the walls. I pat the bed, sounding like Gung. "Sit."

He sinks onto my tiny bed, and the mattress feels like it might split.

"I like it," he says. Shuffling closer. Shoulder to shoulder. Hip to hip. "It's like a time capsule." He picks up a music box and turns it over in his hands. He turns and grins, and I'm too focused on his mouth. *I don't know what's wrong with me.* "It's about the same size as one too!"

I laugh, leaning my forehead on his shoulder to hide my crooked smile.

He shirks me off, brings a finger to my chin, and pulls my face to the light. "Don't hide. I love it when you laugh."

I blink. Wait. Watch him close his eyes, and then I close mine.

The brass doorknob squeaks, and we fly apart. An un-kissed kiss on our lips.

"Sunny! You left this in, er, in bathroom," Ama shouts, slotting herself into the room. She's being less than subtle. She waves plastic Jesus at us, and I roll my eyes. *Sure thing, Ama. I always bring Jesus into the bathroom with me.*

She places it on my bedside table and pats his head lovingly.

Even plastic Jesus looks at me like he's unimpressed with her lack of ingenuity.

Breaker glances at his watch. "I have to go," he says, jumping up. "Thanks so much for having me, Mrs. Douglas. I mean, Annie. Um, Sunny, see you tomorrow?"

I nod. And then I glare at Ama, who stares back unapologetically.

Ama waves as Breaker hurries down the hallway, thanking Gung as he leaves.

Once she's gone, I touch my lips. They burn, unfulfilled. Ama fills every space from floor to ceiling. She's taking moments away, and it makes me angry. This part should belong to me. I don't feel like I should have to share it with anyone.

Every day for the rest of the week, Breaker picks me up from school.

Tuesday

He leans in to touch my hair… and Ama bursts into the lounge. "Break Ah! Come try my rendang. Tell me if too spicy."

Wednesday

I take his hand to go for a walk through the field… and Ama's voice pulls us back inside. "Break Ah! You move George's chair to window. Winter sun good for his bones."

Thursday

I curve over a book and Breaker leans in, reading over my shoulder.

Ama cuts in… "Break Ah! Don't you think Sunny should go to NYU? Then she close to you." It's a shrewd and completely expected move. "Now." She claps her hands. "Come help George stack wood in workshop."

Friday

Breaker and I sit in the kitchen, his hand going to my knee.

Like a hound that caught the scent, Ama calls out… "Sunny! You look tired."

I am tired… of you!

And then, "Break Ah. Come tell me word on *Wheel of the Fortunes*. That band with floppy-haired men and big noses. Is it B-E-A-T-L-E-S or B-E-E-T-L-E-S? I never remember!"

She's a sniper. A ninja. A catholic virtue protector. And she's driving me crazy.

There's only one thing I can think of. One sure way to find some uninterrupted time with Breaker. Otherwise, this will stall and breakdown like a truck on the highway. I'm not ready for that to happen. Not just yet.

51

The phone rings twice before Red answers. "Hello? Sunny! Hey! Guess what? I'm going to soccer camp this weekend. It's going to be so cool. Jake and I are gonna bunk together..."

I snatch the phone from his hands, watching Mom's face twist into a sour expression at the mention of Jake. I stretch the cord as far as I can, turn around the corner, and hide half-stooped in the linen closet. "Sunny, hey," I whisper.

"*Allo*. I mean, hey," she whispers back. "So, I've been thinking..."

"Yeah? You know that can be dangerous," I joke, and she laughs.

"I have an idea I'd like to run by you. Can you meet me at your place around ten AM?" she asks.

I scratch at the cheap carpet. Dirt cakes under my fingernails. "My place? Um..." I really don't want Mom to see her. Not yet.

"Yeah, I can stop in there before work. Cara's dropping me in," she says cheerily.

I tell myself I'm protecting her. "Um, that's no good for me. How about I meet you at the store, after work?" I say too sharply.

"Uh. Okay. Three o'clock?"

"Sure."

She looks cute and kind of wrong in her mustard smock. And seeing her like this reminds me of my bad behavior when we met. Seeing her face from this distance, her head bowed, reminds me of the half faces in the fields, the curves of straw hats covering their eyes.

Water droplets reflect only green. Always green. My heart rushes down.

"Don't be fooled by their innocent smiles and all that bowing," Sarge warns, eyes aflame with caution. "Under one of those hats could be a murderer, a commie with a gun hidden under his shirt." He grabs my collar and pulls me so close I can smell his unclean teeth. "Assume they're all the enemy. It's the only way you'll survive out here."

I swallow. Throw my cigarette butt on the ground and crush it under my boot. She lifts her head, waves, and I try to pack my trauma away in a box marked 'Irrelevant'. I stride toward her and take her face in my hands. "Say something."

She blinks, confused, suspicious. "Like what?" she says in her unique accent.

It's enough. My hands release and relax, so I can move past the memory. For now, at least.

"Sorry. What did you want to talk about?" I say, trying to skip over my weirdness. But I don't think she's buying it.

We get in the truck and she clasps her hands in her lap, staring straight ahead. "I had one thing to talk about, but now I have two," she states.

Two things. I imagine what they are. One—*Breaker you are great, but this is too complicated.* And two—*let's end it now before it gets worse.*

"Do I want to know?" I ask, shakily feeling like an avalanche is moving toward me, ready to bury me.

She keeps staring ahead, her full lips pursed. "You can't like the white part of me and just forgive the rest." Her voice gets smaller and smaller, a dot on a page. She turns to me, water in her eyes. "Are you capable of liking all of me?"

It's more than that, but I can't say it.

I trace her eyes. Her dark skin. Her straight, dark brown hair. I think about Chinatown. Annie and George. Their miraculous family. A family I'm jealous of, if I'm honest. "I do, Sunny. I really like all of you and your family. I'm sorry that I hold onto your voice as an anchor sometimes. It's not so I can remind myself that you're part white. Maybe it was at the start, but now, it's what brings me home. Because it's uniquely yours. I can't help when memories are going to attack me. But when I hear your voice, I can pull myself out."

She's listening. Sorting out my words and weighing them to decide if she can believe them. "I don't know," she whispers, playing with her fingers.

How can I explain it? I don't fully understand it myself. "It's like there I am, stuck in the jungle again or wading through a rice paddy, and when you speak, your voice, well, it's like a chopper swooping down to lift me out. Do you understand?"

"I'm your diamond of sky," she says with a nod, a revelatory tone to her voice.

"Huh?"

She draws a diamond on the condensation of the window and taps twelve dots inside it. "When I was trapped under the rubble of the consulate building, what gave me hope was that I could always see a diamond of sky, even through the layers of bricks and twisted iron. The greater world was out there still, even if my own little world had been destroyed."

"So you do understand then." I exhale relieved clouds of jungle mist from my lungs.

"I understand, but I don't really like it. If this is going to work, I can't be your magic fix. Your anchor. I want to be your girlfriend, not your therapist."

I take a breath and hold it. Then blow out a breath that's packed with unmarked boxes of uncertainty and fear. I try to let them go, chase them from the car. I can do this. I do want this. "Girlfriend?"

She crosses her arms over her chest stubbornly. "*Oui, bien sûr*. Yes. Girlfriend. Think you can handle that?"

I take her hand in mine and bring it to my lips. I remind myself that she is light, golden and warm. She floods my heart with good things. Sound, solid, beautiful things. She's everything I'm not. I bite my lip. Wanting to punch myself for what I'm about to say. "I don't think I deserve you."

She looks at me fiercely, shades of Annie Douglas radiating from her eyes. "You don't get to decide what I deserve."

I salute her, grin like a goofball, and say, "Yes, ma'am."

"I do have one condition." She raises her finger in

the air. "While I'm at school, you're going to join a veterans' group or something."

I roll my eyes and groan.

"I want you to tell me about your experiences, but I also think you need to talk about it with people who have been through the same thing."

I tell myself she's worth it. She *is*. "Okay, okay. Geez, you're one bossy chick."

"Don't call me a chick," she says, trying to sound serious, but the line of her mouth is fading to a smile.

"All right. So, what's the second thing you wanted to talk to me about?"

Gestures fly wildly as I release her hands from mine. I watch the display with amusement and affection as she tells me how annoying Annie is and how we will never get any privacy.

"We could go on a date?" I suggest.

She shakes her head. "There's nowhere nearby where she won't find us. And we can't drive to Manhattan every time we need time alone. No. I know what we need to do. It feels like it's the only logical option."

I think I know too, but I let her say it.

Her mind is made up. "We go to the tree. We sit north-south so that a short walk to Ama and Gung will be hours for us."

"We go to the tree?" Time alone with Sunny. This can only be a good thing, right?

She drops her chin definitively. "*Oui!* Yes!"

I have doubts, but when I look in her eyes, so sure and brave, those doubts grow wings and flap into the sky.

52

"Ama, I'm going for a walk," I say. "I'll only be ten minutes."

"*Baik baik.* Okay. Be careful. Tell Gung to come inside. I make bread-and-butter pudding."

The air is weak. Like dying hands trying to hold onto life but always slipping, slipping. The smell of smoke, however, is easy to follow. It curves around the house and down the side near the water tank. I poke my head around to see floating red embers. A curdled cough. Gung startles. "Sun!"

"Gung!" I whisper. "What are you doing out here?"

The red ember moves from head height to waist height. "I need peace. I need smoke."

I should tell him no, turn him into Ama for punishment, but I understand. I'm sneaking out for the same reason. I sidle up to him and touch my cheek to his worn face. Inhale the sweet, pungent smell. "I won't tell Ama. This time. But Gung, please, you need to stop or it will kill you."

"Bah! I live through war." He chuckles. "I live with Ama."

Sadly, I whisper, "Just get inside before she comes looking for you, okay?"

"*Baik.* Okay."

I leave him puffing unhealthy clouds into the starry sky. I try to leave my worry tacked to the timber walls too.

My toes touch the edge of the woods, and I wait for it to tell me which way to go. The air feels warm, but not like before. It wanes and falters and I put my hands out, searching for it in the dark. The tips tickle my fingers and I stumble forward, the signal getting stronger the deeper I go.

It feels urgent. Pulling me to it desperately. And as I break through the trees into a clearing, I understand why. Our ugly tree is dying.

The soil is light and flyaway as paper ash. The ends of the branches are crumbling like they're slowly being erased. The deep brown of the trunk has faded to a sickly gray. Breaker bursts through the brush to my left and curses.

In his arms, he carries a blanket, a thermos, and a backpack. I take his hand. We approach the tree carefully, ducking under the brittle arms and making sure we are in the right position by using the marks Breaker made on the day we tested it. The moment we rest our backs against the solid trunk, the warm honey buzz starts. Softly. Rising from the ground like we're the batteries that just recharged the earth.

Swirls of dust push out from where we sit and, I swear, the tree sighs happily.

"We're the batteries," I whisper, leaning my head against Breaker's shoulder.

"Looks like it," he says as my thoughts start down

a logical, problem-solving path. If we're the batteries... I yawn. He places a finger under my chin and lifts my mouth to his. My lips part, allowing him in, letting him give me parts of himself that I'll keep. Crushing and warm. Sweet and endless. Because we are here. And here, time is endless.

He pulls back, touches my temple, his fingers coming back sticky. "This may get messy."

I laugh. *He said it.*

He yawns and holds up the thermos. "Coffee?"

I nod and recline, my back resting against what was once dry, cracked wood and is now damp and mossy. The bitter dark liquid does little to keep me alert. The only thing that wakes me is Breaker's hand on my knee, his other arm around my shoulders. The way he leans his chin on my head and kisses my hair.

I don't think about Ama or Gung, college or the future. Here in our refuge, I don't need to. Time stands still. Time is ours. And we make the best of it.

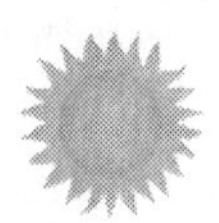

We untangle, breathless, hearts pounding, grins stretching our faces. I keep trying to find this track of thought, but it's like the rails have been pulled up. There's nothing left but a few rotting sleepers.

I reach up and scratch at Breaker's eyebrow. Small pieces of bark are embedded there, and I flick them away. My bones are tired and tied down. It's Breaker who stands, peels himself from the trunk, and offers me his hand. "We should go," he says, brushing dirt and sap from his fingers.

I take his hand reluctantly, feeling like I want to stay here forever.

It would be easier…

Distance makes me feel cold. Uncomfortable. I hug my chest and shiver. Breaker brings me into his arms, holding me close. "What the hell?" he says into my ear.

I turn around and watch as moisture returns to the earth under the tree roots. Leaves begin to sprout. A trickle of water can be heard behind it. My brain winds around a thought, trying to pull it out like a stubborn weed. *If we're the batteries…*

A strong gust of warm air blows my hair back and, with it, the thoughts from my head. "Wow!" I whisper.

"Yeah, wow," Breaker repeats.

The sun was mostly set when we got here. Hours later, the sun hangs just one shelf lower in the sky. It worked.

We trudge home, both feeling pulled back. Like it's an effort to walk forward, not backward. I'm more sluggish than Breaker and he scoops me up, carrying me to the edge of the field.

He drops me on a rock so I'm standing level with him. He kisses my nose. "Tomorrow night?"

I nod. "Yes. I want to hear how your first veteran get-together went." I wink and jump from the rock, landing with a thud.

As I'm climbing the stairs, Gung joins me. "Quick walk," he mutters, dropping his pipe into one of his boots at the door.

"Yes," I reply, shivering from cold and lying. "It's too cold to stay out for long."

Sunny

53

Counting the minutes to no minutes. I add up the customer's total and don't even look to see if she gave me the right amount.

A bag of marshmallows comes flying at my head. "Snap out of it!" Cara shouts.

Kez growls at her for throwing merchandise. "Calm down, Kez, they're *marshmallows.*" She points at the pack in an exaggerated way.

He shrugs and wanders out the back.

"So," Cara starts. "I got my curriculum from Vassar. Sooo exciting! They've just added this new subject called Women's Studies. It sounds dope. Have you got yours?"

I sigh. Minutes will dissolve like sugar in tea. *A timeless place.* "Not yet. I don't think they send them until you're actually enrolled."

"Oh, right. Have you decided where you're going?" she asks, leaning over her register to catch my eyes.

I yawn. Crack my neck. "Not yet."

She groans loudly. "How's George? And don't say *not yet.*"

I pause mid-yawn, find my friend's face, and pull a horrified expression of my own. Because I don't know. These past few weeks, I have passed Gung like a breeze through an open window. Kissed his cheek. Done my homework. Eaten dinner. Let Ama's nonsense pass in one ear and float out the other. And then I've been out the door. I've been living in minutes.

"He's okay," I reply, unsure.

I try to remember how many times I've seen him smoking by the side of the house, heard him coughing. A warm breeze ruffles my hair, and anxiety liquefies and drips from the counter. I'm sure he's fine. If I can't remember when I last heard him cough, maybe that's because he hasn't been coughing much. Warm whispers comfort my ears. *Yes. That must be it.*

Cara gives me a strange look. "Sunny in love is a weird creature."

I throw the marshmallows back at her.

BREAKER

54

I knock on the open door even though I can see him sitting at his desk. A slick of hair has fallen from its place and sways back and forth over some kid's transcript. "Mr. Delquin?"

He glances up, smiles. Stands. "Breaker Van Winkle! I was hoping I'd see you again. Have you changed your mind about college?"

My legs are cemented to the ground. *Move forward*, I scream in my head. I run a hand through my hair. "Um. No. Actually, I was wondering if you knew of any veteran groups in the area. You know, um, a place where soldiers get together… To talk." I wince at my words. Embarrassed. Soldiers shouldn't need help. I half spin on my heels, ready to exit.

"I certainly do. And I think it's great that you're thinking of joining." He scribbles down an address and a time, hands it to me. I want to scrunch it up. I want to pretend that I'm not that person. But I promised Sunny.

"Thanks," I mumble.

"Anytime. Hey…" Delquin stands, his sport coat too short and his tie too long. He looks like a Ken doll. "The next meeting is not for a while. Would you like to grab a beer? We can talk…" I know I make some sort of face because he says, "Or not. We can just drink. No talking necessary."

I cut him a break. "Sure. One beer."

He looks kind of giddy at my acceptance, which make me want to take it back. "Great! I get out of here at four thirty. Meet you at the bar just after?"

I nod. Give him a thumbs-up.

I don't tell Red about our plans. He would die of embarrassment.

The bar glints depressing in the afternoon light. I open the door, the soles of my shoes sticking to the floor. The smell of booze and stale air swaddles me, and I pause. My heart takes a step down a long flight of stairs, hovering on step two. Green is the color of vomit.

"What is this shit?" Grims spits the liquid on the ground, and the others laugh.

"It's snake vodka," Sarge says, passing the mug to me. I sniff it suspiciously, swirl it in the mug, but with all eyes on me, I have to drink it.

I do better than Grims and don't spit it everywhere, though that may have been the better choice. My throat burns as my head swims through mist.

"Aw. Isn't that cute? Iceman's first hard liquor."

I punch him in the arm. "Shut up!"

When Sarge holds up the bottle, shaking the pickled snake coiled in the bottom, I vomit in my mouth.

It feels strange to be in a bar when it's still light out.

Delquin perches on a barstool, two beers in front

of him. "Thanks, man," I say, reaching for a glass.

He grabs my arm. "Who said that was for you?" He manages to keep a serious face for two seconds before breaking into a cheesy smile. "Just kidding." He clinks his glass with mine, and we drink.

Beer one is sloshing around the bottom of the glass, and we've probably talked about everything except the thing we're supposed to talk about. Neither one of us knows how to bring it up. Like... *Hey, man, remember that time you watched your friends get torn apart by bullets? Remember dragging a dead body hundreds of feet away from the fight just so you'd know where to find it later when the medicos came?*

It's not easy. It's three beers too early.

"It's the looks they give you..." Delquin starts. I look up from my pile of peanut shells. "You know, like they feel sorry for you but they don't want to show it because you're a soldier. You deserve respect; you don't need their pity."

I nod. "That or they disagree with the politics, and then it's a whole other kind of look."

He smoothes his hair back and signals for another drink. I pass. "They don't understand. They don't get that no one *wants* to fight in a war. But sometimes, you don't have a choice. It's not as simple as they'd like to believe."

"But it's easier for them to make it simple. Good guys and bad guys, nothing in between," I finish.

He points at me like I'm a student who got the right

answer. "Exactly."

We both face the bar and sigh. I run my finger around the rim of my glass, thinking about the way the world changes and how, in a lot of ways, it doesn't change at all. Two different wars. Two similar experiences.

"But it's been years for me. I'm finally getting my civilian life together. Got a wife. Two kids and another on the way." I clink my empty glass with his full one. "Those demons I brought home with me, they're quieter now." He raises his glass. "This helps!" He winks slowly.

Those demons dance around the rims of his irises. Soldiers can never escape the things they've done. The horrible things they've seen. But maybe building a new life helps build a foundation over the old one. *Maybe…*

I want to believe him, but an uncomfortable feeling settles over the bar as I wonder if my demons will ever be silent.

He senses my discomfort and turns toward me. "Friends help. Family sometimes doesn't get it. They want you to be the man you were before. They don't understand that he doesn't exist anymore. That you buried him over there. That he's never coming back."

I laugh bitterly. "You're so right there."

He slaps me on the back. "You just have to keep marching forward. No matter how much your neck aches to turn around. To look behind to see if they're still chasing you," he says, staring at the sticky bar, the damp towel crusted with peanut shells and chip crumbs.

Move forward. That's what I'm trying to do.

I just hope I'm marching in the right direction.

55

"Are you always right?" Breaker asks, his arms wrapped around my middle, sap smears staining my t-shirt into a camouflage pattern.

I stare up and find my stars. "Yes. Always."

He chuckles. and I want to live inside that sound. That rare, beautiful sound. The tree breathes and new leaves, green as Kermit the Frog, shudder. The brook babbles over rocks, chattering happily about nothing and no one. It's serene, perfect.

"I talked to someone. Someone like me," he whispers against my ear. The air is sweet, the atmosphere full of temptation.

I turn in his lap. "And it helped, didn't it?"

His eyes wax. Going to a place I can't reach him for a moment. Then he's back and smiling. "Yes, it did."

"It always does. Knowing you're not the only one."

The cluster of nurses close ranks as people pass, but I hear them say, "She's waiting for her family. She refuses to leave."

"I feel bad for her. Poor girl has lost everything."

I have lost everything. These people, broken and torn like the building I was buried in, are all I have left.

"Soleil!" Gung's voice is never loud, but it thunders through the halls of the crowded hospital. I turn to see my

grandparents standing real and solid before me, and I run. I run into their arms and let the grief pour out of me like water from a bucket.

We are three corners of a sad triangle, but we are strong.

We understand each other. Because only the three of us understand what it is to lose my parents. This binds us.

And everything is not the word. I haven't lost everything. Because they're finally here.

Now I have them.

And now I have Breaker.

I kiss his jaw as he recounts his conversation with Delquin. His plans for the future. I half listen as he tells me he's thinking of asking for a job at the school. I'm half awake and dreaming of his lips. He stops talking and moves me closer, bringing my legs around his waist. We yawn together, swallowing mouthfuls of the peaceful air.

"Do you have any…er, *cicatrices*, scars?" I ask, my hands pressed to his chest, feeling the contours of his body underneath his clothes.

He lifts his shirt up and places my hand on his stomach, tracing a jagged raised line about two inches long just under his ribcage. "I have two. This one's from my appendix being taken out."

His skin is firm. Radiating heart.

"Where's the other one? I want to see it," I say. I want to *feel* it.

He starts unbuttoning his jeans, folding down the corner of his boxers and placing my hand just below his hipbone. I stop breathing. My heart twisting in my chest. This is so close. So intimate. I run my finger so gently along a small, puckered scar. A round dent in his skin.

"This is my bullet wound," he states. "It was a graze really. I was lucky."

His voice is wistful. Blown around by the warm breeze.

"Did it…" I yawn again. Try to find my words around the sleepy comfort. "Did it hit the bone?"

He begins to answer, "It chipped the bone… It wasn't…"

Leaning in over half-open jeans and exposed skin, I kiss the corner of his mouth, and then his eyelids, which are snapped open while mine are half closed. He groans impatiently and takes my mouth. We are slow and fluid. We are heat and crumbling walls. Every kiss is brighter and darker at the same time, pulling me in deeper, making me want more.

I open my eyes. My fingers feel cramped and stiff, and I pull back to look at them. Bark grows like a second skin to my first knuckles. I scratch at it.

Breaker tries to pull me in again, but I pause. Try to shake my head loose of the tangle of leaves and branches growing over my thoughts.

"I'm not going to sleep with you," I say firmly.

His hands freeze under the back of my shirt and then withdraw. I step off his lap and sit beside him, leaning my head against his shoulder. In the corner of my vision, I see a bud forming on the end of a branch.

Embarrassed, he says, "I wasn't expecting…"

"Look, I know you probably have already." I twist up to catch his eyes. When they dart away, I take that as confirmation. "But I'm not ready. You're my first real boyfriend…"

He grabs my hand, brushes each knuckle with his lips. "I'm not ready either," he whispers, and I can't stop my eyebrows rising in surprise. My understanding was that boys always wanted to have sex. Like *always*. "Sunny. I'm in no rush."

And I guess, right now, we have all the time in the world.

BREAKER

56

First times. The brush of fabric on skin. The heart wanting to retreat. Forget.

"Give him a break," Grims warns, ruffling my hair. "Poor kid enlisted fresh outta high school."

They're all giggling like schoolgirls and jostling each other as we stand outside the brothel on one of our rare passes. I try to make myself smaller. Pull my shoulders in, bury my feet in the mud, but it isn't working. The boys are on a mission. A mission to get the virgin laid.

I feel completely stuck. If I don't go in, I'll never hear the end of it. They treat me like the scared kid all the time as it is. Acid rises up my throat. I didn't want 'It' to be like this.

One of the girls wanders over to us, smiling seductively and walking a circle around me like she's sizing me up. My hands shake. Can I just add this to the list of uncomfortable, crappy things I didn't want to do? The list is getting longer and longer. I could just go in and pretend.

I let the girl take my hand and lead me away from my troop, trying to close my ears to the hooting and catcalling. One of them yells to the girl, "We want confirmation, lady." I turn to glare at him, and it only eggs him on further. "We're paying, so report back to us that the deed was done."

The girl nods and says, "Ya huh," while squeezing my big hand in her tiny, delicate one.

I stare at my feet.
I feel sick.
I want to go home.

It's dark and smells of incense and cheap perfume. The girl leads me to a door, releases my hand, and knocks. Suddenly unconstrained, I freak. I thought she was the one. But now the door is opening and black lashes are batting at me. A bowed head and an open arm beckon me inside. I gulp.

"No kissing. No hitting," the first girl states before gently pushing me inside.

Red candles, the smell of wax burning.

The woman with her head bowed looks up. Beautiful dark eyes smeared with thick black pencil make her look like a cartoon. Her silk robe is parted. I can see the curve of her small breasts and her olive skin down to her navel.

I'm starting to sweat. Nervousness and something else. This isn't what I wanted, but I feel the desire growing as she pulls me toward a lumpy mattress scattered with cushions. Her robe slips away and she stands before me naked, unembarrassed.

A tear slides down my face and she reaches down, catching it with her finger. "This is my first. I mean, I've never done this before…" I start.

She doesn't speak. She kneels down and unbuttons my shirt, rubbing her hands over my chest. The desire swoops around my heart like Saturn's rings.

I want. I don't want. This.

They're waiting outside. They won't let it go. I have to. I want to.

She undresses me carefully, gently, and guides my hands to her breasts.

And I cry.

She teaches me to do the things I'm supposed to do. Shows me how to move, how to hold her.

And when it's over, I think I should have kissed her. But then a hollowness deepens in my chest. Because we're not allowed to kiss them.

When it's over, I don't feel freed or relieved. I just gave something away I shouldn't have. Now, it's gone. Swept away in minutes. I will never get it back.

I am no longer a virgin, and I feel as empty as her eyes.

Sunny

57

A piece of paper slides under my chin. A 'B' is circled in red marker with three question marks after it.

"Mademoiselle Soleil." Madame Moreau pouts with blood-plum lips, her dyed black hair framing her unimpressed face like quotation marks. "A *B*? How could *you* get a *B*?"

I yawn, try to think of a good reason, but come up with nothing. Truth is a B is fine. A B maintains my GPA, which is all that really matters. I yawn again. Thinking about the future is a drag. Madame Moreau catches my chin with her painted fingernail and closes my mouth for me.

"Je suis, je suis…" I start.

Cara finishes my sentence. "Désoleé. She's sorry, Madame. She'll do better next time."

Madame turns swiftly, a swathe of perfume flapping the air in her wake. I gag, and the students around me giggle. I don't see what the big deal is. A *B* is a good grade. It's good enough.

Warm air caresses my cheek, seeping under the cracked window. My eyes turn to the view. From here, the woods are thick, dark green blankets, layered over each other in patchwork. Hiding secrets. Hiding time.

I sigh loudly, and Cara kicks my chair. I barely notice. My thoughts have traveled to the tree. My fingers are sticky with sap, and I breathe in the sweetness. The life.

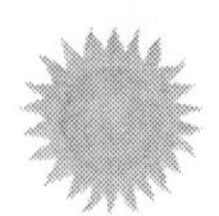

"Where Sunny?" Gung waves chopsticks in front of my eyes as I gaze out the frosted window at the naked spindly trees. The last of the leaves decomposing at their feet. When I don't respond, he carefully collects a single strand of my hair in the chopstick and gives it a tug.

"Ouch!" I rub my scalp where the hair was plucked.

He grunts, triumphant to get my attention. I look down at my book; it's opened to a page I don't remember reading.

"I don't like you like this," Gung says, folding his arms slowly across his brown cardigan. His stomach bulges, the wooden button straining to stay done up. "You too, uh, *apa?* Head in sky. You boy crazy."

I snort. "Gung, I'm not boy crazy. *C'est nouveau*. This is new. The whole boyfriend thing. But I'm not crazy. I'm just...happy."

He leans back and considers my words. "I think maybe you not need a boyfriend right now. No." He shakes his head, conferring with himself. "You need focus on school and college." He points at my brain. "It going soft. Soft like scrambled egg."

I frown. This side of Gung is unfamiliar.

A rustle down the hall. I think I see Ama's head retreat into her bedroom. "What are you saying?" I ask, closing my book with a snap and standing.

He straightens, gives me a stern look. A disappointed look. And instead of feeling shame, I feel anger. My fists clench at my sides, and I step back from the table. "I saying you see less Breaker. You wait until school over. Then..." He points at the table. At his imaginary list of requirements. "Then you can have boyfriend."

A tick. A flick of the switch. A wrong way to act. It didn't used to be me. But maybe I'm not the same person anymore.

Gathering up my books, I slam them into my bag. When I turn back, Gung's expression is hidden. He's playing a role I don't recognize. That I don't accept.

I stamp my foot and wish I hadn't. His eyebrows rise, and it's like he's thinking I've confirmed I'm a child. It turns the dial of my anger up to full flame.

"You don't get to decide that for me!" I shout, looming over him. Sparks fly from my eyes; my words are broken pieces of glass. "You're my grandfather. You're *not* my father."

He rises suddenly, the chair flying backward. For a moment, he curls over. One second and a sharp breath. And then he's up, standing straight and sure. "No! Your father dead," he snaps. "I not your father, but you will listen to me."

I will not listen to you.

I suck in a breath, shocked. Gung has never raised his voice to me. Never. He has never looked at me with anything other than love and pride. Now he stares down at me like he is ashamed. I twist in my place. I fight against myself.

Threads of warm air snap around my head.

I smell oil, tobacco, and tiger balm. I bow my head.

"I'm sorry, Gung."

He stares at me. A few seconds pass as he catches his breath. Then he reaches out to pat my head. He looks at his hand and shakes his head. "Annie!" he shouts. "I going for smoke. Don't you dare try stop me!"

Ama is suspiciously quiet.

I'm sorry that I raised my voice, but I think he's wrong. This is a new thing. And maybe I'm not in control. Maybe I don't know what I'm doing. But I don't believe that something that feels this good could possibly be bad.

"I got my first *B* today," I confess as Breaker kisses my neck. My eyes are heavy, my head bobs down, hazy, happy, uncaring.

Every kiss plants a seed on my skin that blooms into subtly scented flowers, bringing life to my body. I could lie here forever. I could not care about anything but this.

"A *B*?" he says into my neck. "That's not that bad, is it?"

I sigh. No, a *B* is not that bad at all. Gung's overreacting. I wind my fingers through Breaker's hair, soft, dark waves. There were things I was supposed to care about, but now they seem…unimportant.

He makes his way to my mouth, and I let him push open my lips. Let his tongue move inside. Warm air seems to press against us like palms on our backs, pushing us closer together. My heart slows, steady, sleepy.

Pulling back, hands in my hair, breath ragged. "Are you worried about your grades?" he asks, eyes bright. Cheeks flushed.

I shake my head lazily. "No, not really."

I lay my head in his lap, and he strokes my hair. I yawn and close my eyes. *It would be nice to just…rest.* Just for a moment. I could forget the arguments, the expectations. I let the buzz of the tree lull me to sleep.

I give in.

Sunny

58

Her face is a perfect slope. Her cheekbones high and round like scoops of ice cream. Her skin is a warm, sunshine tan. I sweep the hair from her face and listen to her soft, delicate breathing. I could stay wrapped in this slice of peace forever. *I want to.* But I know she needs to wake up. She needs to go home. She needs to finish school, go to college. Do the things she planned.

I shiver. This is not the first time cold air has poked my chest since Sunny suggested we come here. I feel alert. I don't feel like I used to. Lazy and uncaring. And that's a good thing.

Something clicks over. The arm of a clock. The seconds actually move for me as I understand.

I need to have my own plan.

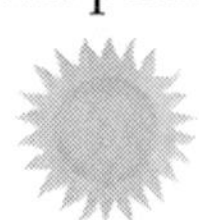

When I rock her shoulder gently, she rolls like a log on the ground. "Sunny, you need to wake up."

She groans. Doesn't wake. I touch her face, and it feels gritty. I push bark from her eyelids in alarm. We've stayed too long.

"Sunny!" I say louder, shaking her shoulder more vigorously. Nothing.

I pull her into my lap. Her body is slack, supremely relaxed. The corner of her mouth drips sap like blood from a dead man's lips. I twist the lid of my thermos and pour lukewarm tea on her face. She blinks lazily, wipes her mouth in confusion.

"*Que se passe-t-il*? What's going on?" She swats at her face like a fly is buzzing around her, her hand resting on her neck, which is now drenched in tea. She sniffs her fingers and looks at me in confusion. "Breaker!" She gets off my lap, each limb moving slowly, like they're unwinding.

"I'm sorry. You wouldn't wake up. You've been asleep a while," I blurt. "I was worried."

Her face cracks into a long, lazy smile, and it's like breaking open a fortune cookie. She stretches her arms wide. "Don't worry. I feel great. That was the best sleep I've had in years."

I tilt my head, trying to match this Sunny with my Sunny, but I come up short. "Annie and George will be wondering where you are. With time slowing, we've still been gone a while."

She frowns, but even that seems like an effort. "Oh, they'll get over it."

Standing, I pull her up. "Annie doesn't strike me as the forgiving type."

She laughs. Cracks her back and rolls her shoulders. "No. You're probably right."

I tug her arm, breaking the bubble of air and panicking a little when I see the sun has already set. Sunny seems nonplussed. I have to yank her along as she drags her feet, about as elegant as an elephant, in the leaf debris.

Without a torch, I use my instincts to find our way back to Sunny's house. It's strange because it's not that hard. Rather than being pulled back to the forest, I feel like the outside world is calling me to it.

Sunny, on the other hand, is a tetherball, constantly straining to get back to its origin.

Finally, after too long, I see the yellow squares of light that the Douglas' windows make as we hit the edge of the woods and the beginnings of the field.

Sunny stops, breathes in hard like she's just realizing how much trouble she's going to be in. I squint through the dark, searching for Annie's impatient shadow at the window, but it's clear.

She faces me, suddenly nervous. Leaning back toward the forest, she says, "How do I look?" Smoothing her hair, she scratches the bark from her fingers. She peels a small piece from her curl of an ear, which kind of terrifies me. "Huh…" she whispers curiously, turning it over.

I smudge the sap from her forehead and straighten her clothes, then lean in and kiss her on the cheek. She tastes like earth and bitter toffee. "You look beautiful. Dirty but always beautiful."

She smiles and hugs me tightly. "See you tomorrow."

"Do you want me to come in and help explain?" I ask.

She laughs again. "And how on earth would you do that?"

I chuckle. "Good point."

"Goodnight, Breaker," she whispers. Then she turns her back to me and walks slowly toward her house, swaying in zigzags across the dirt like she's more breeze than person.

I lean back on a tree and watch. Ready to back her up if she needs me.

59

I exhale, my breath joining the cool wind, slipping and dipping between the plants and rocks and wandering back into the forest. *I miss it already.*

Ama must be watching me from the window, although I can't see her. So I go slowly, hands grazing the frostbitten stalks on long-dead grass. Each end stabs and scratches me, but it makes me more alert and helps me compose my story.

The red embers of Gung's pipe don't float by the side of the house, but I'm later than usual. I reach the steps and kick the baseboard softly. I miss the place where minutes mean something different, where time is in my control.

Sighing, I climb the stairs. With each creak, I become more nervous, I know she's biding her time. She's going to pounce on me the moment I step through the doorway.

Slipping off my shoes, I hold my breath. *One, two, three…*

I close my eyes, ready for the sting of rosary beads slapping my arms. Or Ama's high-pitched scolding. The house shudders with empty spaces. She must be hiding.

Padding inside, I survey the house. The TV is on, and I use the noise as cover to creep to my room. Maybe they never noticed I was gone. I can pretend that I was here the whole time.

But when I open my bedroom door, I know there will be no escaping, no pretending. *They know.*

My new bed sits in place. Freshly made and smelling of furniture oil. I run my hand over its polished frame as guilt splinters me. I have been absent, selfish, and lazy.

I bow my head and pick up the person I used to be. She's dusty from lack of use, but she still fits. I clean her off and go to thank Gung, to apologize to them both, and promise to be a better grandchild.

Armed with these resolutions, I march to their bedroom door, knocking determinedly. "Ama? Gung?" The light is on. I lean into the door so it will ease open. My eyes land on an unmade bed, glasses on the bedside table. A pair of slippers not tucked neatly under the bed. My breath wraps around my ribs and squeezes. It doesn't exhale. It stays there, slowly strangling me. "Ama? Gung?" I whisper, taking a step into the room.

Something's wrong.

I don't run. Something inside is denying my legs. It tells them to walk slowly. *Don't panic. Don't panic. Don't panic.*

Woodenly, I click off the TV and turn on the living room light. A cup of tea sits on the coffee table. I pick it up, hold it carefully in my hands like it's a baby bird.

It's still warm.

There's a place. A place where time stands almost still. Where I can pretend the world doesn't turn at an alarming rate. Where I can pretend that bad things don't happen...

A chilling breeze hits me like a right hook, and my eyes go to the ajar front door. Moving faster now, I chase the breeze, collecting it in my hands like a magician's scarf. Following it like a piece of string. I bring it to me faster, closer, tumbling down the stairs to where the Cortina should be, but only deep tire tracks sit in its place.

My eyes land on my old bed, one corner buried deep in the mud, the other side balancing awkwardly on a log that must have rolled from the woodpile. It's abandoned. It's a frame around a scene that's already played out. One I missed.

I curve around the bed, running now, the cold air pushing sharp things into my lungs. A burn I feel like I deserve. Wet leaves shatter under my feet. Mud cakes my shoeless feet. Turning at our driveway, I run. I run for fear. From fear. For answers. From the truth.

Our neighbor stands by his car like he just arrived there, dropped from the sky like a seed from a bird's claw. And when I see him, see the sorry—*I'm sorry. I'm so sorry*—expression, it turns my legs to jelly. They fold beneath me, and he rushes to my aid. Nothing will grow from this moment.

"Sunny, sweetheart, are you okay?" he asks, pulling me up roughly under my armpits. I try to catch my breath, but it's too late. It's a balloon floating to the stars.

I say one word. "Gung?"

And he says too many words. Words I don't want to hear. I wish for bark to grow over my eardrums, sap to fuse my eyes closed. "Oh, honey. George had another heart attack. I was helping him carry your old bed out to his workshop, and he just seized up." He clutches his chest, fisting his shirt. Swirls of blue and green checks. "I'm sorry. The ambulance took him, and Annie followed with the Cortina to the hospital."

I back away. He's saying something more. He's looking at me with those *I'm so sorry* eyes, but I can't hear it. All I can hear is blood rushing in my ears and those splinters of guilt breaking channels in my veins.

Taking off down his driveway, I head for the woods.

I need…

I don't know what I need.

I just need to find Breaker.

BREAKER

60

I wait about ten minutes, my eyes searching for an animated shadow shaking thin, strong limbs at a smaller, calmer one. But I don't see anything except lights switching on, and then off.

Maybe she got away with it.

Turning around, I head home cutting through the woods. My feet light. My memory focused only on what just happened minutes ago. A kiss. Sunny's smudged face lit by stars and a quarter moon. I inhale, breathing in the cold, pressed air of the forest. Pines, the mushroomy scent of decomposing leaves.

I feel content for a moment, picking out the seconds and replaying them one by one like pulling cards from a hat. Then Sunny's panicked cries tear my content to the ground. Shreds it into flakes.

She's crashing through the woods, screaming my name. A shadow, a banshee, a spirit.

Following the noise, I run to meet her, jumping over a log and slamming hard into her body.

The hollow sound of me winding her is so much better than the two words she says next. "Gung," she whimpers, barely able to breathe. "Hospital."

I take her hand, operating on salvage mode. *Take what you can carry. Get to safety. Save who you can.*

Branches reach out and slap us, adding injury to

heartbreak. I put my arm up to shield her as long fingers reach out to scratch our faces. As I drag her down the street, her wet socks squish on the concrete. Sad streetlights light the way. Sickly yellow shining down on us from above, giving a stage to our panic.

Taking the rundown stairs two at a time, I barge through the front door. Mom stands from the couch, her eyes wide with surprise. She takes in Sunny, attached to my arm, a mess of dark hair and sap-covered skin. I know she wants to say something, but I don't give her time. I just bark, "Car keys!" at her.

"In the bowl on the hallstand," she says, her shocked eyes on Sunny as I pull her across the carpet, grab my keys, and drag her back out the door. I snatch Red's rubber boots from the porch as we tumble down the stairs.

We jump in the car, and I look up to see my mom standing under the porch light. She stares at us with her mouth twisted in judgment as we back out the driveway and speed down the street toward the hospital.

Half an hour of misery.

Sunny doesn't know what to do with herself. Clasping and unclasping her hands. Leaning against the window, and then shuffling forward. Hands on the dash, hands in her lap. She bites her lip. I shouldn't be thinking how beautiful she looks right now, but I am.

She turns to look at me, opens her dark pink lips to say something, but her words seem to dissolve on the tongue like aspirin.

One eye on the road and one on her, I say, "There's a box of Kleenex in the glove compartment. You should clean your face."

She sighs with gratitude. She needs something to do.

I flick on the radio, keeping it low. *Killing Me Softly* pushes sad, sweet notes between us. We can't speak. We can't give voice to our fears yet. We're holding on. Because even though we really know it's not going to be okay, we can pretend it is until we reach the hospital.

Five minutes before we arrive, Sunny sucks in a breath and whispers, "What if he's…"

I shake my head and take her tiny, trembling hand. "We don't know that. Okay?"

She bows her head. Barely able to respond with an, "Uh-huh." She holds herself together with bits of bark and unwarranted hope.

61

Two.
One. Two.
Deux.
Un. Deux.
Two heart attacks.
People don't survive two heart attacks.

62

We scream into the ambulance drop-off area, and I stop the car. "Go," I urge. Sunny skids off the seat and out the truck before I can say more.

I don't know what I'd say anyway. *It'll be okay. Don't worry*. Stupid things that are said when there's nothing we can do. When we're helpless.

I park the car.

Run across the parking lot. Misty rain cools my hot face.

I get to the doors.

Hand on the handle.

Sunny's unsheltered back faces a doctor. She goes from standing to crouching on the ground. Cracking over like a dehydrated tree. She plants her hands on either side, hair falling over her face, her back rising and falling. Her small feet fitting perfectly into Red's blue rubber boots.

Annie crouches down too, arms around Sunny, binding her. Together, they breathe and stare at the floor. Too fast. Too much.

My heart squeezes and bleeds as I watch a family disintegrate behind the glass.

Sunny

63

Could I have stopped it?

If I'd been there, could I have helped him in some way?

They tell me no. Nothing could be done. Massive cardiac arrest. Acute Myocardial Infarction. Death of the heart.

They did everything they could. So sorry. So sorry for your loss.

No matter what they say, those fragments of guilt travel up my veins and pierce my heart like pins in a pincushion. Because I wasn't there. And I should have been.

I hold Ama up. She's a collection of bamboo sticks and broken twine. She moans. She cries. She clutches her heart. Her heart—my heart—is dying.

I hold her up because without Gung, she might disappear. The sane part of her might evaporate. "It not true!" she wails. Searching for someone to confirm her hope.

And I have to keep saying, "I'm sorry, Ama. So sorry. But it's true. Gung is gone." I have to keep smashing her hope to the ground, stomping on it until there's no life left.

Finding a chair, I arrange her frail limbs to sitting. She makes horrible, horrible noises. Noises of agony, of heartbreak. Of loss. I haven't cried. I can't. Not yet.

"No! I don't believe it. I need to see George. Sun, I want to see my husband," Ama says, a voice of withering reason cutting through the grief. I wish I could stop her. I want to say no. But this is her right.

Breaker stands, a mess of hollow eyes and sadness. *How long have we been here?* I run my tongue around my mouth. It feels dry and tastes of acid. I think I threw up. I look down at the stain on my shirt. Pieces coming back. I threw up. Breaker held back my hair. Ama screamed that the devil was trying to take me over.

This day is endless and looping.

"I'll get the doctor, Annie," he says, stalking away. Big, certain strides.

We all want to be useful.

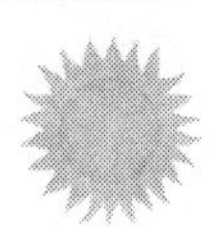

It's dark in the room. I smell Betadine. I see blood spots on the blanket that's tucked up under the man's armpits. I see a car crash of equipment shoved in the corner. The things that couldn't save him.

Breaker stays by the door, guarding us. Ama grips my arm. Her eyes on the ceiling. Watching, hopeful for ghosts.

I look up too.

The priest will be here soon.

Ama steps forward, her eyes lower, and she whispers, "George," as she reaches out to touch his face timidly. "Don't leave me here. George, come back."

I force myself to face him, what's left behind. My eyes fly over a shadow of a face. Sunken eyes and a pulled-down mouth, and then I bow my head. I bow my head and pray to a God I don't really believe in for things to be undone. For it not to be too late.

But it is.

And now he has left me alone with Ama.

The person talking is some wooden imitation of me as I say, "Yes. This is George Douglas, my grandfather." My breath is hickory smoked. The doctor nods. I sign some forms and force Ama to sign them too.

Pink light forces its way through the blinds of the common room. The endless day is over. But I find myself not wanting it to be. I want to go back. I want to undo this day. Undo the last few weeks.

But Gung is dead.

There is no undoing it.

BREAKER

64

Sunny told me to go home and get some sleep. I didn't want to. But she said, "Please, Breaker," with eyes that couldn't take anymore and a body that was sapped of all effort. So I left.

I've seen a lot death. I've watched people die in extraordinary circumstances. Brave, sacrificial deaths. Lives cut short. But this death is so ordinary. So run of the mill. I hit the steering wheel with the heel of my hand. Pain shoots up my arm. This *ordinary* death has destroyed the Douglas family.

I want to ask why. But I know the answer. Because. Just because.

I wipe an angry tear from my eye. He was a good man. He deserved more time. Sunny deserved more time.

Driving down the highway, I watch people commute to work, watch them get on with their day. Today is just another day for everyone except Annie and Sunny. For them, it's one of the worst days of their lives.

When I pull up to our house, Mom is waiting, standing on the porch with her arms crossed like she never left, like she's been there all night. Her face is dark and thunderous as storm clouds. Her forehead is creased with deep lines like tidemarks.

I get out and slam the car door as she says, "I sent Red to the neighbors."

Red. I need to tell Red.

"What? Why?" I ask stupidly. I mean, I haven't had a lot of sleep. When I think about it for a moment, I know why.

Mom opens the door. "Get inside," she says between clenched teeth.

From the bottom of the stairs, I say, "No. I'm not doing this with you now."

Her eyes are fire. Her tone is pure anger but as soft as steam. "Get. Inside. Now."

I wish I were anywhere else. I would rather be in the jungle than here.

I stomp up the stairs and into the living room. Mom slams the door behind me.

When I turn to face her, she's already in my space. Glaring at me with eyes that have been crying. She pokes me in the chest with her finger. "You've been lying to me."

"About what?" I challenge.

She throws her hands in the air, summing it all up with big gestures. "Everything, Breaker. Everything! Did people see you? How long have you been seeing that, that..."

She's acting crazy. And not good crazy like Annie. This is hateful, irrational crazy. "That what?" I ask, stepping back from her because she's emanating heat and hate.

"That gook!" she spits.

In a quiet but stern voice, I say, "Her name is Sunny." My hands fist at my sides. "And don't you ever use that word in front of me again."

She pulls at her hair, looking at me like I'm a stranger. And maybe I am to her. "What's wrong with you?" Her mouth forms an ugly arch, a scream about to happen. "What changed? I thought you were like me, like our family. That you shared our values." She's pleading now. Begging for me to buy into her prejudice.

I loom over her, but I don't like how she cowers, so I step back. Collapsing on the couch, I sigh. "I was never like you. I had trouble when I came back, I'll admit. I found it hard to face people like Sunny because they brought on bad memories. But that wasn't about them. It was about me, and I hated myself for it. You think it's a *value* to treat people of color like dirt? It's not. And with Sunny's help, I'm working through my problems." My arms are splayed out, entreating.

Mom shakes her head. "I'm so ashamed of you. I can't believe you would do this to your family."

I snort. "You're ashamed of me? That's freakin' hilarious. You're ashamed because I'm trying to make myself better. That I'm trying. That I found a girl I love and I'm finally happy. Get bent, Mom. *I'm* ashamed of *you*."

"You love her?" Dread drips down her face.

Of course I love her. *I. Love. Her.* "Yes, I love her. She's incredible. Can you give me one good reason why I shouldn't?"

She's shaking. Confused and bitter. "Because she's not your kind. Her kind is untrustworthy. They come to this country and take American jobs. They don't belong here." She's grasping at nothing. Because there is no basis for her attitude.

I could defend the Douglases, tell her how George lived off a Malaysian police pension and made extra cash selling his woodwork. That Annie was a teacher in Malaysia and she now tutors Chinese and French. That Sunny is amazing, intelligent, and better than pretty much everyone I know. But Mom doesn't deserve to know them.

All I say is, "You should hear yourself," with a sad laugh, and then I go to my room and pack my things.

Mom's waiting for me in the living room when I emerge from my room. Duffel bag over my shoulder. She wipes her nose with her sleeve, her face streaked with tears. I do feel bad, but then I don't. How can someone be so good and so wrong at the same time? I shake my head and stalk toward the door.

"Of course you're leaving," she says, pushing hurtful into her voice. I turn, let the bag hang from my hand. "That's what Van Winkle men do. Lazy, useless sons of bitches. They all leave. When things get too hard, they always take off."

I step one foot onto the porch. "What are you talking about?"

"Your dad, his dad, and his dad before him. And now you. They always abandon their families. They're weak," she spits bitterly.

I want to tell her I'm not leaving. I could never abandon Red. But I do need a break. I need space and time to think. But I don't say a word. I leave the truck keys in the bowl so she can take Red to school, and I walk out on her. It's not forever, but I'm angry. Right now, I want to hurt her the way she's hurt me. It's not lazy, but it is weak.

65

I drive us home, despite not having a license. Ama is a silent sack of bones, shaking beside me, refusing to talk. And I don't try to talk to her. I don't know what to say. We are both in that walled up hell of grief. A muggy feeling where the brain doesn't know what to do except cry silent tears and *wish, wish, wish* it wasn't happening.

Easing the handbrake up, I kill the engine. Car doors closing sound lonely. We walk around the dropped bed, slumped in the mud. I put my hand at Ama's back and help her up the stairs. She moves sluggishly, clasping her hands together, head bowed. Her speed has slowed to a snail's pace. She has no energy.

I take her purse and fish out her keys. Open the door. Focus on mundane, easy-to-process things. Key in lock. Turn. Push open.

We stare at the inside shell of our house.

Wishing for ghosts to fill it.

"Ama, avez-vous faim?" I ask.

"No, not hungry." She shakes her head, hangs up her purse, and walks to her room.

My stomach gurgles, so I find some leftovers in the fridge. The food hits my stomach like a stone, and I nearly vomit. I drink some water. I try to breathe. I try not to think the thoughts that keep pushing at my brain. But it's no use.

I wasn't with Gung when it happened. I was kissing Breaker at the tree. While Gung was clutching his chest, hot pain searing through his body as his heart struggled to live, I was joking around about my grades. I got caught up in this new love, and now Gung is dead. I slam the bench with my fist.

This is all Breaker's fault.

The light clicks on at about one AM. "Sun! Why you on the floor?" Ama asks.

For a second, I forget that our family is broken again.

I roll to my back and stare up at the ceiling, blinking at the harsh lightbulb. My back aches, and then I remember. I'm on the floor because I can't bring myself to sleep in my new bed.

Again. My family is broken. *How many times can you break something before it can no longer be repaired?*

I yawn, watching Ama swing excitedly from the doorframe. When I prop myself up on my elbows, the hard floor bites into my bones. "Ama, it's the middle of the night," I say in confusion.

"I know. I know," she says animatedly. "But I want to tell you Gung here!" Her dark eyes are ringed with purplish circles radiating out like ripples in a sad, sad pond. The brightness in them seems false.

Hope. Then logic. Then hope crushed to pieces.

I rub my eyes and get up, taking Ama's outstretched hand.

"Come," she says, a spring in her step.

She drags me past their bedroom, past the wall of family photos that are now all we have left of him, and shoves me into the bathroom.

The water is running in the toilet, and Ama points to it. "Gung only one who get up in night for toilet. See," she says. "Still running. He just been."

Blowing cold, dead air through my lips, I try to calm my anger. My frustration at her. My heart hurts. It hurts so much I feel like it might explode.

I push the stuck button of the toilet. The water stops running.

Resting my cold cheek against her hot one, I say, "You need to go back to bed." I turn off the bathroom light, and she turns it back on.

"He be back soon," she whispers with a strange, greedy sound to her voice.

I look up at the ceiling. *How am I going to do this?*

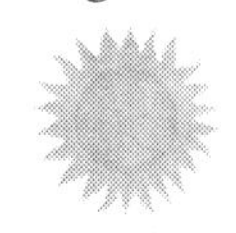

Ama stands in front of the mirror, applying a thick layer of waxy red lipstick, a houseplant balancing on the thin hallstand. I shuffle toward her in my pajamas. "*Ou?* Where are you going?"

Her eyes dart to me and then back to her reflection. "Gung's spirit need place to live." She puts down her lipstick and holds up the plant. "I take to hospital. Then Gung's spirit jump in." She makes weird flying gestures with her hands.

"But I thought he was in the bathroom?" I say, bewildered at myself for playing along but not knowing what else to do.

She turns to me like I'm as dense as one of her butter cakes and says, "Don't be stupid. He visit. It was a, uh, a message."

I cross my arms over my chest, weak scaffolding for a failing heart. "To bring a plant to the hospital for him to jump into?"

She grips the plant tightly under her arm and nods. "Gung likes ficus."

I've heard this legend before. How a spirit can jump into a plant or animal. Usually it's not something the family wants. They want their loved one to move on, whatever that means. I should be surprised or maybe try to stop her, but I don't have the energy. My mind is filled only with sadness and a deep need to sleep. Deeper than a black hole.

Briefly, I picture her running around the hospital with the houseplant, and I snort.

Then I look to Gung's chair to share my amusement with the one person who understands, and my ribs shatter like ice. My chest squeezes like an accordion, and I feel like there's no air in the room. His empty chair screams hollow.

I barely notice Ama leaving.

I think maybe I'll sit in Gung's chair, that it might bring me comfort. I think it might also hurt like a pike to the chest...

The door opens, and there Breaker is. Looking devastated and worried, cold light wrapping around his body. I step back into the shadows where I'm more comfortable. I want to hide in the dark, away from the sun, away from reality. I want to close my eyes and escape.

66

Sunny shields her eyes from the light like a night creature, stepping back and away. She finds a dark corner and stands next to George's chair, hanging arms and hollow eyes. A face so stripped of its normal nature that she's almost unrecognizable. She runs a hand across the green arm slowly, staring at her fingers. Disconnected, turning them like they're not her own.

"I spoke to the school for you," I say, talking to a shadow, another ghost. "And I told Cara what happened. She's real worried about you and Annie."

Her head dips as she whispers, "Cara." She shakes her head slowly, sorrowfully.

"Sunny. I'm so sorry," I say, approaching her.

Her head snaps to me, a sudden bolt of energy that seems to exhaust her. "Don't."

I come closer, arms ready to fold her inside, but she looks at me with anger. Grief. Grief clothes her from head to foot. "It's not your fault." I say the useless words because there aren't any good ones. Good words don't belong in this moment.

She tries to breathe, and it catches on a sigh. Something's breaking inside her. She touches her chest lightly with two fingers and I can almost hear her heart crumbling away. "I let you take over my life," she says in a dead whisper. "I let you change me into someone else. I was happy before I met you. Without you. Our family was happy." Her voice sounds shredded, grating against her throat.

I'm within arm's reach of her, but the air between us has become as thick as concrete.

"I'm sorry. Blame me. You can blame me," I say, a tear pricking my eye. Because I cared about George. I'm going to miss him too. "But please, don't push me away." This is not the time, I know, but if I don't say it, maybe she'll slip away for good. I can feel it happening, the bond between us stretching thinner and thinner. "I don't want to lose you." I threaten the words to wait, but they escape my mouth like breathing. "Sunny, I love you."

She steps toward me and I close my eyes, thinking she's going to collapse into my arms. And then, I can hold her. I can comfort her. Together, we can work this out.

Her palms slam into my chest, hard, and I stumble back. The sound is empty. "Don't say that! Not now. *Ce n'est pas juste*! It's not fair! I don't want it. I can't… I can't handle it," she shouts, pushing me again.

I stand rigid; the collision of palms on my chest brings a flash. A jolt like defibrillation. Green dots in my vision.

His hands are so small, but they slap at my body like paddle bats. He tips, I tilt. We're a mash of arms and legs. A mash of two wills to survive. But there can only be one. There are no words. This language is unspoken. Mud slaps, dirt spatters. Groans and shifting feet. Desperate fingers scratching, clawing, trying to bring me down. There's no finesse in this fight, no training remembered. This is life against life.

I have to decide. Do I want to die here in the mud, thousands of miles and several seas from home? Or do I kill a man?

His shin slams into my stomach, hard, fast. I won't. The words—I can't. I can't. I can't—come with my gasps as I grab his hair and jerk him back. Wild, fearful eyes. A conversation identical to mine, shining in his expression.

All choices today are bad choices.

But I have to.

I don't want to die.

"*Allez*! Wake up! You're not even here. Damn you, Breaker. Get out! Get out now!" she screams, her hair falling loose from its braid, her tears wetting the carpet. She swipes her running nose, a shrieking pain in her eyes, and clasps her hands together in prayer. "Oh, God…" She's sinking, her knees giving out on her. She sweeps the room, searching for him. Her hand goes to her mouth a sharp cry hitting her palm. Her hand drops, plants on the ground like a root searching for water. "He's dead. He's gone." She mutters something in French that I can't understand, wobbling on her haunches and curling over her stomach.

I bring her in as she folds, even as she whispers, "I hate you," into my chest.

We climb into George's chair, and I let her expel what sadness she can.

And when she's cried all she can cry, when she can finally breathe a single breath without shattering, she stares up at me and says, "I love you."

In the next breath, she says, "Please get out of my

house. Please leave and don't ever come back."

And then it's my turn to shatter.

BREAKER

67

I love you. I hate you.

She said both. Blames me. Is that fair? Maybe. I don't have enough evidence stashed in my pockets to prove otherwise. I storm down the street, passing wooden shacks and stripped trees before I stop, grab a smoke from my pocket, and light it up. The moment the tarry taste hits my tongue, I gag and spit it out, working it into the pavement like it's done me wrong.

She did this. This and so many other good things. It never occurred to me that while she was a good influence on me—light in the dark, coaxing me from the shadows—that I might have been a poor influence on her.

I don't want to believe it. She said *I love you.* That has to count for something. I run to the phone booth and dial the Douglas' number. It rings so many times I nearly hang up, but then I hear her beautiful voice, or at least the last shreds of it. "Allo?"

I clear my throat. "Sunny, please," I beg.

She hangs up before I get to the S end of the word, and my heart drops to the ground.

Cursing, I pull out my smokes and throw them in the trash can. I also kick the trash can. I want to run back to her so bad. Convince her that she needs to let herself love me.

I put a coin in the slot and dial again.

It rings twice, and I'm surprised when someone answers. "Hello?"

"It's Breaker," I say.

"Breaker. Wow. I haven't heard from you in forever. What's happening, man? How are you?" Dad asks with as much enthusiasm as someone with no care can have.

"I'm good," I reply, almost laughing at how inaccurate that is. "Look, Dad. I can't talk for long, but I wanted to ask you a question."

He coughs. "Shoot."

I slam a hand in my pocket, take a breath, and say it, "Why did you leave Sundown? Was it just because of Mom or was there another reason?"

The phone crackles. He sighs. "Well, dude, the simple answer is that I wasn't strong enough to stay."

"You couldn't fight it?" I ask, hoping he knows what I'm talking about.

He sighs again like he's bored. "I couldn't. You know I've said it before, but the offer still stands. You ever need a place to crash, I've got you," he offers.

I don't need to think about it. I don't feel it anymore. "I think I'm strong enough. I'm strong enough to stay."

"Well, good for you, man," he says genuinely. "You go break the mold."

Okay. I will.

"Bye, Dad."

"Bye, son."

I hang up and wait for the warm air to curl around me and pull me to the woods. It gathers loosely at my hips, but it can't get a grip and slowly fades away. I *am* strong enough.

"How is she?" Delquin asks, pouring me a cup coffee from his fancy French press in his pale blue kitchen. He boiled the water in a microwave. No one has a microwave in Sundown.

"Leave the boy alone, Marcus," Mrs. Delquin says, shooing at him with a tea towel.

My head is heavy in my hands. I run my finger along the edge of the mug and gaze into the black liquid. "She's not good. She doesn't want to speak to me. Right now, I don't blame her."

"It's not your fault he died, Breaker. Sounds like he had a lot of health problems," he says, adding cream and stirring.

Their windows frame a neat view. This house is perfect, fresh-cut lawn, picket fence, kids playing at the bottom of the stairs. It's a nice family in a nice neighborhood. It would be easier to take him up on his offer to stay here and live in their spare room. It would be easy, but it wouldn't be right.

Easier is not always better.

"I know. But it's my fault she wasn't there when he died. And I spoke to her friend Cara. She said her grades had slipped. That she had changed a lot over the last month, and not in a good way. So I get why she's angry. I get why I'm not good for her. Not how I am now. That's kind of what I want to talk to you about..."

Delquin's smile is like white-out on a dark page. "You want to apply for college?" he asks, clapping his hands.

I nod. "Yes. But I also want you to give me a job."

It would be easier…

But easier is not what I want anymore.

68

I knock on the front door and wait like a traveling salesman. I don't have anything to apologize for, but I have to work this out with her.

The door opens, and Red's beaming grin greets me. He runs into the screen door in his excitement. "Ugh!"

"Red, you're gonna break a hole through the fly wire!" Mom shouts, a laugh in her voice. It reminds me that she loves Red. She probably loves me too. *I think.* Maybe we can work on the rest together.

I try the handle, but it's locked.

"Mom! It's Break! It's Break! And the door's locked. Mom!" Red shouts.

She comes to the door, eyebrows raised in surprise. "You're back," she says, almost like a question, almost like a joke, unlocking the door. I step in and she steps back, staring at the stained carpet in embarrassment. It's a good sign.

Red wraps his arms around my middle and squeezes. And I don't try to peel him off. I don't feel like his hug is going to strangle me. I hug him back. Then I look up at Mom, who's staring at us with a guilty expression.

"Mom said you took off fer good," Red says, releasing me. I hate that she put pain in his voice when she didn't have to. "She said you weren't coming back."

"I never said I was leaving for good." I connect with her eyes. "Mom was wrong." Her face falls back to the floor.

Red cranes his neck around my body to look outside. "Is Sunny here?" he asks. "I haven't seen her in ages."

I laugh. He saw her three days ago. Then I gulp.

Mom retreats to the kitchen. I think the best she can do right now is keep her mouth closed.

I take Red to the couch, and we sit down. "Sunny and I are on a break. She's going through a bad time right now, and she's not very happy with me."

Red turns on the TV, starts flicking through channels. He's ten. He has the attention span of a ten-year-old. "What'd you do?"

I was drowning and dragged her down with me. And when I stopped drowning and started swimming, I only saved myself. I forgot to pull her from the water. How could I forget to pull her from the water?

"Red, Sunny's grandfather died." I feel the choke, the grief wrapping around my throat.

Red blinks and tries to absorb the information, but it's a lot to ask. He turns to face me. "You didn't do that though, did you?" A high tone at the end.

"No. Of course not. But she's grieving. She's upset, and I need to let her be angry with me for a while."

I do, I tell myself, even though I want to charge to her door and demand she see me.

He nods. "Okay. But not forever, right? You'll fix it?"

I put my arm around his shoulders and pull him close. "I'll fix it."

"That's sad that George died. Sunny must be really, really sad." He stares at his fingers for a while, his lips set in a frown. "Wanna watch *Tom and Jerry* with me?" he asks.

"Sure."

69

Salmon-colored carpet is a strange choice for a funeral parlor. Although, I don't know what would be a good color. Is it supposed to be reassuring? Distracting? To me, it looks like the color of Haw Flakes. Or fish food. The two are very similar in color, very different in flavor. I lick my lips, thinking of Chinese candy. Then saltwater stings my eyes as I remember Gung fishing packs from his pocket and giving them to Red, to any of the neighborhood kids who came by to see the progress on their dollhouse or rocking horse.

Ama hangs from my elbow. The funeral director was talking, but I missed it. He opens a side door and ushers us inside. He says something, something, "Viewing," and now it's too late to back out of the room.

Ama lets go and approaches the coffin. I'm frozen in place, wiggling my toes in black court shoes on the Haw Flake carpet. She gets to the coffin and stands on her tiptoes. It shouldn't be funny. It's not the time to laugh, but she jumps slightly and a small chuckle rises in my chest. "I can't see," she says crossly. "You make it too high. This not made for petite Chinese people. This made for Yankee cowboy."

My eyes roll to halfway and can't be bothered to finish the rotation.

Flustered, the funeral director disappears, returning with a footstool I assume is for children. It's a horrible thought.

She steps up and lifts the lid. "Ai ya!" she shouts. "He look funny. He not look like George." She doesn't seem very upset, just put out. She crosses her arms. "Lucky he not here to see this."

No, he's not here because Ama thinks she trapped his spirit in a houseplant. Water spills from my eyes as I let out a loud laugh. I grip my stomach, feeling so wrong and entertained at the same time. The funeral director looks at us like we're both insane.

Maybe we are.

Would it be easier to just embrace the crazy?

Ama calls me over. "Sunny! Come."

I don't want to, but I can see this tipping from funny to disastrous in seconds. I approach the coffin carefully and step on to the stool with Ama. We share it, one foot on, one foot off.

I start as his hands, not ready to see his face. Big, rough hands clasped neatly over his belly, his skin an off-yellow color. Ama points, almost touching him, and I grab her hand. "Ama, no! Don't touch him," I whisper.

She snorts. "Why? He not feel it."

Breathe. Don't laugh. Don't cry. Don't shout at Ama to act normal just once in her goddamned life.

I force myself to look at his face. His skin hangs loosely on his bones. His eyes are closed and sunken. She's right. It doesn't look like him. But I'm glad for that. I press my cheek to hers and say, "It's him, Ama. It's his body anyway. His spirit, the thing that made him George Douglas and Gung, it is not here."

She purses her lips and nods, seeming to accept my answer.

The funeral director steps too close and looks to the ceiling. "He is with God now, Mrs. Douglas."

This makes Ama tense. She's feeling guilty because she's holding Gung's spirit hostage in the ficus on top of the TV.

I look at the ceiling too. *Gung, I wish you were here.*

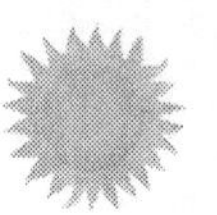

The funeral makes it too real. The hymns. The priest. The earth to earth. The ashes to ashes. The dust to dust. My mind travels outside. It winds its way around the trunks of trees. It weaves across paths and over streams. It nestles in a nice, warm spot where time changes. I don't just feel a pull—I need it.

Ama and I walk out first. In the back row, Breaker stands with his head bowed in prayer. My eyes take him and lay his image into the flower press of stored memories. Maybe one day I can take it out and I won't be angry anymore. But when I look at him right now, I feel robbed. He robbed me of time with Gung.

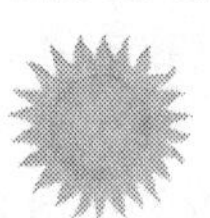

Cara's warm, round shoulder hits my sharp one. "I'm going to sleepover," she tells me.

I watch Ama introducing people to the ficus. I honestly can't tell if she believes he's in there or if she's doing it for her own amusement.

People nod and smile uncomfortably. Most of

them know she can be a little eccentric, but this is too much. And it's because there's no one here to rein her in. The thought that I should be the one rises and falls like a mist too lazy to become a cloud.

"It's okay, Cara," I say as both of us track Ama flitting around the room, forcing people to try her food. Crying, then laughing, and then crying again. She's collecting handkerchiefs. I can see her sleeves bulging with them.

Cara elbows me. "Seems to me you could use some backup."

I sigh. "Breaker was there. Did you see him?"

Usually, I'd lean my head on her shoulder, but something stops me. This pain… it's my own. I don't want to share it.

"I did. What's going on with you two?"

I don't answer. Ama is cracking open her harmonica case, and I stand in a panic. "*Mon dieu!* My God. She's acting completely crazy!" I slap a hand on my forehead. It's like a two-by-four.

Cara chuckles. "She's just being Annie. I mean, she's pretty upset. Maybe we should just let her have this one, Sunny."

New anger fires in my stomach. "You have no idea what it's like to live with her like this, Cara. Without Gung."

Cara puts her hands up in defense. "I'm sorry. I just meant…"

She doesn't understand. Her family is normal. Boring even. How could she possibly understand? "You don't get it," I snap. "How could someone like *you* possibly understand what I'm going through?"

Cara looks like I just stabbed her in the stomach, and she holds her palm there to stem the blood flow of our dying friendship. She whispers, "I'm just trying to help."

I leave Cara whimpering on the couch and stalk toward Ama, gently prying the harmonica from her hands. "Maybe another time, Ama. It's getting late." I eye as many people as I can and say loudly, "People probably want to get home before it gets dark."

They take the hint. Soon, almost everyone has left.

Cara still sits on the couch with Ama beside her. Her eyes hopeful, Cara says, "I could still stay over. If you want?"

Ama pats Cara's blonde head and flicks on the TV. "Yes. You stay and watch *Gilligan* with me. I don't know why Skipper so fat. Where he get food from on desert island? You no get so fat from eating only coconuts. He hoarding food." She shakes her finger at the screen. "I think they should eat Skipper. Serve him right for being a glutton!"

Yawning exaggeratedly and tapping my mouth, I say, "I'm pretty tired. I think I'm just going to go straight to bed."

Ama waves at me. "*Baik*. Okay. Go."

I go to my room, pull all my sheets from the bed, and sit on them. Pressing my ear to the door, I listen and wait for Cara to leave.

BREAKER

70

A week without Sunny is like a North Pole winter. I pull the timber from the bleachers with little effort. It crumbles in my hands and falls beneath me. I shake my head. I can't believe a kid or parent hasn't fallen through. These bleachers are held together with old chewing gum and bird shit.

The weather is starkly cold, the football field vivid green. And me? I'm the lack of color in between. Beige coveralls. The high-school handyman. It's not glamorous, but it beats moping around at home. Avoiding Mom and itching to pick up the phone.

Sunny hasn't been at school. I watch for her when the bell rings, but she's not in the flood of bored teenagers pouring from the building. I write wishes in the clouds.

Sunny, I hope you're okay.

Climbing down from the bleachers, I try to feel *it*. The call. The warm air. I think I have it and walk to the edge of the field, but then it disperses and disappears. I can't get a hold of it. I've tried a couple of times, but I can't find the tree. Or maybe it can't find me.

I shrug, pick up my toolbox, and walk to the elementary school to get Red.

"When do you have to leave?" Mom asks, stirring something that smells like burned cheese.

"Half hour. I just want to finish reading these notes," I say, trying to absorb the information Delquin gave me about college essays.

"I'm so glad you're applying to college, Breaker, that you listened to me," she says, leaning on her wooden spoon. I sniff the air, burned cheese and cat food. It's Tuna Mornay. I think about Annie's cooking and frown.

"It was Sunny, Mom. She's why I started this. I think it's turned into more. Like more for me in the end. But Sunny…Sunny lit the fire," I blurt.

Red punches my butt, and I wobble on my stool. He laughs and croons, "Breaker lurves her."

Mom turns away from me, and I ignore my very accurate younger brother.

I don't know exactly how this will work. But I'm not going to leave Red alone with her. His heart and head are untouched. They're like the crystal waters of the falls. I'm not going to let her muddy them.

"Also, I'm going to start paying rent from next week, okay?" I ask.

Her shoulders, which were up around her ears, relax by half an inch. "Thanks, Break, that will help a lot."

"No problem." I pack up my papers and slot them into my bag. "Red?"

His freckled face appears from around the living room door. "Yeah?"

"Tell Jake to meet us after school tomorrow for a kick around."

"Yes!" Red squeals. Jumping up on the couch, he

sinks between the cushions, which are so old and pummeled they're beginning to disintegrate.

A crack in the kitchen as Mom hits the spoon on the edge of the sink.

I throw a cushion at my trapped brother and turn to Mom. "Times are changing, Mom. You either change with them or you get left behind." I linger in the doorway, picturing her standing at the back, the world shifting without her. I don't know if she's got it in her. I just know I'm not going to bend myself to fit into her way of thinking anymore.

"Jake's gonna be stoked!" Red shouts as I start to close the door. "Can I call him?" he asks Mom.

And she actually says, "Maybe..."

Sunny

71

I should feel better. I've read the pamphlets handed to our shaking hands by bowing, faceless people, and I've been through the stages of grief. I accept that Gung is gone. But I feel him. Not in the ficus. But in the house. His strong voice is caught in the corner cobwebs. The fabric breathes tobacco. I touch the arm of the chair and it's warm, like he just got up. Like he'll be back soon.

Every day, I have to *accept* that Gung is gone. Again. And it's crushing my spirit. It's flattening it to the thickness of rice paper. Once water touches it, it will lose its strength and dissolve.

I want to throw the ficus in the trash.

A flannelette shirt flies through the air and dive bombs into a pile of clothes in the hallway. It perfumes the air briefly with tobacco, sweet and heartbreaking. "Ama! *Que*. What are you doing?" I ask, kneeling to touch the heap of shirts and jackets.

Her head pokes out from ~~their~~ *her* room. "Father say donate clothes. It healthy." She holds up a wool coat, wooden buttons still shiny and buffed. "You think Break Ah want this?" she asks.

Breaker. Anger has been replaced with shame. But I can't call him. I can't deal with any more feelings. I'm so sick of feeling. Anything.

Ama stomps from the room, stepping over the pile and into my doorway. She tries to grab at my arm fat, but comes up empty. She tsks and shakes her head. "Ah. I don't know what to do, George. She no eat." She points at her tearstained cheeks. The saltwater has created riverbeds in her makeup. "I sad, but I still eat." The ficus she's addressing stands predictably still.

I groan. I can't be bothered with her nagging either. I grab an armful of shirts, lifting them to my face. The soft feel of the fabric, the smell, the… *Gung, I need you.*

Putting them on the bed, I start sorting and folding. I put some on the dining table, but keep three, placing them in the back of my wardrobe.

Ama hums in the kitchen. Off key like someone slamming paws on a piano. Then she cries out. I lift my head too quickly and bang it on the hanging rod in the wardrobe. The coat hangers clang against each other. When I step back, I see a sweater that wasn't there before. The glaringly white NYU letters push my anger back into place. I yank it off the hanger and throw it on my bed.

"Sunny! Help!" Ama shrieks.

My anger has to stay, splayed on the bed I won't sleep in. Festering for another time.

Something smells dark and black.

I run to the kitchen.

Flames lick the range hood, which Ama is leaning toward rather than away from. "Ama, get back!" I shout. The kitchen is a mess. Three different dishes on the stove and oil flaming from a saucepan. I want to cry. I want to throw my arms up and scream. Because she's not like this. Not when Gung is here. Something's snapped in her brain or she's stopped caring. I don't know. But she's pulling me down. Exhausting me to the point where I soon won't care anymore either.

I grab the lid for the saucepan and drop it on the oil, starving the flames of oxygen and flicking the stove tops off. Ama holds her wrist gingerly, and I pull her arm under my eyes. "*Merde!* Shit! What have you done now?" I ask in exasperation.

"I make prawn cracker," she whispers, her eyes downcast like a naughty child.

Her skin bubbles red and yellow. I turn on the tap and shove her wrist underneath. "Don't move!" I order while I quickly clean up the kitchen.

I bite down. I can't fall apart. I can't get cross at her for hanging that NYU sweater in my wardrobe. I can't, I can't, I *can't* do anything I want to do. My life is my responsibility to Ama now. My eyes ache to cry. My chest constricts with panic. I'm trapped.

She cries as the water runs, and I touch her shoulder. "It's okay, Ama. It's okay. It's not that bad."

But it is bad.

What happens to the mind of a free spirit when there's nothing left to hold it to earth? It simply flies away.

I want to hold it together. I want to be strong. For her. For Gung.

I try to talk myself into it. But there's a call. There's warm air pushing between us. Pushing us apart. Pulling me away.

After I dress Ama's wounds, I put her to bed.

I walk out the back door and sit on the porch steps. I want to see an ember floating in the dark from the corner of my eye. A spot of orange in the absolute black.

You would say something short and quiet and comforting. I would know just by the tone of your voice that I am loved. I am safe. But you're not here. You've been torn from my family. There's no comfort, only pain. It's on all sides, and I can't run from it.

I don't think I have the energy to.

I squash my fingers together, trying to feel anything other than this crushing, concrete feeling. Dust clouds don't just hover in the background—they *swarm*. They over take the air until I can't see. I sink below the surface, arms at my sides. I don't fight. I don't kick my legs or move my arms. I let it drown me.

My head drops between my legs, and I weep.

BREAKER

72

"Are you ready for this?" Delquin asks, his hand on the horizontal bar of the door.

No.

He's going to push down on it either way. The door *will* open.

His blue eyes are painted with concern. I said I'd try. I promised Sunny.

I nod, running my sweaty palms down my clean army jacket. My mind prepares itself for a drag back, a shock of green sweeping in from the sides like a theater curtain.

The door creaks open to a rumble of men's voices. Swept together in groups, talking, laughing, holding cups of coffee that smell bitter and tinny like it used to back there. I wait. I brace. Something claws at my back, but a voice pulls me forward…not backward.

"Richard, this is Breaker. He served seventy-one to seventy-two." We list our various platoons, squads, company names, like a second surname.

Richard offers his left hand for me to shake. I try not to stare at the jacket sleeve pinned up with a nappy pin, hiding a missing arm from the elbow. Richard laughs. "It's okay, son. You can look. We don't have any secrets here." He pulls a flask from his pocket and flips the lid with his teeth. "As long as I can still do this." He takes a swig. "I'm good." He winks at me. He clinks his flask with another man's paper cup as they pass.

"Nice to meet you," I say, standing too upright, my hand aching to salute. "Sorry."

Delquin pats my back and moves me through the group, making introductions. They range in age from mid-twenties to seventies. I'm the youngest one here. But I don't feel out of place. Their faces all tell a similar story. My story. Their eyes are pooled with things no one should see. We all have that in common. We've all seen death in a different way to the rest of the world. Death on a large scale. We've been in a place where death means something different. It means less, and it means more. Less—because there's too much of it. More—because it always felt like we could be next.

I think about George for a moment. I imagine he would have been pretty comfortable here. These people are his people too. *Were*, I guess.

Delquin wanders off to talk to his Korean War buddies, and I go to the table to get a cup of coffee. I snatch up the tin of condensed milk, pouring a blob into the bottom of my cup and adding the strong coffee. I watch the milk swirl like a thick tornado up and around the blackness, warming the color to caramel.

"It's funny the things we bring home with us, right?" a man says, taking the condensed milk and doing the same thing as me. We both swish our cups around instead of using a teaspoon.

I follow his arm up to his almond eyes. His tan skin is spotted with freckles and they move when he smiles. In a perfect American accent, he says, "I'm Tien."

My heart stays steady. It beats out a rhythm it has learned the music to over the last month. I take the hand he offers and smile back. "Breaker."

We find two plastic chairs and collapse into them. Tien blows on his coffee and takes a sip, holding it with both hands. "Ahh, a Vietnamese coffee. I like it when I get a blob that hasn't dissolved yet," he says, still smiling. "Gives me an excuse to get more coffee."

I laugh in an unsure, awkward kind of way as I swirl the coffee some more. I'm okay, but I'm not sure what to say to this guy.

Tien rests his elbows on his knees and surveys the room. "You know the other thing that I can't seem to shake since I've been back?"

I want to know. I want to hear that he's just like me. I force myself back into my chair. *Relax*. "What's that?"

"Sleeping without a pillow," he says, grinning with neat, narrow teeth.

I let myself nod, agree, and smile. "Yeah, I get ya. Same here."

An older man in full uniform approaches us, looking stern and judgmental. He frowns at Tien, and I feel like I want to stand and defend him. Tien stands and salutes the older man, whose crinkly face cracks into a smile. "No need to stand on ceremony here, Tien," he says gruffly, ruffling his spiky black hair. Then he looks at me. "Don't let his looks fool you! Tien will take care of you. He's one of the good guys."

I frown then. Not sure how to take that. Tien doesn't seem to mind though.

When the old guy is gone, I nudge Tien. "Are you cool with that? I mean, shit, this must be a little awkward for you sometimes," I mutter, watching all the white men strolling between groups, their uniforms in varying states of spit and polish.

He shrugs. "It was at first. And yeah, looking like I do, I have to work harder at getting some people to accept me, trust me, but once you know me, well…" He gulps down the rest of his coffee and crushes the cup in his hand. "You can't help but love me!"

It doesn't seem fair that he has to work harder. "Doesn't seem right, man," I say, shaking my head.

Tien knocks my leg with his knee. "Nope, it isn't. But what you just said. That right there is enough of a reason to keep trying. Things will change. Name by name. Face by face. I like you already, Breaker!" He's intoxicatingly hopeful.

I run a hand through my hair. Who would have thought I'd be on this side of the argument?

Tien knocks my knee again. His laugh is full of light. Not sunshine exactly. More like the light from a cluster of stars. It sparkles with magic.

Heart steady. A smile, tinted green, but a smile just the same.

The sun hits the sand, and it sparkles. Palm trees bristle in the warm breeze. If I squint, if I look past the stacks of wooden crates piled on the beach, the dirty men draped over them, it looks like a postcard.

I snap that image for later.

Booze is poured into tin cups, and we sip. We wipe our brows of sweat and tell stories, swap the most mundane details of our lives with each other, building something. This foundation we have to rely on.

Kicking my shoes off, I bury my toes in the sand, watching it cascade over my white, shriveled skin. My feet look like they've been in a bath for hours.

I'm staring at them when a disk with colored feathers sprouting from it lands at my feet.

I look up into the expectant grin of a kid, about the same age as Red. He beckons me with his hand, asking me to join the game he's playing with his friends.

Sarge nods an okay.

Towering over these little Vietnamese kids, I jog to where they're playing. Quickly, I realize the aim of the game is to keep the feathered disk in the air using whatever I can.

The kids are amazing, back-flipping, twisting, slapping at it with their hands and feet. I try to keep up, and they laugh but encourage me to keep trying.

We're just kids, playing a game.

Our shouting rattles across the waves. We kick and slap at the ball, we laugh when someone falls over, but offer a hand to help them back up.

My smile cracks open my chest as some fear spills out onto the sand to be collected by the sea.

Some of the other guys join us, and we play until it's too dark to see.

The sun sprays red and orange over the water, and the kid who invited me slaps my back and winks. He hands me the feathered disk and runs away, laughing and shouting at his friends.

Tien taps my back gently. "Breaker. Where'd you go?"

My mouth feels strange, turned up into a smile.

I'd forgotten about that kid. That good memory.

"Sorry. I was just remembering something," I mutter.

"Must've been a good something," Tien says, pointing at my mouth.

I chuckle. "Yeah, it was."

Sunny

73

I wake to Ama moaning in pain and praying for Jesus to take her. I'm a sloth. My arms and legs stapled to the floor. I pry them off one by one and wearily pull on clothes, not really noticing what I'm wearing. I shuffle to her room in odd socks, one striped, one polka dot.

"Oh, Lord," she wails, both hands in the air. "Take me to Heaven." She waits, papery lids closed. When her prayers are not answered, she mutters something in Chinese under her breath. Curse words. I lean my head against the doorframe, watching her. She's sitting up in bed, dressing gown on, hair sticking up at all angles. In her hand is a clear, glass bottle. She pulls her sleeve up, and I shout, "Ama, stop!" before she pours Kwan Loong oil on her burn. My heart sputters and chokes like a lawn mower trying to start.

She scowls at me for interrupting her. "What matter?" she asks, still poised and ready to pour. "Kwan Loong good for everything."

"It's menthol and eucalyptus." It's mostly pure alcohol. "It will sting like hell." I flap my hands about. "You'll make it worse! Please!" I think about diving onto the bed. Thankfully, she places the bottle back on the table with a sharp bang before I can move.

She glares at me, her eyes darkening in the corners

like an oil spill. "Don't say hell!"

I help her out of bed. Bowing my head, I apologize. "Sorry, Ama."

She clucks her tongue. "George never let you speak to me like that."

When Gung was here, there was no need to speak to her like this.

Emptiness carves more hollows in my heart. I'm Swiss cheese. I have a Swiss-cheese heart.

I lift her wrist and inspect the wound. It looks a lot worse than yesterday. "We need to take you to the hospital," I say, sighing an empty, apathetic sigh.

Ama shakes her head vehemently. "No. George die there."

I breathe in and hold it, hoping the bursting pain in my lungs will somehow spark my will to care about her fussing. She'll only get worse if I don't take her, and that means more effort, more fighting later. I channel Ama. "If you don't go now, your skin could get infected. It will rot and smell and then they might have to amputate." She looks at me like she doesn't understand. "They'll get a big saw and cut through the flesh and bone. They will cut off your hand!" I do a sawing motion as I speak.

She looks at her hands and then back at me, seemingly weighing up whether she is ready to lose a limb. Finally, she decides she would like to keep her hand and concedes.

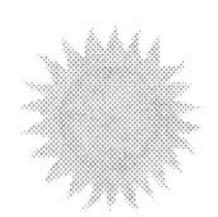

She wanted to bring the ficus but I wouldn't let her,

so now she's not speaking to me, which is a welcome relief.

I sit in Gung's seat, unable to take his place but having to just the same. The radio moans about love. Ama nurses her sore wrist, poking it every now and then and letting out cries of discomfort and prayers, which sound more like threats, to Jesus. I steer one handed and take her wrist, placing it above her heart to help slow the blood flow and ease the pain.

We pull into the hospital parking lot, and I breathe in deeply. I count to three before I get out. *Un, Deux, Trois. Je suis si fatiguée.* I'm so tired.

She lets her hand fall and then winces. "Ah! It beating like a heart. A heart in my hand." She pokes it again and shrieks.

I roll my eyes. My head to the sky. "Hold it up, Ama, then it won't hurt so much." She frowns at me, but does what I ask.

We get to the doors and I stop, scared to enter. The ghosts of my heartbreak warn me this will hurt. This will break me again. I place a hand on my heart and steal what little stamina I have left. Just walk. *Use your bones and joints. Your ligaments and muscles to move forward.*

Breathing ineffectively, I drag my body across the threshold.

A nurse greets us and tells us to wait.

"But my hand could be am-potatoes!" Ama screeches holding her thin, bubbled wrist in the nurse's face. The nurse snickers, and I stare at her with large, vacant eyes until she stops.

I'm swept clean, empty as a shell that's lost its owner.

I'm as thin as a cockleshell. I picture treading on them. The crunch and the shattering into a hundred small, sharp pieces. That's me. Soon, the sea will come and drag me under. At least there, it's dark and quiet.

When the doctor comes, he scolds me for waiting so long before bringing Ama in.

How old?

Eighteen.

No, your grandmother.

Seventy-one.

Do you have any other family?

No.

There is no one else. Just us. Me and Ama now.

Next time, he tells me, waving a stern yet friendly finger. *Next time.* The cage shrinks until my feathers are caught between the bars, and I can no longer move. I'm responsible for her now. The bars get closer together, stripping them from my wings. Flight may be impossible now. I have to accept that.

He puts burn cream on her skin while she tells him he looks like a white Bruce Lee. "It's your eyebrow," she says, tracing them in the air. "Sharp and thick like Chinese writing."

He raises his calligraphy brows and smiles at her. A little confused but mostly amused. "Just be careful when you're cooking Mrs. Douglas. One dish at a time, perhaps."

She cuts the air slowly with her good hand, moving gracefully, controlled and fluid. "You know Tai Chi, doctor?"

He shakes his head. "I'm afraid I do not."

"You should learn Tai Chi!" she orders, snatching a

handful of tongue depressors from the jar and putting them in her purse.

"I'll think about it," he says, humoring her and ushering us from the exam room. "Bring her back in a week for a checkup," he directs at me.

While she's talking to the receptionist, I put the tongue depressors back in a jar.

As soon as the doctor is out of earshot, she whispers sharp as a cobra's tongue, "Who is he to tell me how to cook, Sun? You make better doctor in sleep." She waves her purse at me triumphantly. "I got kindling!"

I sigh. "He's right, Ama. You need to slow down. At least until you've…"

We break into the cold outside air.

"Until what?"

"Until you've dealt with your grief. Ama, you could have burned our house down last night. You're distracted and tired." *God, I'm tired.*

She breathes in sharply through her nostrils and folds over. "George," she cries. "I am half. I am half."

I rub her back. Absorb all her pain, lump it together with my own. "I know, Ama. Me too." We are two halves that don't fit together. We don't make a whole. We don't heal. The open side is just bleeding and raw.

On the way home, I let her prattle about the need to introduce Tai Chi to all schools. And Gung. And plants with spirits in them. And Bruce Lee. I take it all. Layer it over my skin like an uncomfortable coat and let *it* wear *me*.

Sunny

74

I part the curtains in my room. They flutter with warm air, trying to squelch under the window sash. It raps on the window, beckoning me to come outside.

You're tired. You're so very tired...

Air like a hand, curled into a lazy fist, knocking gently, enticingly.

Come rest. You've done enough. Now it's time to close your eyes. Rest.

Pulling on my dressing gown, I creep down the hall, feet like liars, a mouth showing an ache that can't be cured. The family in the pictures on the wall has blank faces in the dark. Just pale against dark, smudges for eyes and lips. Ama snores loudly. The painkillers she was prescribed have knocked her out.

I'll just go for a few hours. Get some time alone to recharge.

Slipping into my boots at the door, I sneak down the steps on tiptoes and hit the field with flattened, exhausted legs. A channel of air is visible in the moonlight. I let it wrap around me, swallow my body and lead me into the forest.

I'll just go for a little while. Get some peace from this horrible time in my life.

My feet dip gently into the soil. I'm coursing along

like a stream over rocks, barely here, barely touching the ground. The air is golden. It's in my ears, my eyes, my mouth, just brushing away the pain gently like a paleontologist brushing dust from an ancient bone. It tells me to forget. It tells me it knows a way.

Just for a little while.

Dip, drag, dip, drag. Boots crusted in dirt. Furrows like a plowed field.

I feel alone in this. Like it wants me and only me.

The ugly tree's arms bulge with lumps and bumps as it seems to reach for me. Call me home. It hums a soft tune, a lullaby, as I check my axis and nestle into the north / south side of the trunk, the side where time at the tree slows down. The trunk seems to contract, the bark pulling closer together, the moisture retreating. It moves away from my ear as I press my cheek to the warm, damp wood like it's rejecting me.

The temperature drops, and I shudder. The warmth is withdrawn, leaving me huddling, truly alone, and a sour smell floats in the air. I hug myself, bringing my knees up and pulling my dressing gown tightly around my body.

This was supposed to help. It was supposed to give me peace. Yet, even here, the care I need is snatched from me. I'm deserted. Cold. Alone. Again.

Picking at the crumbling trunk with my fingernails, I rest my forehead against the cooling moss. I lift my head and bang it against the stupid tree that refuses to help me. Tears hotter than fresh tea sprout from my eyes as its leaves curl and shrivel away from me in disgust. Branches part and fold back from my pathetic, shaking body like it's packing up and going home.

"Please," I whisper. "I don't want to feel like this anymore."

But, of course, the tree doesn't answer. There's no escaping this pain. It drips down the walls. It fills our mouths, our lungs, with mud. Ama is changed, and I don't know if she'll ever change back. Wailing. Then hyperactive. Hurting herself. Searching for a ghost that's not there. She is untied and wasting.

I would give anything to make this stop. To get to the other side of grief before it completely devours me. Because right now, I can't help her, reach her. And she can't reach me. People say time heals. It just has to be moved through. But I don't feel like I can. I'm buried up to my knees in grief. Without Gung, I don't even want to try.

The tree relaxes. The warmth returns. Tiny, white flowers shaped like stars, *my stars,* dot around the trunk. A path to follow. I trace the line of flowers with my finger, shuffling over roots and dirt a quarter, until I'm sitting on the east/west axis of the trunk. A heated complacency floods my chest like strong ginger. A peace in knowing it could all be over soon. I could just rest for a while. Sleep through the hard part. When I wake, I'll feel ready. I'll be able to handle it better.

Coaxing branches bow down to me, and I thread my arms through them. They hold me up. Support me. They whisper calm, breezy words in my ears. They stroke my hair and tell me it's going to be okay. The roots at my feet rise up like a wave and wedge me against the trunk. I smile a blank smile, caring about nothing. Feeling nothing. All I need is rest.

Sleep will cure me.
Time will heal me.
I will just close my eyes and … … …

75

It's been a few weeks of a solid routine now. Going to the VA, working, preparing college applications. But the sun seems permanently set, a heavy weight resting on top of it. My routine is solid, but a large part of it consists of waiting for the sun—for Sunny.

Mom lurks in the window. She's fast becoming a ghost in the house. Outvoted and ignored, she hovers in the background. I should feel bad for her, but it's her choice to act this way.

Jake's a funny, dorky little kid. He makes jokes and laughs at them before anyone else does. He squints up at me, a smile missing three teeth. "Your brother is very tall," Jake says in a mild accent. "He's like a giant." He laughs a gobbling air kind of laugh. Red laughs too. They elbow each other and whisper conspiratorially. About me, I guess. Snickering and glancing up at me and then snickering some more. Stomping around at my feet, saying, *Fee fi fo fum,* and smooshing their sneakers into the icy dirt.

We play in the front yard. Soccer goals set up using old paint tins. It's me against the two of them. I'm ashamed to say that they're kicking my ass.

They weave between my legs, seeming to have a playing rhythm that I'm totally out of sync with. Jake pulls around me and goes for goal, kicking it straight and clean before I can get to defense.

Red and Jake pull their sweaters over their heads and tear around me in circles as they celebrate. Huffing and puffing like the giant they think I am, I try to catch them. Until they decide it would be more fun to tackle me to the ground.

Laughing to the point where they're hyperventilating, they grab both my legs and try to upend me. I lock my legs and grab at Jake, hooking under his arms and lifting him from the ground like a crane. He shrieks and giggles, swinging from my arm.

I stare at him hanging there, this little Asian kid, Red's best friend, and I feel fine. He's just a kid. His face doesn't scare me or drag me anywhere. My eyebrows rise and drop. I know it could still happen. But I'm starting to understand that's okay too. They're flashbacks. They don't control me. They're memories. And by definition, they will always be in the past.

Jake's kicking legs graze my hip, and I drop him in the mud. Red tries to defend his friend's honor by throwing the soccer ball at my head, but he misses.

We scrap and play-fight for half an hour before it's time for Jake to go home.

His mom accepts my apology for him being so dirty with a demure nod.

My brother and I stand there waving goofily as his mom drives him away.

I put my arm around Red's shoulders and scruff his flame-like hair. "Jake's pretty cool."

Red rolls his eyes. "Uh, duh! That's what I've been trying to tell you."

We climb the stairs and I stop in the middle, turning to him. "Hey, little man, I'm sorry if I haven't been listening to you. I promise. I'm going to try harder."

"You're such a pansy ass," he teases, trying to punch me in the side. "And don't call me little. I'm like..." Holding his hand out from the top of his head, giving it quite a generous angle, he lands it at my sternum. "Up to here on you!"

"I might be a pansy, but I'm not above giving my brother an atomic wedgie!" I threaten, lunging for his waist.

He screams like a little girl and runs to the door in a panic, his hands on the back of his waistband.

I laugh so hard that tears come to my eyes. It feels good but not quite there. The needle says I'm three quarters full.

I think I'm ready to go to Sunny now.

I'm ready to stand in the sun.

Sunny

76

I climbed onto a tire swing. I pulled it back as far as I could, my legs straining to the ground to get that maximum height. Heart tripping. Air sweet in my lungs. That anticipation a golden ball of light I could hold in my hands. And then, I let go, my hair streaming behind me, my breath coming in short, giggly bursts. I reach the peak height of the swing and then... Nothing. I stop. My mouth parted on the outbreath. My hair frozen horizontally behind my head. The golden ball turned grey and concrete in my lap.

At night, ice creeps like a spilled drink, spreading slowly from the ground up. It glosses over my feet, my legs, and up, up, up to my heart. When it reaches my lips, they tremble. But it's just the ghost of a tremble. There's a layer between the ice and me. The *world* and me. I feel the breeze, but as if from beneath a blanket. I see the sky as if beneath a layer of lace, my view cut into pieces. There's always something between reality and me. I am sufficiently numb.

In the morning, the sun warms the ice. It melts slowly, drip, drip, dripping down my legs, my sides, streaming down my face like tears. The tree sighs for me. It breathes for me. If I'm awake, I'm only part awake. I don't want to move. I don't want to feel. I like this floating feeling. I like the quiet humming. The soft swish of my leaves. The low creak of my branches. I'm not empty; I'm above that feeling.

I dream more than I don't.

My dreams are sweet and simple. They don't cause an ache. They are biting into mooncake. They are watching steam rise from sun-warmed piles of leaves. They are heavy quilts and summer dresses. They are cinnamon and butter.

Time means nothing now. It's just the sun and the moon changing places.

The crunch of leaves and the arm of torchlight move in front of us. Men's voices. Concerned, serious voices. We don't call to them. They're not ready. They have purpose and can't be tempted. Whatever they're doing, whatever they're looking for, we don't mind. We are buried under layers of bark, and no one can find us here.

Me. No one can find *me.*

Am I losing myself?

Does it matter?

No.

I sigh, and my leaves flutter in the breeze. The water plays over my feet. My branches curl over, hiding me. Protecting me.

Here, I am warm all the time. I never shiver. I never cry. I am perfect nothing.

BREAKER

77

Knuckles on the door. Sharp, bony rapping that doesn't stop. I wrap a towel around my waist and open the bathroom door. Steam clouds my eyes, but I hear Mom unlatching the door.

"Break Ah?" Annie shouts. "Sunny, you here?" Her voice is a sharpened pencil of panic, writing warning lines everywhere.

My heart tears open, and blood starts dripping onto the already-stained carpet.

"Excuse me, who do you think you are knocking on my door at this time?" Mom asks, her voice haughty and rude.

Annie pushes her way into our tiny apartment. "I'm Annie!" she states, like that's explanation enough. And in a lot of ways, it is.

Mom steps away from Annie like she's carrying the plague and tightens her pink robe. "You need to leave," Mom snaps. "Now!"

Ama narrows her eyes at Mom. Sizing her up and deciding she can take her. "I no leaving. I no going anywhere. Sunny? You here?" she calls out again. The sound of Sunny's name. The sound of searching is doing hard and painful things to my insides.

I edge into the hallway and address Annie, gripping the towel around my waist. "Annie, Sunny's not here." I put my free hand up, palm out. "Let me change, and I'll be right with you."

Red's curious face appears in the crack of his bedroom door. I watch his innocent eyes absorbing the scene, his ears soaking up Mom's hateful tone and the panicked sound of Annie's.

Mom's voice is a shrill threat. "Don't you dare leave me here with one of them."

I kneel and put my hands on Red's shoulders. "Let's go to my room. You can pick any record you want to listen to, okay?" His eyes light up at the permission to be in my room, but there's a speck of fear in there. A small dark spot in his cheery blue irises.

I hear Annie growling as I race to my room with my hands on Red's little back. I set him up on my bed, clapping headphones over his ears and throwing on whatever clothes are lying on the floor.

He's chooses Pink Floyd's *Dark Side of the Moon*. A good choice.

I stumble into the lounge as Annie waves her finger at Mom. "What make you so special? You think your skin make you special? I tell you," she starts, snorting in anger. "I tell you. You ugly and dull inside." She points to her heart. "You don't see…"

Mom stands in the corner of the lounge room like a trapped spider, her arms crossed. Her ears closed to Annie's words. "Are you going to let her talk to me like that?"

I look at her eyes, piercing and bitter. The way she glares at Annie like she's not human. "Yes, Mom. She hasn't said anything that isn't true."

Annie huffs triumphantly before turning to me. "Is

Sunny here?" she asks again, her voice suddenly small. A daring-to-hope kind of sound.

I shake my head, pieces of me sliding away with every movement. Mom disappears into the dull, gray wall. Her voice, her opinions, don't matter to either of us right now. I take Annie's hands in mine, noticing a healing scar on her wrist. "How long has she been missing?"

Annie's heart opens and pours all over our joined hands like boiling oil. "She gone one week," she cries painfully. "The police, they no care. They say she eighteen. She leave home. Nothing they can do." Her hands grip mine with the strength of iron. Her head falls. "It my fault. I crazy since George die. I make it too hard for her. She hate me now. Oh, Break Ah, she so sad. George dying, it break our hearts. But I know she wouldn't just leave me like this."

I pull her from her squatting position and onto the couch. "And you haven't heard from her at all?"

Annie sniffs and dabs her eyes with a handkerchief. It has puppies on it.

I should have gone to her sooner. I should have helped her more. I should have realized she was struggling. I gulp down my fears, my blame. I know it will only hurt Annie further.

There is a place. A place to rest. To escape. A place that calls to the suffering and the lonely. "Annie, I think I know where she might be."

Her eyes snap open, pits of fire and determination. "Where?"

"It's a little hard to explain, but I'll find her." I know exactly where she is. But also, not exactly.

Annie brings me down to her level and grabs my face in both hands, pulling me closer until we're almost nose to nose. "Then we go!" she announces, pushing me away forcefully.

BREAKER

78

From my bedroom, I hear sharp slices of conversation as Annie challenges Mom over and over again. There's no rational answer Mom can give to explain her feelings. Each word she utters embarrasses me. *Jobs. Dishonest. Foreign.*

Smashing supplies into a pack while Red watches, I pull the zip too violently. It splits open like my chest. I don't want to stop and think about being too late. I can't. I can't. *Can't.* The word spins in my throat, cutting away at the thing I need to breathe.

I tie the bag together by its handles and pause, sounds of pointless arguing shrinking away to muffled words beneath a gag. *Breathe in and out.* My mind reaches for that warm air, the pull to the woods. I close my eyes and hear Annie chanting in Chinese in my lounge room. I beg for the air; I pray for the air. But there's nothing.

I stopped needing it, and it stopped wanting me.

My eyes sting as I realize something must have changed in Sunny. It wants her now. It *has* her now. I picture bark growing over her beautiful face, and I feel sick.

Red lifts one of the headphones from his ear and says, "Is everything okay?" His scared voice is a hammer crashing to the floor. "Where are you going? You're not leaving me, are you?"

I pull the headphones down and bend down so we are eye to eye. "Red, everything's okay. I promise I'm not leaving you. But Sunny needs me. And so does Annie. Do you understand?"

His mouth turns serious. "Then you should go," he says, pointing at the door.

I pull him to me, crushing him in a hug that's made of so many missed embraces. So many times I've kept him at arm's length. He squirms and protests into my shoulder, and I squeeze him extra hard. When I put him down, he's grinning.

"Love you, you little weirdo," I say, heading for the door.

He shouts, "You're the weirdo!" as he slides the headphones on. He's singing along to electric guitar music as I close the door.

Crashing into the kitchen, I grab whatever long-life food we have. There's not a lot. Tinned beans. Condensed milk. Some candy bars.

Mom and Annie stop circling each other like men in a pit and watch me.

"Where do you think you're going?" Mom asks, all haughty and offended.

Annie's arms relax from throwing fake curses at Mom, and she answers for me, "He go find Sunny. *We* go find Sunny."

Mom scoffs at her proclamation, and I don't know what to do. I can't take a seventy-year-old lady with me into the woods. But as I look at her, I know I'm not going to be given a choice.

I storm to the door, Annie trailing behind me.

"If you leave, don't bother coming back!" Mom shouts.

Turning, I glare, seeing her for the desperate, depressed woman she really is. She is losing every fight we ever had. She has lost me. "Don't threaten me," I say, voice low and sure.

She steps back, her hand slipping from her hips, her face contorted, not sure which emotion to show.

I walk away before she makes up her mind.

Annie and I get in the Cortina and drive away.

Annie keeps no eyes on the road. She turns violently, looks out the side windows and the rearview mirror and at me. Not the road. I grip the door, knowing nothing will save me if a car comes in the other direction.

"Tell me where Sunny go," she says, her elbows up, driving like she might pull the steering wheel from the shaft.

"It's, um, I don't know how to explain it…" I start, my hands trembling. How do I tell her I think Sunny has fallen asleep against a tree that changes time? That maybe it has consumed her? And that it's my fault she's there at all?

Annie purses her lips and swings down the dirt road to their cabin. "Explain!"

Here goes.

The gravel pelts the underside of the car like bullets. Annie stares at me with intense dark eyes. They're not like Sunny's, which are brown but golden. Full of light. These are eyes that know more than they let on. "Okay,

okay." I put my hands up. "But you're not going to believe me."

We bump and bounce into her driveway, and she jumps out of the car with far too much spring for a seventy-year-old. "Talk and walk," she orders.

I follow her up the stairs, watching her bony, cardigan-covered back as I explain. "Sunny and I found this tree... At first, we didn't realize what it was. The kind of power it had. But after a couple of visits, we worked out that it changes time."

She pauses, ears pricked, and pushes open the door. "Magic tree. *Ai ya!* Makes sense!" she exclaims, and I almost fall down the stairs.

I continue as we enter the house. "So, depending on which axis you sat on, time would either speed up or slow down."

Annie grabs a large purse and starts packing it with food, dumping a saucepan on top. "So you think Sunny go there to change her time. She go there to speed up her, uh..." Annie thumps her chest, a look of anguish flashing across her powdered features.

I wish I could feel the call. I stretch out my feelings and try to pick up the trail of warmth. "I think she went there to speed through this part of her life. Skip over the hard parts. But I'm scared she won't be able to wake herself."

There was something Sunny had said, about us being the batteries. What if it needs her life to charge its batteries? "I'm scared it will consume her," I say out loud, the words like a rope that drops down to hang me.

Annie slings her bag over her shoulder and grabs my arm with strong, thin fingers. "We find her first."

Annie

79

I have always had a lot of life in me. When my daughter died, I had to live for her. For two people. I look down at George's boots on my feet. When George died, I had to live for him too. I carry two lives inside me now, plus my own. There is no room for a fourth.

I put on my red beret. It's good luck and warm, soft because it's good quality wool. George didn't like how much I paid for it.

Oh, George.

Shaking my head, I drag the boy down the stairs. He doesn't think I can do this, but I have three lives in one body. I'm strong for an old woman. I'm strong for a young woman.

Yes, I'm strong, but I have no room for more. Sunny ran from me because I'm too much. Too much life, too much love, too much *everything*. I need her to come home now. I need to share some of my life with her.

"This isn't going to be easy, Annie. Are you sure you want to come with me? We're going to be camping on the ground. It will be cold." The boy looks terrified, and he doubts me. But his heart is full of love for Sunny. This is a good thing. Love might bring her back.

"I tough," I say, pumping my arms. "I seen worse." What is the word I'm looking for? Through? Been through or in? "I been in worse." I want to tell him I have slept in the dirt. I've been separated from George by high-wire fences and men with guns who kicked us when we cried. But these things are not easy to say. The words are hard. Words always get in my way here. Every day, though, I'm learning.

"Okay, Annie," he says with a wary smile.

We walk fast across the field. The grass is thick and scratchy like cat whiskers.

Sunny and I are all that's left. We grew from the same seed. I promised my daughter I would look after her. It's my duty.

She will not be consumed. I will not let her.

BREAKER

80

The sun and moon have swapped places. *We* have swapped places. It used to call so strongly to me, but as I sweep my head back and forth, searching the spindly woods, I feel nothing.

I picture Sunny traipsing between these blackened trunks, weaving purposefully on a trail that only she can see, and I gulp down guilt. Her face is clear in my mind, brown eyes red from crying, face pale and forlorn. If she did this, it was because she felt there was no other option. *I left her with no other option.*

Annie stands between the trunks, almost as thin and dark, wearing a black sweater, black cords, and a red beret. "Where we go, Break Ah?" she asks, cold winter light dancing in her eyes.

I don't know. Shrugging, I pick a direction and start walking. Annie crashes through the brush behind me. She's eighty pounds of person, but more like two hundred pounds of force.

I keep hoping the air will change, that I'll sense that sweetness, that comfort and warmth, but it's not happening. So I will just have to search the traditional way. Mark the trees and eliminate areas as I go.

We walk for two hours. I scratch marks into the trees with my pocketknife. Small Xs that bleed. I've done this before. I just need to stick to a system. Annie's strained huffs sound behind me.

"Do you need to rest?" I ask, turning to face her red cheeks pulsing through white makeup.

"No," she shouts stubbornly. Birds flap from the branches above, frightened of Annie Douglas in the woods.

I hand her some water and watch her unwrap a candy that smells like gingerbread, eating it with the inside paper still on. She looks up, chewing. "Sun go down in few hours."

She doesn't need to say it. "We'll keep going til' then," I mutter, opening my arm for her to lead the way.

She nods. Full of fire and persistence.

The light has faded like the ink on my marching orders. We've probably covered seven or eight miles. Annie braces herself on her knees, folded like craft paper. "I think we should camp, unless you want me to take you home?" I ask hopefully. I can't be responsible for killing a little old lady, no matter how tough she says she is.

She snorts. "Maybe I take you home!" she says, jabbing my chest with her finger. "You out of shape."

She forces a laugh from my lungs. Air that's been trapped there for too long. "All right, all right." I put my hands up in surrender. "You win."

She stares up at the sky. The stars appear one by one like eyes opening to watch over the night, and she sighs. "I win when we find her."

Yes. *When* we find her. Not *if*. I need to take a page

from Annie's book. I need to believe we will find her.

I light a fire and we watch it grow, warming the freezing earth around us. Heavy clouds have pulled in over our heads, blinding the stars. It traps the air, keeping the temperature tolerable. Annie pulls her saucepan from her purse, along with things wrapped in foil. Eggs, onions, chilies. I watch her compose a meal from nothing, almost salivating as she spoons some onto my army-issue plate.

"Fuel for what come next," she announces, eating a much smaller serving.

I collect more wood and make sure the fire is high. Then we pull on our respective sleeping bags, and Annie turns her back to the flames.

"Sleep," she orders.

I pull my head under the suffocating nylon and manage, "Goodnight, Annie."

For once, I feel uncomfortable in the dark. I'm wishing for the sun. I don't know if I'll sleep at all tonight.

Then Annie whispers, "Bears," in a hissing warning… and *I know* I won't sleep tonight.

Sunny

81

My lips are cracked and caked. Curled pieces of bark cover my mouth and start broaching my tongue, my nostrils, my ears. There's no sigh in my lungs. My lungs are wrapped in thin vines acting as bronchioles. That word. It feels like it used to be important, like it was a part of something I wanted.

There was this piece of me that cared. That piece is being smothered.

My heavy eyes gaze up, searching for my diamond. But it's not there. The clouds crowd the stars, competing for rule over the sky. It should be cold. Somewhere in the back of my mind, I know I should be cold.

My body tries to shiver, causing parts of me to crack and crumble.

Sh! it whispers. *Sleep,* it tells me.

You don't need to worry anymore. The branches rock softly.

I watch the sky change from black to grey. A blanket of ice layers my still body, burying me, burying me slowly.

There was this piece of me…

BREAKER

82

Terrified, I rattle Annie's shoulder. Flakes of snow tumble from her back, pool in the curves of the sleeping bag that she only takes up precisely one eighth of. When she doesn't respond, I shout at her. "Annie!" My voice carries through the forest, waking creatures buried in snow. Sending birds soaring into the sky like my call was the blast of a shotgun.

Sunny

"Annie!" The sound curls around my blocked ears.

Annie. *Annie.* That word means something. Something I can't put my frozen finger on. I stretch it. Feel bark cracking. Cold, cold air on my skin.

BREAKER

Annie moans, suddenly sitting up. "What?" Her hair is a mess, her made-up face has migrated west of where it should be, and dark freckles have appeared under her eyes.

I breathe a sigh of relief. "I thought… I thought." Oh, crap! I really thought she had frozen to death during the night. I lean in and hug her. It's like squeezing a bag of kindling that's already been lit.

"*Apa ini?* What is this?" She slaps me away with her palms. "Break Ah. You crazy." Her irritated expression is so welcome that I break into a grin.

"Sorry," I say, dusting snow from my jacket and hair as I pack up our gear.

She glances around and takes in the light layer of snow covering, well, everything, and shakes her head. After taking her beret from her purse, she pulls it over her ears. Then she pulls another hat out and hands it to me. It's has purple and pink stripes with a pom-pom on top. It's Sunny's. "Wear this," she orders. I don't argue, pulling the hat that smells like fresh soap and Sunny over my head.

We chew on strange snacks from her weird bag and press on. Move deeper into the forest. The trees clamor. The snow piling between their trunks.

My faith is dwindling with every skinny, non-tumorous looking tree we pass. My heart aches for that warm air. The elastic pull has abandoned me and lies slack in the snow.

After a few hours of trudging and getting buried up to my knees—Annie's waist—in snow, we stop. I cough, my lungs tight and freezing, as I hold onto a trunk, wanting to rip it from the ground from frustration. Annie squats on a rock, resting back on her haunches like she was made for this. She stares up at me and asks, "How you find tree before?"

My lips are turning blue. Frosty clouds form around my words. "I don't know," I say while trying to stop my teeth from chattering. "It always kind of found us." *It's so damn cold.* Annie said she thought all Sunny was wearing that night was a nightdress and dressing gown... My ribs grow icy and harden my insides.

Annie shakes her head, pokes holes in the snow with her finger, and shudders. "We not going to find it."

The hole that was opening inside me becomes a gaping chasm. Hope plummets to the ground and then tunnels beneath the ground.

"No. I'm not giving up," I say, tightening my jaw and my resolve.

She places a hand on my arm, and her coal-black eyes are alight. "No, Break Ah. She find us."

Her head tilts toward the grey sky as she screams, "Sunny!"

I nod, walk forward, my legs sinking deeper and deeper into the snow. "Sunny!" I shout until my lungs hurt. I will shout for Sunny until they stop working altogether.

Sunny

"Sunny!" It's a bellow.

"Sunny!" And then a squawk.

Two voices. A word? No. A name?

That word means something. My brain is thick and syrupy, but those voices. They have a pull of their own.

My casing tightens and pushes me back against the trunk. *Rest. Just rest. Grief can't hurt you here. All that waits on the outside is pain. More pain.*

"Sunny!" a male voice calls. He sounds familiar.

His voice like the start of a map I should follow.

A heart. A *Frankenstein* heart.

Something beats in my chest. What was once moving slowly begins to pulse and flow.

"Sunny!" Her voice is strong, sure. High as an eagle's cry. She calls me home.

Warm. Conflicted. Hopeful. "Sunny!" He *is* my home.

Beat. Beat. Beat.

Tick. Tock. Tick. Tock.

Time.

I pull my eyelashes apart, gritty and crumbling.

Time is not meaningless. Time is equal to life. I knew this once. I need to know it again. Without it, there is no future, no past. Nothing to look forward to, and nothing to hold onto and remember. Time *means* something. It *is* everything. It is right there, waiting for me outside of this bark prison.

Leaning forward, I try to remember my arms and legs, my spine. I rip. *Is it my skin or the bark? What part of me has survived?*

As I tear myself from the warmth, the *rest,* grief floods my heart. My body shakes, weak from neglect, from the power of every emotion hitting me at once.

I crawl forward, branches grasping at my ribs. *Come back, come back, come back.*

Leaves fall with the snow. The heels of my hands are frozen. They plunge into icy water, sending splintered bullets of pain up my arms. Have I taken a breath? My lungs feel fit to burst. My heart wants to seize up, give up.

No.

My arms bow and break, too weak, too wasted. My face hits the cold water with a splash.

It fills my nose, my mouth. It drinks into my lungs, flash freezing them silent.

I watch small fractions of bark float by my eyes, dark sap wash from my skin. The last air in my body compresses and is pushed out by water.

What have I done?

BREAKER

83

Annie screams. It's a scream that fills the forest, strips every leaf from every tree. Her voice fills the sky. "Sunny! No!"

No. No.

I follow her voice, fear biting at my heels, the word *no* clawing at my heart.

No. No. No.

Ahead, Annie's tiny frame crouches low, an icy stream running over her knees while large blobs of snow float by like icebergs. In her arms is a carpet of bark and sap. In her arms is brown hair and almond eyes. Annie scrapes the debris from Sunny's pale blue face.

The sun has lost its fire. It has faded to a charcoal lump in an airless sky.

I run to her side. "Sunny," I say shaking her limp, cold body. I glance at the tree; the scar of where it tried to absorb her is bleeding. Raw, naked flesh bleeds sap. She was strong enough. She ripped herself away. "Wake up!" I rattled her body violently, and her bark-caked arms flop around uselessly. Lifelessly.

Annie throws her head back and wails to the clouds. Praying to God. Praying to anyone who will listen. "Save her! Take me instead," she screams in ten kinds of pain.

I try to pull Sunny from her arms, but she grips her tight. "Annie," I say gently, calmly, though everything inside is breaking apart. "Let her go."

Annie's arms slacken. Carefully, I lift Sunny from the stream and place her on the ground. Annie pulls her wet clothes from her body as I quickly pull out a sleeping bag to wrap her in. I lean down and listen to her heart. It's not beating. She's not breathing. I squash my panic. I do what I was trained to do.

I perform CPR, thanking God I was in the army. That I learned this one skill.

I push on her chest while Annie cries out with every thump.

I blow into her mouth, feel her cold lips on mine. Annie's voice pales to a whimper.

I won't give up. I will *make* her heart beat.

I blow again and sit back. Wait.

We wait.

Her porcelain face, glazed blue, stares dead at the sky.

Breathe, Sunny. Hate me forever. But just breathe.

Sunny turns her head and coughs, water spilling from her mouth.

"She's alive!" I shout. I clasp her face in my hands. "You're alive." I kiss her forehead as she squints at me and frowns.

Annie squeals and crashes around us, pulling us together into an awkward hug. Sunny shudders and whispers against my chest, "I'm alive." There is wonder with threads of determination weaved through it. Then her eyes dip. "It's not over is it?" The color rushes back to her cheeks.

I shake my head, brushing the wet hair from her face. "No." I repeat her words back to her. Ones I refused to hear before. Ones I believe now. "You can't skip through your life, Sunny." I add some words of my own. "You have to live it. Every last painful, joyful, frustrating moment of it."

"That sounds familiar," she says, her dirty lips curving up.

Annie stands, producing a small glass bottle from her purse. She sprinkles it on the tree, which strums and withers in front of us. It reaches for Sunny, desperate to drain the rest of her life, her time away. I turn her to face Annie, seeing the two of them exchange a secret smile. Gold flickers in Sunny's sunken eyes, and the sun, my Sun, shakes off its weight and starts edging toward the sky.

Annie strikes a match, and the liquid sparks to flame. The earth around the tree cracks and rumbles. The branches fold in, almost as if it's huddling away. Soon, it's a raging fire. We watch as individual shadows surge to the sky with every tumorous lump that burns and disappears. Free at last.

Annie steps back, hands on hips, watching with eyes like black diamonds. "See, Sun," she says with a defiant laugh. "I tell you Kwan Loong oil good for everything."

Epilogue

Annie flaps a purple NYU flag in our faces, running back and forth like a kid at a football game. She screams, "N-Y-You! N-Y-You!" excitedly and relentlessly until Sunny finally snatches the flag from her hands.

"Ama!" she groans, but her face is all shining teeth and apple cheeks. She takes the felt flag and pins it up on the wall above her bed, sitting back on her heels.

I stare at the purple-and-white triangle, and it promises hope. "I'm so glad you're staying. Thank you for choosing to stay here…with me," I say, taking hold of her waist and pulling her to me.

She leans in and touches her warm cheek to mine. Rays of sunlight spear my chest. She whispers in my ear, "I didn't do it for you."

Annie's childish face pokes in the doorway. "You two off bed!" she orders sternly, shaking her finger and then using it as a divider, breaking us apart.

I laugh, and the shadows between my ribs melt away.

I know she didn't do it for me. And it makes me love her even more.

ACKNOWLEDGEMENTS

Firstly I'd like to thank my family, Michael, Lennox, Rosalie and Emaline, for nurturing my crazy heart and not just putting up with, but finding affection for the unpredictable life a creative lives. And my parents Bob and Raelene, for the behind-the-scenes support. You're always there when I need you.

Huge thanks go to the lovely ladies at Clean Teen Publishing. Your unwavering belief in my work has given me the strength to keep on writing and the courage to try new genres and push the boundaries of 'commercial' fiction.

Also, I am so grateful to my amazing beta readers. They've always lifted me up when I was feeling a little lost but have also told me the truth when it was necessary. If only every relationship was that easy! You guys rock!

Finally, to my desperately missed grandparents, John and Jeanne. George and Annie are your tributes. They represent all the things I loved about you and even some of your faults. Let's face it, no one's perfect, though you two were pretty close. They are you. They'll live on for you.

About the Author

Lauren Nicolle Taylor lives in the lush Adelaide Hills. The daughter of a Malaysian nuclear physicist and an Australian scientist, she was expected to follow a science career path, attending Adelaide University and completing a Health Science degree with Honours in obstetrics and gynaecology.

She then worked in health research for a short time before having her first child. Due to their extensive health issues, Lauren spent her twenties as a full-time mother/carer to her three children. When her family life settled down, she turned to writing.

Author of the best selling Woodlands Series, she is also a 2014 Kindle Book Awards Semi-finalist and a USA Best Book Awards Finalist.

CPSIA information can be obtained
at www.ICGtesting.com
Printed in the USA
LVOW11s0532130517
534370LV00003B/5/P